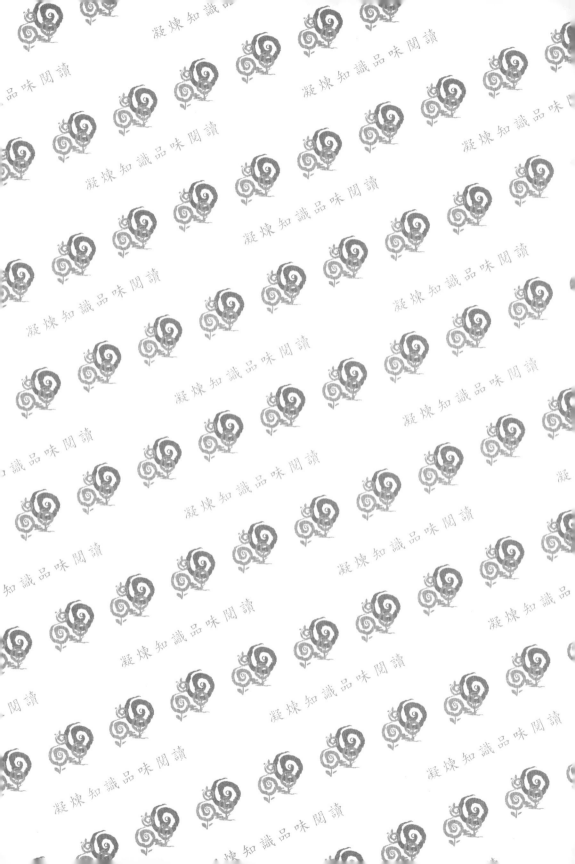

觀光英語

實用旅遊

五南圖書出版公司 印行　　黃惠政 著

推薦序一

　　黃惠政老師的「各層級英文考科考前輔導教學」及「歐洲團帶團實務與教育訓練」兩項專長領域，在國內旅遊業界頗負盛名。多年來，黃老師也在多處旅遊公、協會、科技大學觀光系所、補教界等，擔任一年一度的導遊、領隊英語考照班之考前輔導課程。同時，在帶領歐洲團部份，也不遑多讓，這幾年來，每年也跑了四、五趟歐洲團，其體力之好與敬業，令人敬佩。

　　「最新旅遊實用英語」這本書首創將國外觀光旅遊相關對話例句、旅遊常識等，以完整的英語會話方式，表達出來。配合聽力 QRCODE 的使用，使讀者能夠兼顧英語會話聽、講能力的練習，以及觀光旅遊實務經驗之吸收，一舉數得。

　　本書是黃老師數十年帶團經驗累積的一部份，不論是出國自由行旅遊者、背包客、公司行號國外出差的商務人士、或是公部門派往國外開會、或受訓人士、以及帶領 Out-bound 旅行團出國的觀光領隊人員等，有了本書內容的協助而獲益良多，特別是歐洲團領隊的最佳工具書。本人在此勉勵領隊朋友們，能夠仔細研讀本書，以快速增進帶團功力。並祝各位在帶團領域裡百尺竿頭、精益求精！

中華民國觀光領隊協會理事長

張華坤

2019 年 8 月 8 日

推薦序二

第一次聽到黃惠政老師這個名字，是旅行社的朋友葉先生告訴我的，並不時的告訴我，說黃老師的英文程度有多麼地好。一直到一九九一年底，葉先生傳來了一份，他託黃老師代筆，寫給蒙古田徑協會的一封信，拜讀之後，不忍釋手，很慶幸能看到這麼一本平實通順、文語法正確的好書，令人印象深刻。

一九九二年二月，在葉先生的介紹下，黃老師答應來中華民國田徑協會幫忙，負責對外英文書信之處理。共事一年多以來，更發現黃老師的英文造詣是高水準的。在美國夏威夷求學兩年、工作十餘年的經驗，使他在英語口語的表達上，就像他的英文書信一樣，是無懈可擊的。尤其是黃老師的美語發音，也是一口不帶東方人口音的道地美語。而多年擔任英文教職迄今之經驗的累積，使得他在英文書信的表達上，更是簡單明瞭、層次分明、用字遣詞通俗易懂。另外，黃老師對英文法的特殊詮釋方法，也是令人印象深刻。他能將較難懂的動詞、介系詞、副詞以及形容詞之前後位修飾等，以中外異同之觀點來剖析，循序漸進、簡單易懂，使人霍然茅塞頓開，且讓人有學英文並不難的感覺。黃老師對電腦軟體文書處理之嫻熟與英打每分鐘約 50 字的速度，也是令人羨慕的。

除了英文好之外，黃老師的國學底子也不錯，中文文筆流暢，加上他多年的翻譯實務經驗，使得本協會的許多中譯英、或英譯中文件，都能做得恰到好處。

黃老師的教學態度是認真的，「教學相長」一直是他深信不疑的真理，他教學前所做的準備是紮實的。所以，上過他的課的人，都深覺受益良多。

中華民國田徑協會理事長

2019 年 8 月 14 日

推薦序三

多年來，黃惠政老師一直在「英語文考試教學」與「領隊導遊帶團實務」兩領域，默默的耕耘著，以其在這兩領域的豐富專業知識與經驗，不遺餘力地傳承給年輕人。尤其，十餘年來在領隊協會擔任「導遊領隊考照班」的專任講師，利用獨創的破題技巧，告訴準考生如何以非常明確、快速的方武，僅憑試題句中的少數幾個關鍵字，就可以破解平均 80% 的填空題。這種破題方式對英文程度較差的人，特別管用。而對程度較好的人，則是如虎添翼。

在領隊帶團出國實務方面，黃老師的經驗傳承方式更是生動活潑，輕理論而重實務。很多上過他課程的人皆有一個共同的感受，他們說：很奇怪，經過黃老師的專業資料整理、生動的講解、再佐以大量的實務經驗說明，使學員們聽起來倍感親切，內容的吸收更是久久不忘。

黃老師的為人處事，深具長者風範，且又是「知無不言、言無不盡」的經驗傳承態度，而且為人熱心，學生如有聽不懂的地方，也總是不厭其煩、耐心的講解，直到學生聽懂為止，深獲好評。

在黃老師出版過的多本書裡，內容上皆有平鋪直敘、簡單易懂的特色，非常注重實務性。這一本「旅遊實用英語」也不例外。對有機會出國旅遊但英語文不甚流利人士而言，在國外旅遊期間，所會遇到的問題，如搭機之過境、轉機、入境，領行李，住宿飯店之住房與退房等等說明不勝枚舉，幾乎都可在本書找到，像是把旅遊達人帶在身邊。再加發揮 GOOGLE 等網路資料的方便性，旅遊就會更輕鬆、順利。

中華民國輪船商業同業公會全國聯合會

許洪烈

2019 年 9 月 3 日

自序

臺灣開放觀光這麼多年，國人出國觀光旅行，如果參加旅行團，因為隨團領隊的幫忙，比較不會有太多語言溝通上的困難。如果是自己個人旅行，除非你英語文能力足夠應付，就像時下有很多年輕人三、五好友到國外自助旅行一樣，否則，你在國外可能由於語言上的隔閡或對相關旅遊規定及常識的欠缺，而遭遇到更多的麻煩。

作者從事英語文教學及旅行團領隊實務多年，在這兩方面皆有多年的實務工作經驗。在看到了太多國人在英語文方面遭受了挫折之後，心想，如果能將本人在上述二領域之經驗，與國人分享，那該是一件多麼美好的事，於是，在這個理念的鞭策下，終於將這本「把國外旅遊相關規定及常識，寫成實務性的英語會話」的書呈現給讀者大眾。

這種將旅遊相關規定、常識融入於書內實用英文例句的作法，並且每單元後，配合更多的實務說明，在國內算是創舉。

出國旅行的人，不論有沒有出國旅行經驗，皆可從本書之例句及說明中，了解國外旅行時的相關規定及常識；對英語文程度不太好的人，亦可從書中英文例句之簡單但正確文法、語法、構造裡，去學習怎麼說出簡單，易懂的語句。

為充份發揮本書效果，請務必參閱「如何使用本書」之說明，以便很快的找到你要的相關情境單元及例句。

作者在此要特別感謝，中華民國觀光領隊協會張理事長榮坤、胡專員家寶、中華民國田徑協會前理事長紀政、中華民國輪船商業同業公會全國聯合會前秘書長許洪烈等社會賢達惠賜序文、萬盛旅行社經理葉茂盛等旅遊業人士提供寶貴資料……

作者　於臺北

如何使用本書

　　本書內容，是依國人出國所面臨情況之先後順序，寫成「飛機上」等十二篇，話題單元 108 個，實用例句達一千五百餘句。

　　由於本書是以「英文會話」和「旅遊常識」二者並重，所以在各話題單元後，作者都以若干國外相關的旅遊規定及常識來補充說明（標示＊號者），使內容更趨完整。

　　使用本書之前，請先仔細地閱讀一遍目錄裡各「篇」及其所屬的「話題單元」名稱，確實了解此兩者之間的相關性。那麼，以後要在書中找你想要的「話題單元」及例句，或有關之旅遊規定及常識，就會很容易。

　　茲舉數例說明：

例一：

　　假使你是一位吃齋素食者，在出國搭乘飛機時，不知道在飛機上，可不可以吃到素食餐？我們來看看，上面所說的，是關係到飛機上用素食餐的問題，所以應先找「飛機上」這一篇（第一篇），其中的第 12 話題單元名稱就是「素食者」，在這個單元裡，就會告訴你，在什麼時候向航空公司，預訂你在飛機上所要吃的素食餐。

例二：

　　假使你在飛機上，看到空服員，在分發入境卡旅客填寫，為什麼有些人要填，有些人卻可以不填寫？那麼你自己，到底要不要填寫入境卡呢？這個問題也是發生在飛機上，所以還是應從「飛機上」這一篇去找，此篇的第 25 話題單元「要填入境卡嗎？」就會給你正確的答案。

例三：

　　假使你人在倫敦的旅館房間裡，要撥長途電話回臺北，要怎麼撥呢？這個問題發生在旅館房間裡，所以應找「住旅館」這一篇（第六篇），其中的第 13、14 兩情境單元裡，會有詳細說明。

你不可不知 —— 問卷篇

1. 在機上，親友座位沒劃在一起，何時換位子最恰當、最安全，你知道嗎？
2. 手提行李過大，放不進座位上方櫃子裡，也放不下前座位下方之空間，怎麼辦？
3. 機上有三種狀況，非扣好安全帶不可，你知道是哪三種嗎？
4. 機上使用耳機，要付費嗎？
5. 機內座位把手上的各種開關，你都會用嗎？
6. 機上喝飲料、酒類，要付費嗎？
7. 如果你是素食者，你知道怎麼預訂機上的素食餐嗎？
8. 你知道如何向機上空服員要撲克牌嗎？
9. 你知道「直達班機」和「直飛班機」有什麼區別嗎？
10. 長程班次的飛行時間怎麼計算，你會嗎？
11. 如果你是過境旅客，應該在哪裡等過境呢？
12. 如果你需在某地轉機，飛機落地後，經座艙長允許，你可以比其他乘客先下飛機，以免搭不上後段的銜接班機嗎？
13. 何種狀況之下，才要填入境卡？怎麼填？
14. 何謂 local time（當地時間）？
15. 如果你是轉機旅客，怎麼辦理轉機手續？你的託運行李怎麼銜接？
16. 如果你是個人旅行，到了目的地，飛機落地後，你知道如何辦理入境手續嗎？
17. 如果你是旅行團成員，與他人共用「團體簽證」入境的話，你知道「同進同出」是什麼意思嗎？
18. 你知道簽證種類、單次及多次入境，以及入境他國時，護照有效期，必須有六個月以上之規定嗎？
19. 持有某國入境簽證，是否表示一定進得了該國？

20. 到目的地後，發現託運行李遺失了，你知道可以向該航空公司申請數天的每日補償金嗎？

21. 帶零食入境他國，如果沒申報，會被罰款嗎？

22. 有些國家海關檢查區，有所謂「綠燈通關臺」，你知道那是什麼嗎？

23. 所攜帶物品，不願被外國海關打重稅，可以暫時「存關」（IN-BOND），免課稅，你知道怎麼做嗎？

24. 在歐洲兌換美金時，到哪裡換對你最有利？

25. 在國外，怎麼搭計程車才安全，你知道嗎？

26. 在國外，住進旅館房間後，你有沒有將門後小鐵鍊扣上，以策安全？

27. 如果旅客有懼高症，如何要求住低樓層客房？

28. 貴重物品如果是在旅館客房內遺失，旅館會負責賠償嗎？

29. 你知道「歐式早餐」和「美式早餐」的區別嗎？

30. 你的早餐有沒有包括在房價之內，你知道嗎？

31. 何謂「早午餐」，你聽說過嗎？

32. 歐式的一、二樓和臺灣我們一、二樓說法不同，你知道嗎？

33. 客房內要打長途電話回臺灣，你會打嗎？

34. 從國外打電話回國內，市碼（如臺北 02，高雄 07）前面那個「0」不能撥，你知道為什麼嗎？

35. 在歐洲，使用「歐元」的國家有哪些，你知道嗎？

36. 旅行支票沒簽上聯（等於空白，沒簽字）而遺失的話，可以申請補發嗎？

37. 配偶、父母、子女等人的旅行支票沒用完，家人或他人可以使用嗎？

38. 你知道旅館名片卡的妙用嗎？

39. 何謂「客房服務」？你知道嗎？

40. 何謂「客房維修」？它與你的住房有何關係呢？

41. 你會利用旅館的「叫醒服務」嗎？

42. 旅館房間內電視節目，哪些是免費，哪些是要付費的？你知道嗎？

43. 每天早上，你有沒有留一點錢在枕頭上，當做給清理人員的小費？

44. 你知道有些客房內的冰箱裡，暗藏機關嗎？

45. 旅行時，如果沒有再確認你的機位，會有什麼後果，你知道嗎？

46. 你如何在電話中，清楚報出你的英文名字？

47. 在國外，你單獨一人晚上去逛風化區，會有什麼後果？

48. 護照遺失，怎麼辦？

49. 旅行支票遺失，怎麼辦？

50. 在國外使用信用卡，你知多少？

51. 國外百貨公司，有些稅是外加，不是內含，你知道嗎？

52. 在國外，特別要遵守「財不露白」原則，你做到了嗎？

53. 國外尺碼算法和我們不同，你知道嗎？

54. 在歐洲很多國家，購物可以辦退稅，有些甚至可以當場退，你知道嗎？

55. 國外高級餐廳，用餐時須穿正式服裝，亦須等櫃檯人員帶你入座，你知道嗎？

56. 西餐用完後，咖啡或茶一定免費嗎？

57. 癮君子喜歡飯後一根煙，你將煙灰彈到煙灰缸裡，還是隨性彈到用過的餐盤裡？

58. 有些都市，有兩個以上的機場，你有沒有問清楚才去？以免跑錯機場。

59. 到了機場，你會辦理登機手續嗎？

60. 在國外時，你因故不能搭乘原訂班機，而必須改搭他家航空班機時，你知道怎麼辦手續嗎？

61. 你搭機里程的累積可換取免費機票，你知道嗎？

62. 怎麼防止航空公司將你託運的行李送錯目的地，你知道嗎？

63. 託運行李牌（收據）如果遺失，會有什麼後果，你知道嗎？

64. 你知道託運行李的重量限制是多少嗎？

65. 國內新買 V-8 攝影機帶出國使用，返國後如何避免被誤認是國外所買而課稅？

CONTENTS
目　錄

觀光旅遊實用英語

目錄

(13)

目錄

(17)

第一篇 🎧

飛機上

CHAPTER 1
ON THE PLANE

P ：Passenger

客：旅客

F ：Flight attendant

員：空服員

找座位 🎧
FINDING SEATS

P： Excuse me, miss. This is my boarding-pass.

客：抱歉，小姐，這是我的登機證。

"　Can you show me where my seat is?

"　妳可以告訴我，我的座位在哪裡嗎？

F： Yes, let me take a look at your boarding-pass.

員：讓我看看您的登機證。

"　Your seat number is 51H, an aisle seat.

"　您的座位是 51H，是靠走道的座位。

"　It is on the right side of this air-craft.

"　您的座位是在飛機的右邊。

"　Please go straight on, you will find it.

"　請您直接走進去，您會找到的。

P： Are you the flight attendant for my cabin?

客：妳是我那一客艙的空服員嗎？

F： Yes, I am.

員：是的，我是。

P： Good, my name is Tom, what's yours?

客：那很好，我叫湯姆，妳叫什麼名字？

F： I am Carol, let me know if I can be of help.

員：我是卡洛，如果有我可以幫忙的地方，請不要客氣，並告訴我哦！

P： Yes, I will. Thank you!

客：好的，謝謝！

關鍵字詞 🎧

Miss　小姐；少女
例：Excuse me, miss. Where are you from?
抱歉小姐，妳是哪裡人？
boarding-pass　登機證
例：Can I see your boarding-pass?
我可以看看你的登機證嗎？
Aisle　走道
例：I would like to have an aisle seat.
我要靠走道的座位。

 TIP 小博士

對人之尊稱

　　英語習慣裡，對已知對方姓氏者之尊稱，用 Mr、Mrs、或 Miss 等稱呼之。如 Mr. Smith, Mrs. Smith 或 Miss Smith。但是，對不知姓氏者之尊稱，則直接用 sir, ma'am 或 miss 等稱呼之。如：Excuse me, sir; Excuse me, ma'am；Excuse me, miss 等。但第二種用法，尊稱的第一個字母，不必用大寫。如 Excuse me, miss.（不是 Miss）。

登機證

　　Boarding-pass 是指「允許搭乘交通工具」的搭乘證明，一般是指「登機證」而言，各家航空公司的登機證顏色、尺寸等也許不同，但其內容則是大同小異，皆有記載下述資料：

1. 旅客姓名　　　　　NAME OF PASSENGER
2. 班機號碼　　　　　FILGHT NUMBER
3. 起飛日期　　　　　DEPARTURE DATE
4. 起飛時間　　　　　DEPARTURE TIME

5. 登機時間　　　　BOARDING TIME

6. 登機門號碼　　　BOARDING GATE NO.

7. 座位號碼　　　　SEAT NUMBER

8. 目的地　　　　　DESTINATION

9. 艙位等級　　　　CLASS

10. 是／否吸煙區　　SMOKING/NON.SMOKING AREA

對號入座

　　上了飛機，旅客可依手上的登機證，看出自己的座位號碼是什麼，而去找位子。如果看不懂登機證上的內容，可以請機上的空服員幫忙，他們會很樂意，告訴旅客的座位在哪裡，帶領旅客及早入座。

換座位

　　機場地勤人員，在辦理團體旅客的登機手續時，對團體旅客座位的劃分，通常是按個人英文姓氏的第一個字母順序，來安排座位。有時候，難免會將團體內同一家族成員，如母、女、姑、嬸等，因個人姓氏順序不同，而未能劃分坐在一起的座位。所以，常看到有人在上了飛機之後，就急忙的私下換座位，以致影響後面正在上機的旅客，全部擁擠在走道。在此建議，欲換座位的旅客，應等全部旅客都上完飛機且已入坐，而在飛機尚未滑行至起飛跑道之前的空檔時間，或等到飛機升空至某一高度，機內「繫安全帶」燈熄滅後，才去互換座位。如此，就不會影響他人，而且也比較安全。

 自由行實務及緊急事件處理

機上換座位
Changing Seats On Board

A：Excuse me sir/ma'am, I am traveling with my wife, but somehow we are not sitting together.

A：抱歉先生，我與太太一起旅行，但我們機上的座卻沒有劃在一起。

B： Yes. What do you want me to do?

A： Do you mind changing your seat with that of my wife's?

B： What's her seating number?

A： She is sitting at 16C, the aisle seat.

B： That suits me fine. So I can get up and down more easily.

A： Can I help you with your hand-carry?

B： Yes, you can carry that brown bag for me.

A： This is my wife, Jean. And you are ....?

B： I am Peter. I am on my business trip to Berlin.

A： Bye now. And wish you a pleasant trip in Europe.

B： You bet.

B： 是的？我可以幫什麼忙？

A： 您介意和我太太換座位嗎？

B： 她的座位幾號？

A： 她坐在 16C，是個靠走道的座位。

B： 這位子對我來說很好。這樣我就可以更容易地離座或入座。

A： 我可以幫你拿手提行李嗎？

B： 好。你可以幫我拿那個棕色手提袋。

A： 這位是我太太 Jean. 請問您貴姓？

B： 我是 Peter. 我到柏林出差。

A： 再見了。祝你在歐洲旅途愉快。

B： 你也是。

手提行李太大
OVER-SIZED BAGS

P：Excuse me, sir. My carry-on is too big.

客：抱歉，先生，我的手提行李太大了。

"　It won't fit in under the seat.

"　放不進前座座位底下。

"　Where shall I put it?

"　我應該放到哪裡才好呢？

F：Please follow me. I'll show you.

員：請您跟我來，我告訴您放哪裡。

"　You can leave it here.

"　您可以放這裡。

P：Is it safe to leave it here?

客：放這裡安全嗎？

F：Yes. It is safe.

員：是的，很安全。

"　But be sure to take it with you when leaving the aircraft.

"　但下機時請不要忘記帶走。

P：Sure. Thank you.

客：那當然，謝謝你。

F：Anything else I can help you?

員：還有其他事我可以幫忙嗎？

 關鍵字詞

carry on　輕便手提行李

例：Is this your carry-on?

這是你的手提行李嗎？

be sure to　記得要；一定要

例：Be sure to call me when you get home.

　　到家後記得要打個電話給我。

 TIP 小博士

大件手提行李放何處

　　帶上飛機的手提行李，一般是放在前座座椅下方之空間，但如衣、帽等輕量物品，可放於座位上方之置物櫃（over-head compartment）內，如果旅客手提行李過大，放不下前座下方之空間，或置物櫃內時，在徵求空服員同意後，放於該艙等末排座位後方之空間，或其指定的地方，但下機時要記得帶走。

放大衣
PUTTING UP OVERCOAT

P： Excuse me, miss. I am not tall enough to put my overcoat up there in the over head compartment.

" Can you do it for me?

F： No problem, sir.

" There! Anything else?

P： No. That's all.
Thank you.

F： That's alright. There is nothing to it !

P： You are alright, Carol.

F： Well, I am only trying to be nice.

" This is what I am here for, to serve you folks.

客：抱歉小姐，我個子不夠高無法把大衣放進上面的置物箱裡。

" 請你幫我放好嗎？

員：沒問題的，先生。

" 好了，還有其他東西要放嗎？

客：沒有，只有那件而已，謝謝！

員：沒關係，小事一件。

客：你服務很好喔，卡洛。

員：我只是盡力做好工作。

" 這也是我在這裡的目的，我是來為大家服務的。

 關鍵字詞

there is nothing to it　形容某事輕而易舉

例：A：Thank you for fixing my car.
　　　謝謝你修好我的車。

B：That's alright. There is nothing to it.

　　沒關係，也沒什麼嘛！

 TIP 小博士

置物櫃內不可放重物

　　前面提過，座位上方之置物櫃，是放置輕便物品用的，不可放置過重物品，以免萬一飛行途中遭遇亂流，重物摔出來會砸傷人。以前曾經發生過，旅客將一個之重達一公斤的打卡鐘，放在置物櫃內，因遇高空亂流摔下來，而砸傷人的意外事件，請特別注意。

扣安全帶 🎧
FASTENING SEAT-BELT

P： Excuse me. How do I fasten this seatbelt?

客：抱歉，我怎麼扣這個安全帶？

F： I'll show you, sir.

員：我來示範給您看，先生。

" You just buckle it up around your belly.
Like this!

" 您只需把安全帶繞過小腹，再扣上就可以，像這樣。

" And you can easily losen the buckle by flapping this up.

" 然後你將扣蓋向上翻就可以輕易解開安全帶。

" You see! It's easy.

" 您看，很簡單的。

P： Yes. It's easy alright.

客：是呀，很簡單。

" It works even easier than the car seatbelts.

" 它比汽車安全帶用法更簡單。

F： Yes, it does.

員：的確是。

" And be sure to have the belt fastened

" 記得要把安全帶扣好。

" whenever the "fasten seatbelt" light is on.

" 每當「繫安全帶」燈亮起時。

P： Yes, ma'am.

客：是的，女士。

關鍵字詞 🎧

seat-belt　座位安全帶
例：Please faster your seat-belt.
請扣好你的安全帶。
belly　小腹
例：Your belly is getting bigger.
你的小腹越來越大。

 TIP 小博士

何時須扣安全帶

　　搭乘飛機時，有下述情形之一時，必須扣好安全帶：

1. 上完旅客，機門關起，飛機慢慢滑行至跑道準備起飛，機內之「扣安全帶」Fasten Seatbelt 燈亮起開始，一直到飛機上升到一定高度，機內「扣安全帶」燈熄滅為止的這段時間，一定要扣好安全帶。

2. 在飛行途中，遭遇亂流或其他緊急狀況，足以使機內「扣安全帶」燈亮起時，也須扣好安全帶。

3. 到達目的地，飛機準備降落，機內「扣安全帶」燈再度亮起時算起，一直到飛機安全降落，滑行後且停妥於停機門，機內「扣安全帶」燈熄滅為止的這一整段時間內，都要扣好安全帶。

飛機未停妥，勿爭先離座

　　常見很多旅客，在飛機降落後，飛機仍在跑道滑行，還沒到達停機門停妥，機內「扣安全帶」燈尚未熄滅，就爭先恐後鬆開安全帶，站立起來，開始取出放於置物櫃的東西，準備下機。這樣做是不對的，一定要等飛機停妥於停機門，接好空橋，機內「扣安全帶」燈熄滅後，才可以離座下機。

空位有人坐嗎？🎧
THIS SEAT TAKEN?

P1：Excuse me, sir. Is this seat taken?　　　客 1：抱歉，先生，這座位有人
　　　　　　　　　　　　　　　　　　　　　　　　　　　坐嗎？

P2：Yes. I am afraid so.　　　　　　　　　　客 2：是，有人坐。

"　　My wife is sitting here.　　　　　　　　"　　我太太坐這裡。

"　　She is in the ladies' room now.　　　　　"　　但她現在去洗手間。
　　　now.

P1：I see. What about that seat?　　　　　　客 1：我明白了，那麼那個座位
　　　　　　　　　　　　　　　　　　　　　　　　　　　呢？

P2：That's a vacant seat.　　　　　　　　　　客 2：那是一個空位。

P1：Guess I'll take that one since it is　　　　客 1：既然是空位，我去坐那邊
　　　a vacant seat.　　　　　　　　　　　　　　　　好了。

P2：Suit yourself!　　　　　　　　　　　　　客 2：請坐。

"　　It makes no difference to me.　　　　　　"　　這對我來說沒有影響。

P1：That's good. I can't stand the　　　　　　客 1：那很好，我受不了後面吵
　　　noisy kids in the back.　　　　　　　　　　　　鬧的小孩。

P2：You should have asked for the　　　　　　客 2：你應該事先要求前幾排的
　　　seat in front rows.　　　　　　　　　　　　　　座位。

P1：I didn't know I could request the　　　　客 1：我並不知道可以要求想要
　　　seating assignment.　　　　　　　　　　　　　的座位。

" This is my first trip abroad. " 這是我第一次出國。

P2：No wonder. 客2：難怪。

 關鍵字詞

it makes no difference to me　對我來說沒有差別。

例：Coffee and tea, which would you prefer to have?

咖啡和茶，你要哪一種？

Either one. It makes no difference to me.

任一種皆可，對我來說沒有什麼不同。

要耳機 🎧
ASKING FOR HEAD-SET

P：Excuse me, sir. May I have a pair of headset?

　　客：抱歉，先生，可以給我一付耳機嗎？

F：Yes, we will pass the headphones in a minute.

　　員：好的，我們馬上就會分發耳機給大家。

P：Do I have to pay for the earphone?

　　客：用耳機要付錢嗎？

F：No. You don't have to.

　　員：不，您不必付錢。

"　But we will get the headphones back before arriving Paris.

　　"　但是在抵達巴黎之前，我們會將所有耳機收回。

P：Excuse me. This headset doesn't work properly.

　　客：抱歉，這付耳機有點問題。

"　Can I have another pair?

　　"　再給我另一付好嗎？

F：Just a second. I'll get another one for you.

　　員：稍等一下，我再去拿一付給您。

"　Here you are ! Try this one.

　　"　給您，您先試試看這一付。

P：It works. Thanks. Thank you.

　　客：可以用了，謝謝你。

F：My pleasure, sir.

　　員：我的榮幸，先生。

 關鍵字詞 🎧

head-set　耳機，亦可稱為 head-phones 或 ear-phones
it works　器具可以用了 = 之意。

例：My radio doesn't work.

我的收音機壞了。

 TIP 小博士

機上之耳機

　　飛機上耳機使用要收費與否，要看班機飛行地區，或者航空公司的作法而定。亞洲區的班機，不管哪一家航空公司，都是在機內免費供應耳機，到達目的地之前，空服員負責收回，旅客是不能將機內專用耳機帶回家的。

座位上開關用法 🎧
USING SWITCHES

P : Excuse me. How do I use these switches on the armrest?

客：抱歉，座位扶手上的這些開關怎麼使用？

F : Here, let me show you.

員：來，我來示範給你看。

" This is to select the channel and that is for volume.

" 這個是選頻道的，而那個是調音量。

P : How many channels are there?

客：總共有幾個頻道？

F : There are a total of 12 channels.

員：共有 12 個頻道。

P : What about the movie channels?

客：那麼電影臺呢？

F : The movie channel is on channel #1.

員：電影臺在第一臺。

" And the rest of them are for different programs.

" 不同節目在不同臺。

P : What about this button?

客：那麼這個按鈕是做什麼用的？

F : This button is the reading lamp.

員：這是閱讀燈。

" And the next one is the call-button.

" 旁邊那一個是「服務鈴」。

" You press this button for flight attendants.

" 您有事要找空服員時，就按此鈕。

P : It sure is handy, isn't it?

客：實在很方便，對不對？

F： You can say that again!	員：您說得對極了。
P： Let me try the reading lamp.	客：讓我試試看這個閱讀燈。
" The light-beam direction doesn't seem right.	" 閱讀燈光投射方向好像不太對。
" Can it be adjusted?	" 方向可以調整嗎？
F： Sure, it's easy.	員：當然可以，很簡單。
" You can adjust the beam to any direction you want.	" 您可以將光束調到您要的方向。

  關鍵字詞

channel　頻道
例：How many TV channels are there in Taipei?
臺北有幾個電視頻道？
volume　容量、音量
例：Please turn the volume down.
請將音量轉小一些。

 TIP 小博士

flight attendant 空中服務員

　　例：Is Mary a flight attendant? 瑪莉是空中服務員嗎？

　　機上座位開關，一般是位於座位扶手內側，其各按鈕功能介紹如下：

CHANNEL　頻道鈕

　　機內提供多個頻道，有古典樂、鄉村音樂、爵士樂、脫口秀、亞洲線班機更有國、臺語歌曲等。機內欣賞電影時，亦是使用同一耳機、電影頻道一般是在第一或第二頻道，但各家航空公司作法仍有不同，最好是請問機內空服員。

VOLUME　音量鈕

用來調整音量大小，就像任何耳機的使用方式一樣，千萬不要把音量開得太大，以免震壞耳膜。

READING LAMP　閱讀燈

在長程班機裡，由於飛行時間久，都會有讓旅客閉目養神或睡覺的時候，如果你睡不著想看看書，就可以打開，每個座位都有的個人專用的閱讀燈，避免照射別人。燈光光束照射方向如果偏差，可請空服員幫忙調整。

CALL BUTTON　服務鈴

有事想請空服員幫忙時，可按此鈕，空服員聽到後會盡快前來。

音樂、電影節目 🎧
MUSIC/MOVIE PROGRAMS

P： Hi Betty, how many different music are there on this flight?

客：嗨貝蒂，這架飛機上有什麼音樂？

F： There are classical, Jazz, country music, soft music, and other programs on this flight.

員：我們有古典、爵士、鄉村音樂、輕音樂和其他節目。

P： Don't you have any Chinese music?

客：妳們沒有中國音樂嗎？

F： Yes, Chinese music is on channel 5.

員：有，中國音樂在第五頻道。

P： Is there any program chart?

客：有沒有節目表呢？

F： You will find the music program in this in-flight magazine.

員：這本機內雜誌裡面有音樂節目表。

P： What about the movies?

客：那麼電影呢？

F： You'll find the movie programs in it, too.

員：電影節目表也在這本雜誌內。

P： Do you know what the movie title is?

客：你知道這部電影的片名嗎？

F： I think it is "The Ghost".

員：我想是「第六感生死戀」。

" That is a terrific movie. I have seen it twice.

" 這片子很棒，我自己就看了兩遍。

P： Yes it is. But when are you going to show the movie?

F： We'll show the movie after meal.

客：是的，請問您什麼時候放電影呢？

員：電影在餐點後播放。

 關鍵字詞

in-flight　在飛行途中的；亦即「機上的」……之意

例：This is an in-flight magazine

　　這是一本機上雜誌。

title　頭銜；藝術作品等名稱

例：What's the title of your play?

　　你播放的這部歌劇名稱是什麼？

要飲料 🎧
ASKING FOR BEVERAGES

P： Hello miss, can I have something to drink?

客：小姐，我想喝點飲料。

F： Sure, what would you like to have?

員：好的，您想喝什麼呢？

P： I don't know. What's available?

客：我不知道有什麼可以喝。

F： We carry tea coffee, tomato juice, orange juice, 7-up, and coke.

員：我們有茶、咖啡、番茄汁、桔子汁、七喜和可樂。

P： Do you have any hot milk?

客：有熱牛奶嗎？

F： No. we ran out the milk.

員：沒有，牛奶用完了。

P： In that case, I'll take hot tea.

客：這樣的話，我喝熱茶。

F： English tea or Japanese tea?

員：英國茶或日本茶？

P： What is the Japanese tea?

客：日本茶是什麼？

F： It's a kind of tea with sea-weed flavour in it.

員：那是一種有海草口味的茶。

P： I think I'll try Japanese tea.

客：我就試試日本茶吧。

📎 關鍵字詞 🎧

available　可用的；可行的。

例：Are you available tomorrow?
　　你明天有空嗎？

例：Is there any seat available?

還有空位嗎？

 TIP 小博士

機內飲料

　　機內飲料的供應，有非酒精性飲料（non-alcoholic drinks）（或亦稱為（soft drinks）及酒精性飲料（regular drinks）之分。大部份航空公司的機內所有飲料都是免費供應的，但飛航美洲航班則要收取酒精性飲料的費用。包括酒精性或非酒精性飲料，飲料之總稱叫做「beverages」。

喝酒要付錢嗎？🎧
DO I PAY FOR DRINKS?

P： Excuse me. Do I pay for drinks?

F： Yes, but not for soft-drink.

P： Do you mind telling me what the soft-drink is?

F： The soft-drink is the drink without any alcohol in it.

"　Something like coke, 7-up, and all kinds of juice.

P： What about tea or coffee?

"　I don't think they are considered as soft-drink, but I am not sure.

F： Do you want anything now?

P： Yes, just give me a small canned beer or bottled beer.

F： Here is your beer. That will be two dollars.

P： How come you charge for the drinks while other airlines don't?

客：抱歉，喝酒要付錢嗎？

員：要，但軟性飲料不需付錢。

客：可不可以告訴我，什麼叫做軟性飲料？

員：任何非酒精的飲料都叫軟性飲料。

"　比如說可樂、七喜還有各種果汁等都叫做軟性飲料。

客：那麼，茶或咖啡呢？

"　它們應該不算是軟性飲料，但我不敢確定。

員：您現在想喝點什麼嗎？

客：好，請給我一份罐裝或瓶裝啤酒。

員：您的啤酒來了，請付兩塊錢。

客：為什麼你們要收酒錢，別家航空公司不用收？

F：I guess different airlines carry different policies.

員：我想各家做法不同。

P：Yes, I suppose so.

客：也許是吧！

 關鍵字詞 🎧

> drink　飲料；酒類飲料 n
>
> 例：I am nervous. Please give me a drink.
>
> 　　我很緊張，請給我一杯酒。
>
> 例：Do you drink?
>
> 　　你平常喝酒嗎？

 TIP 小博士

酒的分類

　　酒類的總稱是 liquor 酒的分類大概可分為以下數類：

1. BRANDY（白蘭地）：如 COGNAC V.S.O.P., NAPOLEON A 等

2. WHISKY（威士忌）：如 BOURBON DELUXE, JOHNNY WALKER'S 等

3. DRY GIN（琴酒）：如 CALVERT, HOUSE OF LORDS 等

4. WINE（葡萄酒）：如 WHITE WINE, RED WINE 等

5. CHAMPAGN（香檳酒）：如 MANHATHAN, REMY MARTIN 等

6. RUM（蘭酒）：如 LAMB'S WHITE, OLD SEA DOG 等

7. COCK TAIL（雞尾酒）：如 BLOODY MARY, SCREW DRIVER 等

8. VODKA（伏特加）：如 COSSACK, KOSKENKORVA 等

機上用餐
MEALS ON BOARD

P： Hi Betty, what choice do we have on lunch?

客：嗨！貝蒂，午餐我有哪些選擇呢？

F： It says on the menu.

員：菜單上的都可以點。

"　　The main course is beef steak or fish, with rice.

"　　主菜是牛排或魚，附有米飯。

P： Is that all?

客：只有這些？

F： No, it comes with salad, dessert and coffee or tea.

員：不，還有沙拉、甜點、咖啡或茶。

P： It sounds good. I'll take a beef steak, and a fish for my wife.

客：聽起來不錯，我要牛排，我太太要魚。

"　　By the way, can I have my steak medium well?

"　　對了，我的牛排要七分熟可以嗎？

F： I am sorry, sir. We only serve well-done steak.

員：抱歉，先生，機上只有全熟牛排。

"　　We don't cook in the airplane.

"　　機上是不烹煮的。

"　　We only heat up whatever the air kitchen had prepared for us.

"　　我們只是把空中廚房送來的菜加熱而已。

P： Well, I don't have much choice, do I?

客：那我就沒有太多的選擇囉？

F：	I guess you don't, sir.	員：	我想沒有，先生。
"	Would you care for some wine first?	"	您要不要先來點餐前酒？
P：	That's not a bad idea, Please give me some wine.	客：	這主意不錯，先來點酒吧！
F：	White wine or red wine?	員：	白酒或紅酒？
P：	It doesn't matter.	客：	都可以。

 關鍵字詞

---

course　一道菜

例：I had a 12-course dinner last night.

　　昨晚我吃了一頓十二道菜的晚餐。

---

it sounds good　聽起來不錯；這主意不錯。

對別人建議，說法等很贊同，可用此句。

例：I like your idea. It sounds good.

　　我喜歡你的主意，聽起來不錯。

介紹點牛排幾分熟的說法如下：

WELL-DONE　全熟

MEDIUM-WELL　七、八分熟

MEDIUM　五分熟

MEDIUM-RARE　三、四分熟

RARE　一、二分熟

---

heat-up　加熱；加溫

例：Can you heat-up the soup?

　　請你把湯加熱好嗎？

觀光旅遊實用英語

air-kitchen	空中廚房（負責機場所有進出班機餐飲之單位）

例：Grand hotel restaurant is the air-kitchen for CKS airport.

 TIP 小博士

機上餐飲

　　機上的餐飲都是免費供應，長程航班更是有連續幾餐都是在飛機上吃的。機上的餐飲都是由地面的空中廚房（air kitchen）所負責供應，在飛機上的小廚房（in-flight galley）有好幾個，用來把空中廚房送來的食物加熱而已。所以，旅客在機上如果有機會吃到牛排，是無法要求，要吃幾分熟牛排，因為機上的設備只是把已煮熟牛排加熱而已。

椅背活動桌面

　　機內座椅之椅背，可以調整向後傾斜，以便躺得舒服些。但是，由於椅背背後所安裝的，那一塊懸吊式活動桌面，是設計來給後座旅客，作為用餐或寫字使用的，所以在你調整放下椅背之前，最好能向後座旅客打聲招呼，免得打翻可能放在該桌面上的飲料、食物等。

豎直椅背

　　另外，在飛機準備起飛、降落、或是遇到亂流時，都必須將你的座椅椅背還原豎直，並把你前方的活動桌面，收回原位，以免碰撞，發生意外。

素食者 🎧
VEGETARIANS

P： Hello sir, I am a vegetarian

   客：先生，我是素食者。

"   Have you prepared any food for vegetarians?

   "   機上有沒有準備素食餐點？

F： Let me see. I got two names here on my list.

   員：我看看，我名單上只有兩個名字。

"   They had requested earlier for vegetarian food.

   "   他們事先有預定素食餐點。

"   They are Mr. C.C. Chen, and Mrs. K.K. Kim.

   "   他們是陳先生和金太太。

"   I am sorry, sir. I don't have your name on my list.

   "   抱歉，先生，您的名字並不在我的食物清單裡面。

P： I didn't know I could request the food in advance.

   客：我不知道事先可以訂素食點。

F： Yes, you could.

   員：你是可以事先訂的。

"   Please remember that you can request vegetarian food.

   "   記住，你可以預定素食餐點……

"   But only when you are making reservations,

   "   但那是在訂機位時就要先說好……

"   not to request them on board, it's too late.

   "   而不是到了飛機上才訂，這樣就會來不及。

P : Why is that?	客：為什麼？
F : Like I said a while ago,	員：就像我剛才說的，
" we only heat-up what the air-kitchen brought us.	" 我們只是把空中廚房送來的食物加熱而已。
" In other words, we take what they deliver.	" 換句話說，他們給什麼，我們就收什麼。
P : So I'll have to request the food when making reservation, is that it?	客：所以我在訂位時就必須同時訂素食餐點，對不對？
F : Yes, you are right.	員：您說對了。
P : Thank you. But I didn't request anything earlier.	客：謝謝，但這一次我並沒有事先訂。
" Can you do something about it?	" 你可以想想辦法嗎？
F : Yes, I'll do my best.	員：好，我盡力而為。
P : I appreciate it .	客：非常感謝。

  關鍵字詞

vegetarian 素食者
例：Are you a vegetarian? 你是素食者嗎？
in advance 事先
例：I am afraid that you'll have to pay in advance. 恐怕你得事先付款。

reservation 預定（房間、機位等）

例：Have you made reservation?

你有預定嗎？

in other word 換句話說

例：You don't have to come back anymore. In other words, you are fired.

你不要再來了，換句話說，你已被辭職了。

do something about it 想想辦法

例：Can you do something about it?

你可以設法解決這件事嗎？

 TIP 小博士

何時訂機上素食餐點？

　　如果你是素食者、吃長齋或有特別飲食習慣的人，你可以在訂機位時，向航空公司要求你在機上要吃素食。請記住，一定要在訂位時就訂好你要的素食餐點，不可以等上了飛機再說，那樣就會來不及。因為地面的空中廚房，在準備各班機旅客食物時，是最少在一天前，根據旅客訂位記錄去準備的，起飛當天才說是來不及的。

觀光旅遊實用英語

機上免稅品 🎧
DUTY-FREE ITEMS

P： Excuse me. Do you sell duty-free items on board?

F： Yes. We will do that after meal.

P： Is there any pricelist for your duty-free items?

F： Yes. They are listed on this magazine.

P： Do you know how many cigarettes I can bring in to Hong Kong?

F： I have no idea,

" 　but I'll be happy to find it out for you.

P： How? We will be there in about an hour from now.

F： I'll check with the purser.

" 　He has been around, and I think he think he has the answer you want.

" 　Hi, Mr. Chen, the purser says.

客：抱歉，請問機上有賣免稅品嗎？

員：有，我們將在餐點後販售。

客：這些免稅品有價目表嗎？

員：是的，這一本雜誌上就有。

客：妳知道我可以帶多少支香煙入境香港嗎？

員：不太清楚，

" 　但我願意幫你問問看。

客：怎麼問？我們再過一個小時就到香港了。

員：我來問座艙長看看。

　　他是見過世面的，我想他會有你要的答案。

" 　嗨陳先生！座艙長說……

" You are only allowed to bring in 200 cigarettes and 1 liter of liquor to Hong Kong.

P： Thank you, Betty.

F： You are welcome. There is nothing to it.

" 入境香港時只能帶 200 支香煙或一公升的酒。

客：謝謝，貝蒂。

員：不客氣，這對我來說沒什麼。

 關鍵字詞

duty-free 免稅
例： Is this radio duty free?
find out 找出；查出
例： Can you find out who she is?
你可以查出她是誰嗎？

 TIP 小博士

機上免稅品

　　在國際航班裡，也會出售一些煙、酒及其他小部份的免稅商品，不過由於機上空間有限，所售免稅品數量、種類不是很多，僅有煙、酒、香水等體積較小物品。在座位前袋裡的「機內雜誌」in-flight magazine 上，會有圖文並貌的說明，將機內出售的商品做詳細的介紹。

收臺幣嗎？
ACCEPT N.T. DOLLARS?

P： Excuse me, miss. I want to buy some duty-free items on board.

"　　Do you take Taiwan dollars?

F： Yes, we certainly do. Why ask?

P： It wasn't the case years back.

F： That's right, but it's different now.

P： Taiwan dollars are getting more and more popular.

F： Yes, you are right.

P： Do you take cheques if I don't have any cash?

F： Yes, we accept most credit cards and traveler's cheques.

P： Do you charge more if I pay by credit cards?

F： No, we don't.

客：抱歉，小姐，我想買一些免稅品。

"　　請問可以付臺幣嗎？

員：可以的，為什麼這麼問呢？

客：許多年前機上不收臺幣的。

員：是的，但現在時代不同了。

客：臺幣可是越來越受歡迎了。

員：是的，你說得對。

客：如果我沒有現金，妳可收支票嗎？

員：可以，大部份信用卡及支票我們都接受。

客：如果用信用卡付帳，費用會多些嗎？

員：不會，我們不多收費用。

 關鍵字詞

getting popular　越來越流行；越來越被接受。

例：Kung-fu movies are getting popular.

功夫電影越來越受歡迎。

 TIP 小博士

接受臺幣購物

　　在機上購買免稅品時，一般都可以美金、日幣、瑞士法朗、德國馬克等主要通行貨幣支付。近年來，由於臺灣觀光客出國暴增，漸漸地有些航空公司在機上也開始可以接受臺幣了。

要撲克牌
ASKING FOR PLAYING CARDS

P： Excuse me. Can I have some play-ing cards?

F： Yes. I'll see if there is any left.

P： I would like to have three decks of cards, if possible.

F： I doubt I can find that many.

P： You used to give away playing cards to every passenger on the flight.

" How come you don't do this any-more?

F： We have cut down expenses ever since energy crisis.

P： Yes. I can see that,

" because services are not as good as it was before.

F： I am sorry about that.

P： What for? There is nothing you can do about it. Can't you?

客：抱歉，給我一些撲克牌好嗎？

員：好，我看看還有沒有剩下的。

客：如果有的話，我要三付。

員：可能沒有那麼多。

客：你們以前都會在飛機上每人發一付。

" 現在怎麼沒這麼做了？

員：自從能源危機以來，我們就削減開支。

客：是，可以看得出來，

" 因為你們的服務已不像以前這麼好了。

員：對此我很抱歉。

客：為什麼抱歉，妳也改變不了的，對不對？

F：I guess I can't.　　　　　　　　　　　　員：我想我改變不了。

 關鍵字詞

playing cards　撲克牌（注意：不可稱為 poker cards）
例：Can I have a deck of playing cards? 　　可以給我一付撲克牌嗎？
doubt　懷疑；不認為
例：I doubt it will rain tomorrow. 　　我不認為明天會下雨。
energy crisis　能源危機
例：The business is much affected by energy crisis. 　　生意大受能源危機影響。

 TIP 小博士

正確撲克牌說法

　　撲克牌的正確英文說法叫做 playing cards，千萬不可說成 poker cards.
　　「poker」是撲克牌這種紙牌遊戲玩法的名稱，並非指紙牌本身。

索取機上撲克牌

　　在能源危機前，多數航空公司，特別是飛亞洲線航空公司，在機上都會發給每位旅客一付撲克牌，但能源危機後就不是每人給一付，而改為每一航班上只有幾十付牌，旅客要的話才給（不會主動給你）直到給完為止。

有中文雜誌嗎？🎧
ANY CHINESE MAGAZINE?

F： Excuse me, sir. Since we don't have any cards left,

" can I give you something else instead?

P： That'll be nice. Do you carry any magazine in Chinese?

F： Yes. There are two oriental magazines on board,

" one is in Chinese, and the other is in Japanese.

" Which do you prefer to have?

P： What about newspapers? You carry Chinese papers, too?

F： No. We don't have any Chinese paper on board.

P： In that case, bring me the magazine then.

F： Yes, I'll get it for you.

員： 抱歉，先生，既然我們已經沒有撲克牌了，

" 我給您別的東西好嗎？

客： 那很好，妳們有中文雜誌嗎？

員： 有，機上有兩份東方的雜誌。

" 一份是中文的，另一份是日文的。

" 您要哪一種？

客： 那報紙呢？你們也有中文報紙嗎？

員： 沒有，機上沒有中文報紙。

客： 那樣的話，給我雜誌好了。

員： 好，我去幫你拿。

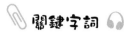
prefer to 較喜某物或某事

例：She prefers tea to coffee.

　　茶和咖啡，她較喜歡茶。

in that case 如果是那樣的話

例：I am sorry, ma'am. We ran out the coffee.

　　抱歉女士，我們咖啡賣完了。

　　In that case, I'll take tea.

　　如果是那樣的話，我要茶好了。

bring 攜帶；英文的「攜帶」有兩種不同的用法：

1. 如果把東西，拿給朝說話的人方向而來，用「bring」：

例：Please bring me some water.

　　請拿些水給我。

2. 如果把東西，拿給和說話者相反方向而去，用「take」：

例：Please take this book away.

　　請把這本書拿走。

then 以後；然後

此處之 then，是口語之轉接，等於中文的「那麼……」之意。

 TIP 小博士

機上刊物

　　國際班機上都會有一些書報雜誌，供旅客閱讀。依飛航地區之不同，會提供一些相關語言的刊物。以亞洲航班為例，大部份班機上都會有中文、英文、日文等刊物。由於臺灣旅客出國觀光呈大幅成長，在國外，不論是飛機上、旅遊風景區、大型旅館、機場等，可以看到的中文刊物標誌等也就越來越多。

病痛用語 🎧
NOT FEELING WELL

P： Excuse me, I think I've got a fever.

客：抱歉，我大概有一點兒發燒。

" My tooth is killing me.

" 我的牙齒痛死了。

" My eyes are very sore.

" 我的眼睛很痛。

" My lips are getting real dry.

" 我的嘴唇越來越乾。

" I've got a terrible head-ache

" 我的頭痛得要命。

" I get chilly every five minutes.

" 我感覺忽冷忽熱。

" I got a diarrhea.

" 我拉肚子。

" I feel sore all over.

" 我全身酸疼。

" My right leg feels numb.

" 我的右腿麻痺了。

" I feel dizzy.

" 我感到頭暈。

" I feel like throwing up.

" 我想吐。

" Do you have anything for head-ache?

" 妳有頭痛藥嗎？

F： Aspirins and bandages are about what' we carry in the First-aid box.

員：我們機上只有阿斯匹靈和繃帶而已。

" Do you want to try some aspirins?

" 您要試試阿斯匹靈嗎。

P： No. I want something to relieve the pain.

客：不，我要的是止痛藥。

F： Yes. This pill can stop the pain for a while.

員：好，這顆藥丸可以暫時止痛。

P： Can you give me some water?

客：可以給我一些水嗎？

F： Sure thing.

員：當然好。

P： My ears are humming terribly,

客：我的耳朵耳鳴得很厲害。

"　because of the altitude pressure.

"　由於高度壓力的關係。

"　Do you know anything to cure that?

"　妳知道怎麼治耳鳴嗎？

F： Yes, please relax yourself.

員：有，請先放輕鬆。

"　And open your mouth and take ten times deep breath like this.

　　打開嘴巴而像這樣地做十次深呼吸。

"　How do you feel?

"　感覺如何了？

P： I feel much better now.

客：已經好多了。

F： Use this waste bag in case you need to throw up again.

員：想吐的話，就用這個嘔吐袋。

P： Can I have an extra blanket? I am cold.

客：再多給我一條毛毯好嗎？我好冷。

F： Certainly, I'll get another one for you.

員：好的，我再去拿一條給您。

"　Here is your blanket, sir.

"　先生，您的毯子來了。

P：I feel warmer now. Thank you.　　客：感覺暖和多了，謝謝妳。

F：It's nothing.　　員：那沒什麼。

fever	發燒	toothache	牙痛
headache	頭痛	dry lips	嘴唇乾
sore eyes	眼睛酸澀	diarrhea	下痢
sore muscle	筋骨酸痛	sore throat	喉嚨痛

 關鍵字詞

my tooth is killing me 字面上是「我的牙齒正在殺我」之意，但真正的含意是「我的牙齒痛的要命」，是一句很道地的美式口語說法。
take a deep breath 「做深呼吸」之意，注意，此字的名詞是「breath」，動詞則是「breathe」。
throw up　嘔吐，正式說法是 vomit. 例：He threw up his dinner an hour ago. 　　他一小時前把吃的晚飯吐了出來。

 TIP 小博士

隨身藥物
　　旅行出門在外，如果生病、不舒服就太遺憾了。在飛機上所準備的藥品頂多只有阿司匹靈之類，根本不夠多。建議有長期服藥習慣的旅客，一定要把自己的藥品帶在身邊，出門在外更應如此。

有華語組員嗎？🎧
ANY CHINESES-SPEAKING CREW MEM-BER?

P： Excuse me. I don't speak much English.

客：抱歉，我不太會講英語。

" Do you have any Chinese-speaking crew on board?

機上有會說華語的組員嗎？

F： Yes. There is one, and she is from Singapore.

員：是的，有一位新加坡人。

" She is busy at the moment.

" 她現在正忙著。

" I'll ask her to come over when she gets through.

" 她一忙完，我就請她過來。

P： Yes, please.

客：好的，麻煩妳了。

F： By the way, what do you need her for?

員：對了，您為什麼要她來呢？

" Don't you think this is a good chance for you to practice your English?

" 您不認為這是一個您可以練習英語的好機會？

P： Yes, I agree with you.

客：話是沒錯……

" But I am afraid that people might laugh at me

" 但我怕別人笑我……

" if I use incorrect English.	" 如果我說錯英語時。
F： You shouldn't feel that way.	員：您不應該這樣想。
" I wish my Chinese is just as good as your English.	" 我的華語如果有您的英語那麼好就好了。
" You should have more confidence in your English.	" 您對您的英語要更有信心才是。
P： I wish I have.	客：希望如此。
F： No one can force you to practice English	員：沒有人能強迫您練習英語，
" unless you are willing to do it yourself.	" 除非你自願去做。
P： I guess you are right.	客：我想你是對的。

關鍵字詞

crew
指整組工作人員而言，如飛機上、火車上、輪船上之整組工作人員等。所以，crew member 是「組員」之意。

Chinese crew member
是中國籍組員，而 Chinese-speaking crewmember 則是會說華語的組員。

get through 通過；完成。
例：I'll call you when I get through here.
我這裡幫完就打電話給你。

TIP 小博士

華語組員

　　國際航班上的空服員，一般來說是包括多種國籍的，主要的目的是為了語言的方便。有些航空公司的空服員，都戴有一個代表自己國籍的國旗名牌，以表示他（她）是那一國人。在亞洲航線幾乎各個航空公司都會派有會講華語的組員在機上服務。

飛行高度、速度 🎧
FLYING ALTITUDE/SPEED

P： Excuse me, sir. What is our flying altitude now?

F： I think we are cruising at about 30,000 feet above sea-level.

P： What about the speed?

F： We are flying with an average speed of 600 miles per hour.

" That is about 960 kilometers ground speed per hour.

P： Oh yes? I don't feel it.

F： Of course, you don't,

" because you don't see anything outside the window

" that makes you feel the fast movement of the aircraft.

" So you don't feel how fast it goes.

P： Yes, sir.

客：抱歉，先生，我們現在的飛行高度是多少？

員：我們是在 3 萬英呎高空上巡航。

客：那速度是多少呢？

員：我們是以每小時 600 英里的速度飛行。

" 大約等於地面速度每小時 960 公里。

客：是嗎？感覺不出來。

員：當然感覺不出來，

" 因為你看不到窗外任何東西……

" 這使你感覺到飛機的快速移動。

" 所以你感覺不出來它飛得多快。

客：是的，先生。

關鍵字詞 🎧

attitude　高度 flying altitude 飛行高度
注意 altitude（高度）和 attitude（態度）二字拼法之區別。
cruise at　定速行進
例：This aircraft is cruising at 600 miles per hour.
這飛機正以每小時 600 哩巡航速度飛行。

 TIP 小博士

飛行高度、速度

　　一般國際航線班機，大約都以三萬五千英呎左右的飛行高度，以及大約 600 哩時速定速飛行。飛行的高度越高，空氣越稀薄，不過機內都有自動加壓設備，旅客不會感到不適。另外，飛機在高空上做高速飛行（時速 600 哩約等於地面時速 960 公里），感覺不出飛行速度有多快，不像在地面上高速前進時窗外都可看到房子、樹木等急速的往後退，才會感覺到前進的快速。

直達阿姆斯特丹？🎧
DIRECT FLY TO AMSTERDAM?

P : Hello. Is this a non-stop flight to Amsterdam?

客：哈囉，這班飛機直達阿姆斯特丹嗎？

F : No. It isn't.

員：不是的。

" It stops at Bangkok before Amsterdam.

" 會先停曼谷，才到阿姆斯特丹。

P : How long does it stop at Bangkok?

客：要在曼谷停多久？

F : It will stop at Bangkok for about an hour.

員：大概在曼谷停一小時。

P : Any particular reason for stopping at Bangkok?

客：有什麼特別的理由停在曼谷嗎？

F : I think it is for refueling and picking up more passengers.

員：大概是加油和可以多載一些客人吧！

P : Is there any difference between the meaning of a non-stop flight and a direct flight?

客：「直達班次」和「直航班次」意思上有什麼不同嗎？

F : Yes, a non-stop flight is the flight flying from ORIGINAL to DESTINATION

員：有，「直達班次」是從「起飛地」到「目的地」……

" without any stops in between.

" 中間不做任何停留。

" A direct flight is the flight flying from ORIGINAL to DESTINATION.

" But it may be non-stop in between,

" or it may have one or more stops.

" Either a non-stop flight or a direct flight carries only one flight number.

P： So you are saying,

" a "non-stop flight" is part of "direct flight".

" A "non-stop flight" may also be called "direct flight",

" but a "direct flight" may not be called "non-stop flight"?

F： Yes, you are right.

" 「直航班次」則是從「起飛地」到「目的地」，

" 可能是中途不停，

" 也可能中途會停一、兩站。

" 不論是「直達班次」或「直航班次」，其航班號碼不變。

客：那麼，你的意思是說，

" 「直達班次」是屬於「直航班次」的一種……

" 所以「直達班次」也可以稱為「直航班次」……

" 但「直航班次」卻不能稱為「直達班次」？

員：是的，你說得沒錯。

 關鍵字詞

non-stop　不停留；直達之意	
例：IM-763 is a non-stop flight to Sydney. 　　IM-763 是直達雪梨的班機。	
refuel　再加油	
例：They stopped at Bangkok for refueling. 　　他們在曼谷停留，加油。	

> stop-over　短暫停留
>
> 例：How long is our stop-over at Rome?
>
> 　　我們在羅馬會停留多久？

 TIP 小博士

直達和直航之別

　　在航空公司廣告裡常常看到 non-stop flight 和 direct flight 的字眼，雖然 non-stop（不停）和 direct（直接）二字在中文解釋沒什麼不同，但在航空公司術語的解釋上是不同的：

1. non-stop flight：表示從「起飛地」到「目的地」，中間不做任何停留之航班，亦即我們所謂的真正「直達」班機。

2. direct-flight：代表的是從「起飛地」到「目的地」，中間可能不做「停留」或「會停一站以上」，通常不必轉機，暫停後還是搭乘同一班機就可以抵達「目的地」之班機。亦即「直飛」或叫「直航」班機。

　　說明：Official Airlines Guide (OAG) 的原文解釋如下：

　　A DIRECT FLIGHT is a transportation from ORIGIN to DESTINATION which may be non-stop or has one or more stops.

全程飛行時間 🎧
TOTAL FLYING TIME

P： Excuse me, miss. What is our flight number?

客：抱歉，小姐，我們的班機號碼幾號？

F： Our flight number is CI-065.

員：我們班機號碼是 CI-065。

P： How long does it take before we arrive at Amsterdam?

客：飛到阿姆斯特丹要多久？

F： It takes about 3 hours to fly from Taipei to Bangkok.

員：從臺北到曼谷大概要飛三個小時。

" And it takes another 13 hours from Bangkok to Amsterdam.

" 而曼谷到阿姆斯特丹還要 13 個小時。

" And there is a stopover at Bangkok for about an hour.

" 在曼谷要稍停一個小時……

" That means it takes about a total of 17 hours all together.

" 總共大概要飛十七個小時才會到。

P： By the way, how many hours more from now before we get to Amsterdam?

客：那麼從現在算起，還要飛幾個小時？

F： Let me see, we just left Taipei 2 hours ago.

員：我來算算看，兩個小時前我們剛從臺北起飛……

" We still have a long way to go yet.

" 我們還有很長的路途呢。

" It takes another 15 hours before arriving Amsterdam.

" So why don't you take a nap or
   something?

P： Yes, I think I'll just do that.

" 還需 15 個小時才到阿姆斯
   特丹。

" 您可以睡個覺或做點別的事
   情。

客：是呀，我應該睡一下。

 關鍵字詞

arrive at　抵達
例：Tom is scheduled to arrive at Taipei at 2 p.m. 　　湯姆預定下午兩點抵達臺北。
nap　小睡片刻
例：He usually takes a nap after lunch. 　　他午後通常小睡片刻。

 TIP 小博士

全程飛行時間

　　全程飛行時間是指甲地飛到乙地所需之時間，包括了中途地面短暫停留的
時間，而實際飛行時間則僅指在空中飛行的時間，不包括地面等候時間。

全程飛行時間算法

　　航空公司時間表上的「起飛時間」和「到達時間」都以「當地時間」來表示，
英國之外的各地時間都是以格林威治標準時間 GMT 作根據。如臺北對 GMT 是
+8，東京對 GMT 是 +9，洛杉磯對 GMT 是 -8，檀香山對 GMT 是 -10 等。所以，
要算出兩地之飛行時間（可能也會包括中途暫停之時間），只要將「起飛」和
「到達」兩地時間各算回 GMT 的時間，再相減即可。茲舉二例說明：

例一 8 月 21 日 KL-878 臺北／阿姆斯特丹 19：35/06：00+1

這是說，於 8 月 21 日，荷航的 878 號班機。19：35 從臺北起飛，於 8 月 22 日 06：00 到達阿姆斯特丹。抵達時間的後方如有「+1」符號，表示加一日，次日之意）

先將上二時間，算回 GMT 時間，（臺北是 +8，阿姆斯特丹是 +2）首先，臺北的 8 月 21 日 19：35 等於 GMT 的 8 月 21 日的 11：35，而阿姆斯特丹的 8 月 22 日 06：00 等於 GMT 時間 8 月 22 日的 04：00。所以，兩個 GMT 時間相減，得知全程飛行時間是 16 小時 25 分鐘。

例二 9 月 1 日 CI.018 臺北／檀香山 14：30 ／ 06：50

（臺北比 GMT 是 +8 檀香山比 GMT 是 -10）

依例一，先將兩地都算回 GMT 時間，臺北的 9 月 1 日 14：30 等於 GMT 的 9 月 1 日 06：30 時。檀香山的 9 月 1 日 06：50 等於 GMT 的 9 月 1 日 16：50 時。兩個 GMT 時間相減，全程飛行時間是 10 小時 25 分鐘。

自由行實務及緊急事件處理

還要飛多久
How long does it take before arrival?

A：Excuse me, miss. How long does it take before we are arriving Berlin?

抱歉小姐。飛到柏林還要多久？

B：It should take another three hours before we get there.

應該還要飛 3 小時才會到。

A：How about the cruising speed now?

那麼，目前的巡航速度是多少？

B：I think we are cruising at approximately 900 kilometers per hour with an altitude of 10,000 meters.

現在的巡航速度大概是時速 900 公里，高度在一萬公尺上空。

B：You know something? You can read all flight information on the monitor in front of you.

你知道嗎？在你面前的顯示螢幕裡，你可找到本航班的飛航資料。

A：Oh yes? Can you show me how to find them?

是嗎？妳可以教我怎麼操作嗎？

B：It's easy. First, to backtrack your monitor all the way to the main page.

那簡單。首先，你必須要將你的螢幕調回首頁。

B：And you'll see three sectors namely "i", "c" and "e",

你就會看到三個區塊範圍，寫著 I，C，E，英文字母，

B：indicating proportionally as "flight information", "communications" and "entertainment".

依序代表「航班訊息」、「通訊」及「娛樂」。

A：Yes, I see it there.

有，我看到了。

B：Then you click "i", and from that on, just follow the constructions shown.

然後你點擊「i」，之後你就依螢幕所出現的指示，

B：You'll find the page showing flying altitude, speed, lapsed time and remaining hours to the destination, and so on.

就會找到有一整頁的文字，會顯示本航班資訊，包括飛行高度、速度、已飛時間、尚餘時間等。

A：Super！You are so professional.

太厲害了。妳很專業耶。

B：Thank you. That's what we are here for. To serve our passengers.

謝謝你。我們的專業就是用來服務我們的貴賓。

過境地氣溫、時間 🎧
TEMPERATURE & TIME AT THE TRANSITING PORT

P： Excuse me, sir. What will be the local time when we arrive at Bangkok?

客：抱歉，先生，我們到曼谷時，當地時間會是幾點？

F： We should get there by 11:10 p.m. the local time.

員：我們應該會在他們的當地時間晚上 11 點 10 分到。

P： I hope that is not too late for me to call my brother from the airport.

客：希望到曼谷機場打電話給我哥哥不會太遲。

F： Where is your brother?

員：您哥哥在那裡？

P： My brother is running a gem factory in Bangkok.

客：我哥哥在曼谷開寶石工廠。

" I am not able to see him during transit,

" 在過境曼谷時雖然見不到他，

" but at least I can talk to him on the phone.

" 但至少可以跟他通個電話。

F： That's right, sir.

員：是的，先生。

P： What about the temperature, do you know?

客：你知道溫度多少嗎？

F： I have no idea about that,

員：不太清楚，

" but I'll check with the the cabin manager and let you know later.	" 我去問座艙長，等一下告訴您。
P：Good, please do.	客：好，拜托啦！
F：Sir, the captain says it's about 30 degrees centigrade now in Bangkok.	員：先生，機長說曼谷現在的氣溫大約攝氏 30 度。
P：Oow, it's still that high at night?	客：哇，晚上了還那麼熱。
F：I guess so.	員：我想是吧！

 關鍵字詞

---

run　經營

例：Tom is running a book-store in London.

　　湯姆在倫敦經營一家書店。

---

captain　機長、船長

例：Are you the captain of this flight?

　　你是本班機的機長嗎？

Centigrade　攝氏溫度說法，又稱 Celsius.

例：Do you go by Centigrade or Fahrenheit?

　　你們是用攝氏還是華氏？

在哪裡等過境？🎧
WHERE TO WAIT WHILE TRANSITING?

P： Hi, miss. Is this flight go directly to Amsterdam?

客：小姐，這班機直飛阿姆斯特丹嗎？

F： Yes, but we'll stop at Bangkok for about an hour.

員：是，但我們將在曼谷停約一小時。

P： I see. But my destination is Amsterdam.

客：是的，但我的目的是阿姆斯特丹。

F： That makes you a transit passenger at Bangkok.

員：那你在曼谷只算是過境旅客。

P： In that case, where do I wait while transiting?

客：這樣子的話，過境時我在哪裡等候？

" Inside the aircraft or at the transit lounge?

" 是在飛機內等還是在過境室等？

F： I am afraid you'll have to wait in the transit area,

員：你恐怕要在過境室等，

" because we are going to clean up the cabins.

" 因為我們要清理客艙。

P： That's alright. Shall I take along my carry-on bags?

客：沒關係，過境時我要把手提行李帶走嗎？

F： You can, if that makes you feel better.

員：如果你認為帶走比較好，你就帶走。

" And of course you don't have to if you don't want to.	" 如果不帶也沒有關係。
P：I don't get it. Why is that?	客：我不明白，為什麼？
F：What I am trying to say is	員：我想說明的是……
" the seat you are sitting on now	" 你現在所坐的位子……
" will be your seat all the way to Amsterdam.	" 到阿姆斯特丹之前都是屬於你的座位。
" That's why I said	" 所以我說……
" you can leave your bags on your own seat while you are gone,	" 你可以去過境室等過境時，把手提行李放在自己的座位上。
" but don't leave anything valuable in it.	" 但裡面不要放貴重物品。
P：No, I won't.	客：我不會的。

 關鍵字詞

transit　經過；路過
例：I am only a transit passenger in Tokyo.
我在東京只是過境而已。
cabin　艙間
例：Mary is the stewardess for the Y-class cabin.
瑪莉是 Y 艙（經濟艙）的空服員。

TIP 小博士

何處等過境？

　　國際長途航班，如果中途有在某機場，作過境停留的話，旅客等候過境的地方有兩種：一是坐在原機自己座位上等候過境，一是全體旅客到過境室等候過境，以便地勤工作人員可以上機來稍做客艙清理工作，以及補上一些機內補給品。

要換飛機嗎（機上問）
CHANGING PLANES

P： Good morning, Carol.

客：卡洛，妳早。

F： Good morning, sir. What can I do for you?

員：先生您早，我可以為您效勞嗎？

P： Yes. It says on my tickets

客：是，我的機票上是這麼寫著……

" I am supposed to change to flight TG-932 at Bangkok, for Stockholm.

" 我應該在曼谷轉搭 TG-932 去斯德哥爾摩的班機。

F： Yes, sir. But can I see your tickets first, just to make sure.

員：是的，我可以看看你的機票確定一下嗎？

P： Certainly, here is my ticket.

客：當然，機票在這裡。

F： You are right, sir.

員：是的，先生。

" You are supposed to change to your connecting flight TG-932 for Stockholm at Bangkok.

" 你應在曼古轉 TG-932 班機去斯德哥爾摩。

P： Do you think I have enough time for my connecting flight?

客：你想我轉機的時間夠嗎？

F： I think so. And we will let you have the top priority to get off the aircraft when arriving at Bangkok.

員：應該夠，到了曼谷後我們會讓你優先下機。

P : That's very nice of you to do so.

F : You are welcome, but we do this to all transfer passengers.

客：你們這麼做很棒。

員：不客氣，我們對轉機旅客都是讓他們先下機的。

 關鍵字詞 🎧

priority　優先順序；top priority 最優先處理之意
例：I want you to do it on top priority. 我要你最先處理此事。
connecting flight　銜接班機

要填入境卡嗎 🎧
FILLING OUT THE CARDS

P： Excuse me, sir. Do I have to fill in any landing cards for Thailand?

客：抱歉，先生，我要不要填泰國的入境卡？

F： It depends on what your destination is.

員：那要看您的目的地是哪裡而定。

P： Does it make any difference?

客：有什麼不同嗎？

F： Sure it does.

員：當然有。

" You only fill in the landing card for the country you go to,

" 只有去您要入境的國家您才填該國的入境卡，

" not for the country you pass through.

" 只是經過的國家就不必。

P： I see. Please show me how to fill in this card for Holland.

客：我明白了。請問這張去荷蘭的入境卡怎麼填？

F： There are so many thing to fill in.

員：要填的項目太多了。

" All the questions are being written in plain English.

" 所有的問題都以最簡單的英文問的。

" You shouldn't have any problem filling in the card.

" 你填表應該不會有問題。

P： What about this one, it says "local address".

客：這一項呢？它說「本地地址」。

觀光旅遊實用英語

" Do I fill in my home address in Taiwan,

" 我是填臺灣的住址，

" or the hotel I stay in your country?

" 還是填這裡住的旅館？

F： Please fill out the name of hotel in this city.

員： 請填寫你住這裡的旅館名稱。

P： What is "maiden name"?

客： maiden name 是什麼意思？

F： It is a girl's last name before she is married.

員： 它是女子婚前的姓。

P： In our country, most married women would carry husband's last name as her family name.

客： 在我們國家，大多數婚後婦女都冠夫姓。

F： Skip this one, you are not a woman.

員： 這項跳過去，你並不是女性。

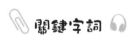 關鍵字詞

fill in 填表，亦可說成 fill out 或 fill up.
landing card 入境卡，亦稱 dis-embarkation card. 或 arrival card.
transiting port 過境地；過境港埠

TIP 小博士

何時填入境卡？

　　出國旅行，如果到了目的國，則必須填寫入境卡才可入境。如果僅是過境某機場，則只是過境旅客，不必填寫入境卡。

入境卡所填項目

　　在機上所填，各國入境卡格式也許不盡相同，但所填內容則不外乎是下列各項，你只要參考對照，據實填寫就可以了。

Full Name	全名	Date of Issue	發照日
First Name	名字	Date of Expiry	效期截止日
Middle Name	中名	Place of Issue	發照地
Maiden Name	女子婚前姓	Male/Female	男／女性
Alias (if any)	別名	Purpose of Entry	入境目的
Sex	性別	Length of Stay	停留期間
Date of Birth	出生日	Port of Embarkation	登機地
Place of Birth	出生地	Flight Number	班機號碼
Age	年齡	Traveling with a group?	參加旅行團？
Occupation	職業	Local Address	本地地址
Nationality	國籍	Signature	簽名
Passport Number	護照號碼		

使用洗手間 🎧
USING THE LAVATORY

P： Excuse me. Where is the wash-room?

客：抱歉，洗手間在哪裡？

F： It's in the rear section of this cabin.

員：在本客艙的後段。

" Come with me. I'll show you.

" 跟我來，我帶您去。

P： You are very kind.

客：妳人真好。

F： Here you are. Do you see the sign on the door?

員：到了，您看到門上的標示嗎？

" The sign of "vacant" means no one is in the toilet.

" VACANT 意思是表示洗手間內沒人。

" The sign of "occupied" means someone is using the toilet.

" OCCUPIED 意思是洗手間內有人。

" Please lock the door after you get in there.

" 進廁所之後請把門鎖上。

" And please put out the cigarette before entering the toilet.

" 進去之前請把香煙熄滅。

" One more thing, please don't use the toilet during take-off and land-ing.

" 還有一件事，當飛機起飛、降落時都請不要使用廁所。

rest room	洗手間，亦可說成 wash room, toilet, lavatory, men's 或 ladies room 等。
put out	熄滅

 TIP 小博士

機上洗手間

　　在商用客機上，每一艙等都設有洗手間，一般來說較廉票價艙等之旅客是不能使用較貴票價艙等的廁所，也就是說經濟艙旅客不能使用頭等艙的廁所，團體艙旅客不能使用商務艙的廁所。

廁所有人嗎？

　　機內廁所是絕對禁止抽煙的。另外，廁所內有沒有人使用，也可以從門上的指示牌看得出來，綠色的寫有「vacant」的，是指廁所裡沒人；紅色的，寫有「occupied」的，表示裡面有人。

空氣亂流 🎧
AIR TURBULENCE

F : Excuse me, sir.

" We are approaching an airturbulence.

" Please go back to your seat, and buckle up your seatbelt.

" Put out your cigarette

" and put your seat to upright position.

P : I got a run. I need to use the toilet badly.

F : Can you wait for a few minutes

" until the turbulence is over.

P : No, I can't. I gotta go now.

F : In that case, help yourself, but be careful in there.

P : I will, don't you worry.

員：抱歉，先生。

" 我們碰上了亂流。

" 請回到你的座位上繫好安全帶。

也把你的香煙弄熄……

" 並把椅背豎直。

客：我拉肚子，我非去廁所不可。

員：您可否稍等一下……

" 等到氣流正常後才去。

客：不行，我不能等，我現在就得去。

員：那樣的話，就請便吧！但在裡面小心一點！

客：我會的，請不用擔心。

upright position　指機內椅背豎直之意

例：Please put your seat in upright positon.

　　請將你的椅背豎直。

I got a run　是「我拉肚子」之意，美式說法。

 TIP 小博士

扣好安全帶

　　搭乘飛機遇到高空亂流是常有的事，這時，機內「扣安全帶」燈亮起，離座的旅客就必須趕快回去自己的座位扣好安全帶，正在上洗手間的人也應設法回去原位，在座位上的人，更應扣好安全帶，並將椅背豎直，以防碰撞。當然，最好是能夠養成坐上座位就扣安全帶的習慣，以策安全。

救生衣及氧氣面罩使用示範

　　班機在上完旅客、機門關上後，在起飛前，機上都會有一段錄影帶，或空服員做救生衣及氧氣面罩使用的示範。這個示範，會詳細告訴旅客，如何拉救生衣扣環充氣，或用嘴吹氣，以及如何先自己戴好氧氣面罩，再幫隨行小孩戴上等細節。

　　座位前方袋子裡，也同時放有，救生衣及氧氣面罩使用的圖片說明，讓圖面更詳細告訴你，緊急逃生時，你必須注意下列事項：

1. 扣好安全帶（fasten the seatbelt）

2. 不准吸煙（no smoking）

3. 椅背須還原豎直（put the seat to up-right position）

4. 座位前之小桌面，必須收回原位扣好（put up the table-top）

5. 如何依圖示，做抱枕低頭的預防撞擊動作（brace for impact）

6. 如何穿救生衣（put on the life jacket）

7. 如何充氣（to inflate the life jacket）

　　（注意：離開機艙之前不可充氣，以免阻塞出口）

8. 如何戴氧氣面罩（put on the oxygen mask）

9. 並且不能使用廁所（using the lavatory is prohibited）

　　不論旅客的旅行經驗多麼豐富，對這數分鐘的示範，絕對不能掉以輕心，畢竟一旦必須使用救生衣或氧氣面罩時，已經是生命攸關的時刻了。

緊急逃生（emergency evacuation）

　　飛機在飛行途中，如遇任何意外狀況，不管是人為或天候因素，而足以使機長發出緊急逃生命令時，機上全體乘客，就必須完全聽從，受過緊急救生訓練之空服員的救生指示，鎮定且守秩序的逃離機艙。

　　緊急逃生時，必須確實遵守下列各點：

1. 百分之百遵守逃生指示：緊急逃生時，必須絕對服從空服員的逃生指示，於此生死交關時刻，多一分的爭執，就等於少一分的救生時間。此時，空服員也可能顧不了，平時所說如「請」、「謝謝」、「拜託」等客套話，取代的可能是一些較具命令式的語句，如「你趕快」、「你必須」、「你不可以」等，以爭取時效。

2. 少拿自己物品，多救他人一命：由於機上緊急救生筏數量少，每筏裝載數量也有限，所以逃生時，除了盡量多穿保暖衣物（因何時獲救，尚屬未知，夜間可能是天寒地凍）外，手上不准攜帶任何物品，不管你的手提物品有多麼的貴重。因為，你多拿一件手提物品，所佔的空間，就等於少救一人。此時，空服員會於機上救生門口，嚴格把關，俾於最短時間內，救最多的人。

3. 隨身金屬、尖銳物等，必須除去：隨身如有配帶任何金屬、尖銳物品，如各形書寫用筆、手錶、戒指、耳環、假牙、眼鏡、皮帶、皮鞋、女用絲襪等，都必須脫下，以策安全。其理由有二：

   (1) 保護自身安全，免於被刺傷或刮傷。

   (2) 保護化學尼龍製品之救生筏或救生滑梯，免於被刺破、刮破。萬一被刺破，就等於減少救生的機會。

   ** 女用絲襪雖非尖銳物品，但穿戴者於跳下救生滑梯時，絲襪與尼龍滑梯會因瞬間摩擦，產生高熱，灼傷力強。先前已有被灼傷的案例。

4. 另外，於此緊急狀況下，男士的領帶，會被要求解下，襯衫的第一個鈕扣，也必須打開。女士如果穿的是窄裙，會被強制剪開或撕開，以利逃生。

5. 搭乘救生筏的先後順序遺，也應遵守空服員指示，長方形救生筏，須以左一、右一、左二、右二、⋯⋯之非字形坐法入座，而圓形筏則必須以東、西、南、北、之對角線坐法入座，以保持救生筏之平衡。

6. 機上組員最後離機時，一定會多帶食物、乾糧、飲水、藥品、毛毯、等物品，如果你是最後一批離機的旅客，說不定也可以幫忙攜帶一些上述物品。

時差 🎧
TIME DIFFERENCE

P : Excuse me. Do you know what time it is now in Amsterdam?

F : Yes, but let's go by Taipei time first.

"   Taipei time now is 11:00 p.m.

"   And Amsterdam time is 6 hours behind Taipei on Daylight Saving Time in summer,

"   so Amsterdam time now is 5:00 p.m.

P : But Amsterdam time is 7 hours behind Taipei time in the winter, isn't it?

F : Yes, Amsterdam time will be 7 hours behind Taipei on winter time.

P : Do I gain or lose one day while arriving Amsterdam?

F : Departing from Taipei for example,

客：抱歉，妳知道現在阿姆斯特丹幾點鐘嗎？

員：知道，讓我們先以臺北時間算起。

"   臺北現在是晚上十一點。

"   而以夏季的日光節約能源時間來說阿姆斯特丹比臺北慢六小時，

"   所以阿姆斯特丹現在是下午五點。

客：而在冬天時阿姆斯特丹比臺北慢七小時對不對？

員：是的，如果在非日光節約時間的冬天來算的話，阿姆斯特丹就比臺北慢七小時。

客：抵達阿姆斯特丹後，算是多了一天還是少了一天？

員：以臺北出發來說，

" by flying west-bound, you normally lose one day while arriving Europe.	" 向西飛，到歐洲時，算是少了一天。
" By flying east-bound, you normally gain one day while arriving America.	" 向東飛，到美洲時，算是多了一天。

 關鍵字詞 🎧

behind　此處是指時間上「慢」幾小時之意
例：Paris time is 6 hours behind Taipei time. 　　巴黎時間比臺北慢六小時。
ahead of　此處是指時間上「快」幾小時之意
例：Taipei time is 6 hours ahead of Paris time. 　　臺北時間比巴黎快六小時。
gain　指時間上增加了幾小時之意
例：You will gain one hour when arrivng at Tokyo. 　　你抵達日本時，是多了一小時。
lose　指時間上短少了幾小時之意
例：You will lose one day when arriving Europe. 　　你抵達歐洲時，是短少了一天。

 TIP 小博士

GMT 格林威治標準時間
格林威治標準時間（Greenwich Mean Time）被認為世界時間的基準。1884年世界天文會議決議，今後所有的經線讀數都以上此為起點。

時區

時區（time zone）：為 1884 年世界天文會議所制定，將地球表面從格林威治天文臺起，按經線分為廿四個時區，每區佔經度十五度，每跨越一時區，時差為一小時。

當地時間

航空公司時刻表顯示的時間，不管起飛或到達時間，都是指起飛地或到達地的當地時間 local time 而言。各地時差不同，如臺灣是 +8，日本是 +9，法國 +2，美國則有本土四個時差，夏威夷一個時差（如紐約是 -4，德州是 -5，猶他州是 -6，加州是 -7，夏威夷州是 -10）計五個時差。（如有日光節約時間，則再差一小時）。

「加一天」表示法

在時刻表裡，如果到達時間的旁邊有「+1」符號者，如 TPE/LON7 月 5 日 20:30/06:50+1 是指七月五日從臺北飛倫敦，晚上八時三十分起飛，次日上午六時五十分抵達。

本篇相關字詞

boarding pass	登機證	smoking area	吸煙區
seat number	座位號碼	non-smoking area	非吸煙區
airplane	飛機	departure	出發
first class	頭等艙	take off	起飛
business class	商務艙	landing	降落
economy class	經濟艙	cruising speed	巡航速度
tourist class	經濟艙	flying altitude	飛行高度
cockpit	駕駛室	temperature	溫度
wing	機翼	Fahrenheit	華氏
galley	飛機內廚房	Centigrade	攝氏

toilet	洗手間	Celsius	攝氏
washroom	洗手間	transit	過境
lavatory	洗手間	arrival	到達
men's room	男洗手間	on schedule	準時
ladies' room	女洗手間	behind schedule	誤點
vacant	廁所無人	delay	誤點
occupied	廁所有人	aspirin	阿斯匹靈
emergency exit	緊急出口	breakfast	早餐
oxygen mask	氧氣罩	lunch	午餐
life jacket	救生衣	dinner	晚餐
cabin	機艙	snack	點心
cabinet	櫃	dessert	飯後甜點
seat belt	安全帶	captain	機長
in-flight magazine	機上雜誌	navigator	領航員
headphones	耳機	flight crew	機上全體服務人員
headset	耳機	pilot	機師
earphones	耳機	co-pilot	副機師
reading lamp	閱讀燈	mechanic	機械員
call button	叫人鈴	purser	座艙長
pillow	枕頭	flight attendant	空服員統稱
blanket	毛毯	window seat	靠窗座位
aisle seat	靠走道座位		

TIP 小博士

GMT 與 UTC 之關係

1. 1884 年 10 月的華盛頓國際會議上，採納了格林威治子午線為量度經度的本初子午線。此子午線亦用於釐定時區，以及原始時間或 GMT（格林威治標準時間）。

2. 由於一天有 24 小時，地球被「分為」24 個經度相差 15°（一個小時）的區份，每區中間的時間決定下一區的時間。GMT 是以中午計算的平太陽時。GMT 系統於 1885 年 1 月 1 日為國際採用。

3. 然而，時區會受到國界影響，有些國家偏離世界時間。例如全中國均採用同一個時間，而印度則一國包含五個半小時的時差。

4. 1982 年 1 月 1 日，國際電訊聯盟（UIT）決定以 UTC（協調世界時）取代 GMT，以修正由於地球在軸心上自轉，故全年每天時長並不一樣的世界時間。按國際慣例，UTC 等同 GMT，但它們的量度時間的方式不同：GMT 從中午起量度，而 UTC 則由午夜起量度。

5. UTC 是法律上依據的世界時間。UTC 本身衍生自國際原子時（TAI），UTC 與 TAI 的差距僅以整數秒計，現為 32。加上閏秒的建議由國際地球自轉服務提出，以確保歷年來太陽平均在 12:00:00 UTC 至 0.9 秒之內經過格林威治子午線。民用時間是一個國家範圍內的有效時間。約 70 個國家使用夏令時間。年中若干期間，在北半球一般為四至九月，而在南半球則一般為十至三月，時間將加上一小時。日本是唯一一個沒有應用夏令時間的工業化國家。

國際換日線在地球另一邊、格林威治子午線的對面。選擇格林威治而非巴黎作為本初子午線的主要原因之一，是巴黎的對極並未橫過任何土地。

 自由行實務及緊急事件處理

兩地間時差問題
Time difference

A： Excuse me, Ma'am. Is there any time difference between Portugal and Spain?

打擾了，女士。請問葡萄牙與西班牙兩國之間，有無時差？

B：Yes. Portugal is in UTC 0 time zone, and Spain is in UTC+1 time zone.

有的。葡萄牙屬於 UTC+0 時區，西班牙屬於 UTC+1 時區。

B：In other words, Span time is one hour ahead of Portugal time.

換言之，西班牙時間比葡萄牙時間快 1 小時。

B：Here is an example. It is now 9 a.m. Spain time, and it's 8 a.m. Portugal time.

舉例來說，現在是西班牙的上午九點，等於是葡萄牙的上午八點。

A：Gee, thank you so much. You've made it clearly understood.

哇，太謝謝你啦。您解釋得非常清楚。

B：With more practice, you'll get used to it.

多練習幾遍你就會熟悉了。

A：Sometime I get confused with "gain" one hour, and "lose" one hour.

有時候我被「多一小時」與「少一小時」弄糊塗了。

A：Take the above "Spain time" and "Portugal time" for instance.

就以上面這個「西班牙時間」與「馬德里時間」舉例來說……

A：Do I "gain one hour" or "lose one hour" when I travel from Lisbon to Madrid?

我從里斯本去馬德里，是「多」或「少」了一個小時？

B：You lost one hour when you travel from Lisbon to Madrid,

從里斯本到馬德里，你「少了」一小時，

B：and you gain one hour on your return trip.

回程時你「多了」一小時。

第二篇 🎧

過境室

CHAPTER 2
AT THE TRANSIT LOUNGE

P ：Passenger

客：旅客

G ：Ground-staff

員：服務員

過境，不換飛機 🎧
TRANSIT W/OUT CHANGING AIRPLANE

P：Excuse me, I'm a transit passenger.

客：抱歉，我是過境旅客。

"　Is there any transit counter near by?

"　這附近有過境櫃臺嗎？

G：Yes, you go straight down,

員：有，您往前直走，

"　and you'll find it on the next counter.

"　在下個轉角您就會看到。

P：Excuse me. Is this a transitcounter?

客：抱歉，妳這裡是過境櫃臺嗎？

G：Yes, sir. Can I help you?

員：是，先生，我可以為您效勞嗎？

P：Yes, I just came in on flight number CI-065

客：可以，我剛剛搭 CI-065 來……

"　and I am heading for Amsterdam.

"　我是要去阿姆斯特丹的。

"　Do I have to change to another airplane?

"　我要不要換飛機？

G：May I see your boarding-pass, sir?

員：讓我先看看您的登機證好嗎？

P：Certainly, here you are.

客：好的，給您。

G：It shows on your boarding-pass.

員：你的登機證上寫明。

" You are going to Amsterdam on the same flight CI-065,	" 您還是搭 CI-065 這班次去阿姆斯特丹，
" so you don't have to change airplane and recheck-in is not necessary.	" 所以不必轉機，也不必再辦登機手續。
P：Good. What time do I board again?	客：好，那我幾點再次登機？
G：The boarding time is 23:40.	員：登機時間是 11 點 40 分。
P：What gate do I go to?	客：在幾號門登機？
G：Please go over to Gate 3 for Amsterdam.	員：在 3 號門登機去阿姆斯特丹。
P：Thank you. Good bye.	客：謝謝，再見。
G：Bye, have a nice trip.	員：再見，祝旅途愉快。

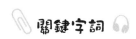 **關鍵字詞**

counter　櫃臺，如 ticket counter　機票櫃臺
airlines counter（航空公司櫃臺）等。
head for　前往，等於「go to」或「leave for」用法
例：I am heading for New York.　　我正要去紐約。
boarding time　登機時間
boarding gate　是登機門之意
have a nice trip　祝旅途愉快，亦可說 enjoy your trip 皆為常用的美式說法。
如果不指旅行而言，只是祝他人玩得愉快，就可說 enjoy yourself 或 have fun 等。

TIP 小博士

過境，不換飛機

　　在第一篇第二十三單元裡，我們提過長途國際航班如在飛行途中有在某機場做 stop over（停留）時，旅客可在機上或過境室等候過境（transit），而這種短暫的過境，主要目的是補充飛機油料，其他機內補給品及上、下旅客等，如果你只是過境旅客，就不必填寫過境國的入境卡，而且也不必在過境地辦理重新看護照，機票等再登機手續，等登機時間到時，就憑原先的那一張登機證，進入原班機坐原機座位，繼續飛往你的目的地，所以這就叫做僅是過境不用換搭其他班機。

轉機，須換航班 🎧
TRANSFER TO DIFFERENT FLIGHT

P： Hello, miss. Is this a Transfer Counter?

客：小姐，妳這裡是轉機櫃臺嗎？

G： Yes, it is. I am Mary. What can I do for you?

員：是的，我是瑪莉，有什麼是我可以幫您的嗎？

P： I just came in on flight TG-763.

客：我剛搭 TG-763 來的。

" My destination is Rome.

" 我的目的地是羅馬。

" Do I change airplane to Rome?

" 我要轉機去羅馬嗎？

G： May I see your air tickets and passport first?

員：我先看看您的機票和護照。

P： Yes, there you are.

客：好，在這裡。

G： The ticket says that you are connecting with TG-972 to Rome at the same day.

員：機票上說明你在同一天要轉搭 TG-972 去羅馬。

" It means you have to change to another flight at Bangkok.

" 意思是說您必須在曼谷換另外一班機。

" Let me take care of it for you.

" 我來幫你辦。

" Here, this is your new boarding pass with the seat number on it.

" 好了這是您的新登機證，上面有座號。

" Please board at Gate 21 for Rome.

" 請去 21 號門登機往羅馬。

P： What about my luggage?

G： All your checked luggage will be automatically transfered to your connecting flight TG-972.

P： That's good, thank you.

客：那我的行李呢？

員：所有託運的行李會自動的轉送到您所轉搭的 TG-972 班機上。

客：那很好，謝謝！

 關鍵字詞

checked baggage　隨機託運之行李

例：Howmany pieces of checked baggage do you have?

你的託運行李有幾件？

 TIP 小博士

轉機說明

　　如果從甲地要去丙地，因沒有固定航班可搭，必須經由乙地轉接其他班機，才可抵達目的地，這就叫做轉機（transfer）。

　　我們以某旅客從臺北到雅典的下述訂位記錄做例子來說明：

5 月 6 日 TAIPEI/HONGKONGEG-2111800/1935

5 月 6 日 HONGKONG/ATHENSOA-4742215/0340+1

　　上述例子說明的是某旅客於 5 月 6 日要搭 EG-211 班機從臺北飛香港，當天再銜接香港至雅典 OA-474 班機飛抵目的地雅典。EG-211 班機於 18：00 臺北起飛，預定於 19：35 抵香港；約四個小時後（航空公司規定兩機銜接的所謂轉機時間至少要有兩個小時以上才行）再轉搭 OA-474 班機從香港 22：15 起飛，隔日的 03：40 到目的地雅典。以此例子來看，該旅客在香港轉機搭 OA-474 續飛雅典，是因為臺北並無飛從希臘雅典的航班，所以才須由香港轉。至於該旅客的隨機託運行李，如果在出發地臺北，已經向航空公司聲明直掛到雅典的話，該旅客到了香港後，只須辦個轉機手續就可以上飛機續飛，不必擔心隨機託運行李之事，因為，原先搭乘的航空公司地勤人員會依旅客行李牌上寫明之目的地，將行李轉送到銜接班機的貨艙裡，續運往旅客的目的地。

機場免稅店 🎧
DUTY-FREE SHOPS

P： Excuse me. Where can I find the duty-free shops?

客：抱歉，請問免稅店在哪裡？

G： Turn to the right after you get through this escalator.

員：過了這條電扶梯後右轉。

"　You can't miss it.

"　您就會看到的。

"　Good morning, welcome to our duty free shop.

"　早安，歡迎光臨免稅店。

"　Can I show you anything?

"　需要為您介紹嗎？

P： Yes, I am looking for something for my wife.

客：要，我想買些東西給我太太。

G： What do you think of this perfume?

員：您看這個香水怎麼樣？

"　This is the brand new model came out only a week ago.

"　這是上個禮拜才上市的，最新產品。

P： It sounds good. How much is it?

客：那很好，多少錢？

G： It's only hundred and twenty dollars.

員：只要 120 元就好。

P： Okay, I'll take it.

客：好，我買了。

G：May I have your passport and boarding pass?

員：我可以看您的護照及登機證嗎？

P：What do you need them for?

客：為什麼要看？

G：Only foreign passengers are qualified to buy duty-free items.

員：只有外籍旅客才可以買免稅品。

"　That's why I want to see your identification.

"　所以我需要看你的身份證明。

P：That sounds okay to me. Here is my passport and boarding pass.

客：好吧，這是我護照和登機證。

G：Here is your perfume and receipt.

員：這是您的香水和收據。

"　Is there anything else you need?

"　還需要其他東西嗎？

P：No. This is all I want, thank you.

客：不用，這個就夠了，謝謝。

 關鍵字詞

duty-free　免除關稅之意
elevator　電動升降梯，英國人則稱為 lift。 另外，各大百貨公司、機場、車站等所用之電扶梯（樓梯狀，不像 elevator 是箱形狀）則稱為 escalator。
look for　尋找 例：What are you looking for? 　　你在找什麼？
brand new　全新 brand new model 即最新款式之意。

TIP 小博士

機場免稅店

　　世界各主要國際機場裡面，都會有「免稅店區」，duty-free 二字的招牌，很容易辨認，一般而言，免稅品主要是賣給外國旅客，外籍旅客在某免稅店購物必須出示護照、登機證等旅行文件才可以。除了在機場內的免稅店之外，像新加坡、香港等國家，地區也在市區設有免稅商店，讓旅客先在市區的免稅店先預付買免稅煙、酒的錢，再憑著收據（上面寫明了你買的煙酒品名、類別、數量之外，也加註旅客所欲搭的飛航班次號碼、日期、起飛、時間等）去機場的免稅煙酒店提貨。不過，上述市區內免稅店營業的另一個目的，是希望旅客購買免稅煙酒以外的各種商品，如珠寶、鐘錶、糖果、餅乾、衣物、鞋類、化妝品應有盡有，由於國人出國旅遊人口增加太快，為了肥水不落外人田，桃園機場這幾年來已開放了小部份的免稅煙酒店，讓從國外回臺灣的本國人在飛機抵達臺灣辦理入境手續之前，有最後機會可以買些免稅煙酒。

 本篇相關字詞

transit	過境	ticket-counter	機票櫃臺
transit card	過境卡	airline counter	航空公司櫃臺
transit lounge	過境室	passport	護照
transfer	轉機	carry-on bags	手提行李
connecting flight	轉機班次	luggage	託運行李
Gate No.	登機門	checked baggage	託運行李
re-board	再登機	baggage tags	行李牌
check-in	辦登機手續	seat number	座位號碼
recheck-in	再辦登機手續	basement	地下室
boarding pass	登機證	duty-free shops	免稅店
destination	目的地	escalator	電動扶梯
counter	櫃臺	elevator	電梯

第<u>三</u>篇 🎧

護照查驗

CHAPTER 3
PASSPORT CONTROL

P：Passenger
客：旅客
O：Officer
員：官員

排哪一列查護照？🎧
WHICH LINE TO GO?

P： Excuse me. I am from Taiwan.   客：你好，我是臺灣來的。

"　Which way shall I go for immigration?   "　我要去哪裡辦入境手續？

"　Do I go to "CITIZEN" or "NON-CITIZEN" area?   "　去「本國人」區還是「非本國人」區辦理？

O： For any citizens other than Americans,   員：美國人之外的任何人，

"　please go to "NON-CITIZEN" area.   "　都請去「非本國人」區辦理，

"　And once you are in the non-citizen area,   "　一旦您到了「非本國人」區後，

"　it makes no difference which line you go to.   "　就沒有所謂排哪一列的區分了。

"　You'll just follow the zig-zag line.   "　您只要跟著曲折線排隊即可。

P： What is the zig-zag line?   客：什麼叫做曲折線？

O： That actually is an extra long single line formed in zig-zag way.   員：那實際上是一種以鋸齒狀排列的超長單線排法。

"　When it comes to your turn,   "　當輪到您的時候，

" you can go to any available officer for passport check.

" 您就可以去讓有空的官員檢查您的護照。

" That is a very good way of lining up. It saves a lot space.

" 這是一種很好的排隊方式。並可省下很多空間。

P： Yes, it is.

客：是的。

" And it reminds me of the same way they do at Disneyland.

" 這使我想起了，在迪士尼樂園也是這種排隊法。

 關鍵字詞

citizen	市民；公民即「本國人」，而 non-citizen 為非公民，即「非本國人」之意。
zig zag line	鋸齒形排隊法，亦即曲線排法多用於大型遊樂場、車站、碼頭等可節省很多空間。

 TIP 小博士

如何辦理入境手續？

　　如果不是參加旅行團出國，相信很多人都滿擔心的是到了目的地，下了飛機要怎麼辦理進入他國的入境手續。

　　下飛機後，必須看懂 ARRIVAL（到達）、IMMIGRATION（移民關）CITIZEN/NON-CITIZEN（本國人／非本國人）、BAGGAGE CLAIM（領取行李）等幾個指示牌的意思，依序前進，茲詳細介紹如下：

1. ARRIVAL：這是下機後，旅客會看到的第一個大型指示牌，此牌尺寸很大，並附有箭頭指示，告訴入境（或到達）的旅客，只要循此牌箭頭指示行進，就會找到入境移民關護照查驗之處。

2. IMMIGRATION：移民關，護照查驗之處。（在歐洲國家則用 PASSPORT CONTROL 代替 IMMIGRATION 一字）此關負責檢查入境旅客是否持有有效護照簽證，確認過機位的機票等入境。

此移民關將所有入境旅客分成本國人（CITIZEN 或 RESIDENT）及非本國人（NON-CITIZEN 或 NON-RESIDENT）二區，分開檢查。

(1) CITIZEN 或 RESIDENT：CITIZEN 是公民，RESIDENT 是居民之意，不管那一個，都是指本國人之意。

(2) NON-CITIZEN 或 NON RESIDENT：二字皆指非本國人之意，如果你到了外國，你就是「非本國人」（有雙重國籍者例外）。

3. BAGGAGE CLAIM：這是下機後旅客要找的第三個大指示牌，是領取行李之意。護照查驗後，就可以去領行李。循著此指示牌箭頭方向，就可找到行李區。再查行李區內行李輸送轉盤上方之螢幕顯示器，顯示你的班機號碼是在第幾號行李轉盤，然後依指示去該號行李轉盤，找尋你的行李。

4. THE CUSTOMS：此為「海關」的意思，海關是負責檢查旅客有無攜帶違禁物品入境、或有沒有攜帶必須繳納關稅的物品？海關檢查臺也是分成好幾個。通常這些檢查臺位於行李區的旁邊，方便旅客在行李轉盤找到了行李後就近檢查。

5. EXIT：「出口」之意，下機後護照、簽證等經移民關查過了，行李找到且也經海關查過，甚至繳了稅了，這時你必須找 EXIT 指示牌，經 EXIT 出口離開海關區。離開海關區後，外面就會有很多人來接飛機，如果沒人接你，可搭計程車、機場巴士等前去旅館。

「移民關」和「海關」之區別

很多人不清楚「移民關」和「海關」兩關之區別，如上所述，移民關是負責查驗護照等文件；而海關則是負責查驗旅客攜帶品有無違禁品？需不需打稅等。

「本國人」和「非本國人」區

大部份國家的入境護照查驗，都開放成「本國人」和「非本國人」二區，美國的入境港埠（port of entry）之入境區就會很明顯看到 citizen（本國人，也就是指持用美國護照或居留證的人）和 non-citizen（非本國人，亦即沒用美國護照或居留證的人）兩個大招牌，臺灣去的觀光客，當然要在「非本國人」區去接受護照查驗。

查驗排隊方式

　　臺灣的入境查驗排列法，採用「一個窗口排一行」的作法，這種作法無法真正達到「先到先查」的公平性，萬一你碰到排你前面的某位旅客，因故被查的時間拖了很長，你也只有眼睜睜的看到比你後到，但排其他排的人，因同排各人檢查順利而比你先完成查驗手續。第二種排法，叫做曲線排法（美國式排法），是將排隊受查的旅客，用粗尼龍繩或其他欄杆等，將排隊者以曲線排法（或稱弓形排法）限制，只留最前面的一個唯一的出口，輪到出口的旅客，看到前面若干個查驗窗口，任何一個空出來，你就可前去受檢。此法真正做到排隊者「先到先服務」（first come, first serve）的公平性。

護照查驗
PASSPORT CHECK

P：Good morning, sir. Here is my passport, visa, and air-tickets.

客：你早先生，這是我的護照，簽證及機票。

O：Have you been in the USA before?

員：您以前來過美國嗎？

P：Yes, I've been here twice before.

客：有的，來過兩次。

O：When was your last visit to this country?

員：您上次是何時來的？

P：It was in October, 1992.

客：在 1992 年 10 月份來的。

O：Do you carry any meat, plants, or seeds with you?

員：您有帶肉類、植物、種子之類的東西嗎？

P：No, I don't.

客：沒有。

O：Have you ever been in any farm area in the last six months?

員：這六個月內您去過任何農場嗎？

P：No, sir.

客：沒去過。

O：What about cash?

員：那麼現金呢？

"　Do you have more than ten thousand dollars cash with you?

"　您身上有沒有帶超過一萬元的現鈔？

P：No. I have about two thousand only, and some traveler's cheques.

客：沒有，大概有二千元現鈔，其他還有一些旅行支票。

觀光旅遊實用英語

關鍵字詞 🎧

have you been to ....? 現在完成式的用法，是問人有沒有「去過」或「來過」某處的用法。

例：Have you been to Paris?

　　你去過巴黎嗎？

例：Have you been to Taipei?

　　你來過臺北嗎？

例：Have you been to Taipei zoo?

　　你去過臺北動物園嗎？

cash　現鈔

例：How much cash do you have?

　　你有多少現金？

兌換支票

例：I like to cash this 50-dollar check.

　　我要兌換這張 50 元面額的支票。

TIP 小博士

憑簽證入境

　　各國的入境護照查驗，是要看看入境外籍旅客有無持有有效簽證？（如果對某些國家，同意免持簽證，可憑護照入境者，那就另當別論）或者旅客的護照有效期有否六個月以上？或者旅客機票上已確認離開該國之離境日期是否仍在簽證有效期之內？上述答案如果是否定，就無法入境。

團體簽證

　　參加團體旅行，如果持有的是「團體簽證」的話，限制更嚴格「團簽」限制旅客必須同進同出，亦即團簽成員必須依團簽上規定的期限入境或出境，不然就有不能入境或出境的麻煩。所以建議想參加團體，但在某國有可能因探親或商務等欲多做停留的人，一定要申請「個人簽證」（費用較團簽貴一些）就可以在該國不必和其他團員同進同出。

落地簽證

有些國家，可以讓旅客入境後，才辦理入境簽證，這就叫做「落地簽證」，有些要繳交照片及費用，有些不必，僅填寫簡單表格就行。不論如何，還是建議各位讀者出國時，一定要帶許多二吋半身照片，有很多突發狀況時都會用到照片。

入境簽證之種類

一、簽證之種類頗多，茲分述如下：

1. 個人簽證 individual visa：依個人名義核發之簽證。

2. 團體簽證 group visa：依團體名義核發之簽證。

3. 商務簽證 business visa：依商務目的核發之簽證。

4. 觀光簽證 tourist visa：依觀光目的核發之簽證。

5. 公務簽證 official visa：依公務目的核發之簽證。

6. 學生簽證 student visa：依求學目的核發之簽證。

7. 移民簽證 immigrant visa：依移民目的核發之簽證。

8. 非移民簽證 non-immigrant visa：依非移民目的核發之簽證。

9. 落地簽證 arrival visa：入境時才辦理的短期簽證。

10. 過境免簽證 Transit Without Visa：簡稱 TWOV 意即只是經過，不必辦理入境簽證的意思。

二、對上述簽證，尤其是商務簽證和觀光簽證裡，又可依入境之次數分為單次入境和多次入境改為，解釋如下：

1. 單次入境 single journey 或稱 single entry：意指在簽證有效期間內只准入境某國一次，用過這一次之後，該簽證自動失效。

2. 多次入境 multiple journey 或稱 multiple entry：意指在簽證有效期間內，可以入境某國多次，直至簽證失效。

三、不管持有任何簽證，多數國家有共同的要求是：入境者在入境時，其護照有效期必須仍有六個月以上。才准予入境。舉例來說，某甲於某年三月一日入境某國，其護照截止日期必須是在同年九月一日以後，才准入境。

有簽證就一定可以入境嗎？

很多人以為持有某國簽證就一定可以進入某國，這個觀念是錯誤的，我們以美國為例來做說明：

旅客持有美國駐外使領館單位所核發的 visa（簽證），僅表示你可以去美國，但是，真正決定你可以不可以進入美國的，不是憑一個 visa 就可以，而是由美國各處入境港埠（port of entry）熔墨薨 x 員來決定。如果他們發現欲入境旅客說話不誠實，或其他足以讓他們覺得不應讓你入境時，他們是有權拒絕你入境，而以下一班有效班機（the next available flight）把旅客遣送出境。

攜帶現金的限制

很多國家對入出境旅客，所攜帶的現金額度，皆有一定的限制。如臺灣對現金的限制是，臺幣四萬元、美金八千元或等值外幣。美國對攜帶現金，必須申報的上限是一萬美元。而入出境澳洲的上限，是五千澳幣或等值外幣。如帶超過五千澳幣或等值外幣入出境，沒有申報而被查到的話，根據澳洲海關官員告知，有可能會被處以一萬澳幣（折合臺幣約十九萬元）以下之罰款，不可不注意。所以，最好事先問清楚，以免違反規定。

 自由行實務及緊急事件處理

入境護照查驗
Passport control

A：Excuse me. Can you tell me how I go to the "Passport Control" Counter?	請問一下，您可告訴我「護照查驗櫃台」怎麼走？
B：Yes, but it's quite a distance from here.	可以。不過走到那邊還有一段距離。

B：All you have to do is, follow the huge signs says "PASSPORT CONTROL". It'll take you there.

你只要依照那個寫著「護照查驗」大型指示牌的方向走，就會找到護照查驗台了。

A：Do I need to fill out any "Arrival Cards" or anything like that?

我要不要填寫入境卡之類的表格？

B：No, you don't. By the way, where are you from?

不必。順便請問一下，您是哪裡來的？（哪一國人之意）

A：Oh, I am from Taiwan.

我是台灣人。

B：To my knowledge, Taiwanese citizens don't need a visa to visit any Schengen Country.

據我所知，台灣人入境申根國家不用簽證。

A：What about the baggage? Where do I claim my bags?

那麼行李呢？我要去哪裡領取行李？

B：It's more or less the same, just follow the "Baggage Claim" signs.

做法差不多，還是要先遵循「行李申報」指示牌的方向走，

B：You can't miss it.

不會找不到。

來訪目的 🎧
PURPOSE OF VISIT

O：Sir, what's the purpose of your visit to the States?

P：I am here on business.

"　This is the name card of my business associates in Miami.

O：How long do you intend to stay in the USA?

P：About three weeks, I think.

O：If you do get any chance, do you intend to work here?

P：Absolutely "No",

"　because I have a good business of my own in Taiwan.

"　Things will be a lot easier back home.

"　And I don't want to start all over again here.

O：That is good. I like to hear that.

員：先生，您來美國的目的是什麼？

客：我來經商的。

"　這是我在邁亞密的客戶名片。

員：您會在美國停留多久？

客：大概三個禮拜吧！

員：如果您有機會的話，您會想在美國工作嗎？

客：絕對不會。

"　我在臺灣有自己的事業。

"　在自己的家鄉做事會比較方便。

"　而我也不會在你們這裡重新來過。

員：那好，我喜歡聽到您這麼說。

P：I plan to stay here for about two weeks if that is alright with you.

客：如果你允許的話我想在這裡停留二個禮拜。

O：I guess you could.

員：我想可以吧。

 關鍵字詞

business associates　指生意往來對象，合夥人等
intend to　想要；計畫要做某事。亦等於「plan to」之用法。 例：Do you intend to stay here long? 　　你要在此久留嗎？
back home　「在家鄉」之意，美式說法。 例：We work only 40 hours a week back home. 　　我們那邊每週只工作四十小時。

 TIP 小博士

入境所問問題

　　一般來說，很多國家的入境移民官員，對外籍旅客的詢問不外如以下各項：

1. 來訪目的？（purpose of visit?）
2. 要停留多久？（length of stay?）
3. 帶有違禁品嗎？（any fire-arms or narcotics?）
4. 帶多少現鈔？（how much in cash?）
5. 有無親戚朋友在該國？（any relatives?）
6. 有確認過的有效離境機票嗎？（a confirmed ticket leaving the country?）
7. 在該國要暫住那裡？（the local address?）

　　不管被問到什麼問題，最好的方法就是據實答覆，不要說謊。

暫住哪裡？🎧
WHERE TO STAY?

O：Mr. Lee. Where will you be staying at this time?

P：I will be staying at Miami Hilton for a few days.

"　I'll visit my son in Seattle after that.

"　This is the piece of paper with his phone number and address in it.

"　I will be staying with him for about a week,

"　and probably do some sightseeing there.

O：That is good. I'll let you stay for four weeks.

"　I think that should be sufficient.

P：Oh yes, that's plenty. Thank you.

O：Don't mention it. Enjoy your stay.

P：You bet!

員：李先生，您這次會住哪裡？

客：在邁亞密我會住在希爾頓飯店。

"　之後我會去西雅圖看我兒子。

"　這裡有他的電話號碼及地址。

"　我大概會住我兒子那裡一個禮拜，

"　也會在他們那裡四處觀光。

員：很好，我讓你在美國停留四禮拜好了。

"　時間應該夠了吧。

客：那足夠了，謝謝。

員：不客氣，祝你愉快。

客：你也是。

stay　指短期停留而言，出國旅行，每地所停留之兩、三天，甚至十
　　　天、八天，只要不是長期居住，都稱為 stay，長期居住則稱為
　　　live。

例：How long did you stay in Berlin?
　　你在柏林停留了多久？

 TIP 小博士

暫時停留之地址

　　在被入境移民官員問到你到該國要短期停留，你的「當地地址」是哪裡時，
你要講在國外當地所住旅館名稱或親友地址，而不是臺灣的地址。

 本篇相關字詞 🎧

citizens	公民	dis-embarkation card	入境卡
non-citizens	非公民	traveler's cheques	旅行支票
designated area	指定區域	signature	簽字
zigzag line	曲折線	counter sign	對簽
passport control	護照查驗	relatives	親戚
passport number	護照號碼	phone and address	電話及地址
issue date	發照日期	purpose of visit	來訪目的
expire date	有效截止日期	length of stay	停留期間
place of issue	發照地	on business purpose	經商目的
visa number	簽證號碼	on family reunion purpose	依親目的
air-tickets	飛機票	on visiting relatives purpose	探親目的
immigrant	移民	on convention purpose	開會目的

E/D card	出入境卡	on pleasure purpose	休閒目的
departure card	出境卡	on sightseeing purpose	觀光目的
embarkation card	出境卡	baggage claim	領取行李
arrival card	入境卡	souvenir	紀念品
landing card	入境卡	jade carving	玉雕刻

領取行李及海關

CHAPTER 4
BAGGAGE CLAIM & CUSTOMS AREA

P：Passenger

客：旅客

O：Officer

員：官員

在哪裡領行李？🎧
WHERE TO GET BAGGAGE?

P： Excuse me, I've just arrived on flight CI-065 from Taipei.

客：抱歉，我剛搭 CI-065 從臺北來的。

O： Yes, what can I do for you?

員：是，我可以為您效勞嗎？

P： Can you tell me where I go for my luggage?

客：請告訴我去哪裡拿行李？

O： Yes, you just follow the

員：好，您隨著取「領取行李」

" BAGGAGE CLAIM sign.

" 指示牌的方向走。

" You'll have to go down stairs first.

員：您需先下樓。

" You'll see luggage area with many carrousels.

" 接著您就會看到行李區有許多行李大轉盤。

" There is a flight display board above each carrousel,

" 每個大轉盤上面有一個航班顯示板，

" indicating all in-coming flight numbers,

" 顯示抵達班機的號碼，

" and I am sure you'll find CI-065 on one of those displaying boards.

" 其中某一個顯示板上會打出 CI-065 這班飛機。

" When you find it, just wait there for your luggage.

" 找到了之後，就在那裡等您的行李。

P：Thank you so much for your patient.

O：My pleasure, sir.

客：謝謝你這麼耐心地解釋。

員：這是我的榮幸，先生。

 關鍵字詞

baggage 大件行李，隨機託運行李之意，美式說法稱 luggage. 小一點的手提行李稱為 carry-on 或 hand-carry bag.
baggage claim 「領取行李」之意，在各機場下機旅客領取行李之處，皆有大型「baggage claim」（領取行李）招牌，指出行李區所在。
carrousel 馬戲團、遊樂場等之旋轉木馬，亦是機場行李轉盤之意。
schedule board 班次顯示板，是指機場內置於牆上，顯示飛機班次起飛或到達時刻、目的地、登機門等資料之大型顯示看板或螢光幕之意。
schedule monitor 是指與上述班次顯示看板有同樣功能，只是體積小，外表看起來，就像大型家用電視機模樣的東西，叫做班次顯示幕（schedule monitor）。

 TIP 小博士

何處領行李？

　　下了飛機，辦完入境之護照查驗，即進海關區領取行李，但是有些海關區很大，輸送行李之轉盤也很多，到底在哪裡找自己的行李呢？方法是，進入海關區之後，應首先找行李轉盤顯示器，（不管是大型或小型，可顯示某些班機號碼的行李從第幾號行李轉盤轉出來的顯像裝置），看看你的班機號碼是在第幾號行李轉盤，如果找到了你剛抵達的班機號碼，就表示你必須在該行李轉盤邊等你的行李轉出來。

行李遺失時

到達目的地，如果找不到自己的隨機託運行李的話，應馬上通知該航空公司地勤人員，填寫行李遺失表格，通常在三天內都會有回音的。在這三天內，航空公司會給遺失行李的旅客，每天若干美元的賠償金，以便購買簡單換洗衣物等。

 自由行實務及緊急事件處理 🎧

行李通關
Customs clearance

A：I came in with LH3611, can you tell me which baggage carrousel is for my flight?

我搭乘 LH-3611 航班剛剛下機，請問這個航班的行李轉台是哪一個？

B：Can you see a huge "Baggage Carrousel Directory" over there?

你有看到那邊的大型「行李轉盤指引」看板嗎？

B：You just go there, and I am sure you'll find your Flight No. listed with Carrousel No. on the directory board.

你只要過去查看那個指引看板，那上頭會有你的航班號碼、以及該航班的行李從哪一號轉台轉出來。

A：Do I have to claim any duty?

我要不要報關稅？

B：It depends on what you have.

那要看你帶的是什麼東西。

B：You can ask someone else about paying duty.

拿到行李後，再問其他人關於付稅的事。

A：Thank you. You've been so help-ful.

謝謝妳，妳幫了很多忙。

B：Don't mention it. Have a nice trip.

不用客氣。旅途愉快。

臺灣零食
TAIWAN GOODIES

O：How many pieces of the luggage do you have, sir?　　員：先生，您有幾件行李？

P：I've got a total of 3 pieces.　　客：總共三件。

O：Please open up your suitcases.　　員：請打開您的行李。

P：Certainly.　　客：好的。

O：What are these?　　員：這些是什麼？

P：These are dry eatingseeds.　　客：這是瓜子。

O：You eat the whole thing?　　員：整個都吃嗎？

P：No, we split it off, and only eat the tiny flesh inside.　　客：不，咬開後只吃裡面的小果肉。

"　This is Chinese tea. We call it Woo-long tea.　　"　這是中國茶，我們叫烏龍茶。

"　This is dry plum.　　"　這是話梅。

"　These are goodies from Taiwan.　　"　都是臺灣的零食。

O：What are those?　　員：那些是什麼？

P：This is dry turnip.　　客：這是蘿蔔乾。

"　It is hot and spicy.　　"　它味道辛辣。

觀光旅遊實用英語

〞　Normally we eat them with congee on breakfast.

〞　平常我們是將蘿蔔乾和稀飯配著吃當早餐。

〞　That is shredded cuttlefish for my daughter.

〞　那是魷魚絲，給我女兒的。

〞　She loves it very much.

〞　她很喜歡吃。

〞　How would you like to try some?

〞　你要吃吃看嗎？

S：No, thank you. It smells funny.

員：不，謝了，味道怪怪的。

關鍵字詞

eating seeds　可吃的植物種子，即我們國人愛吃的「瓜子」。
goodies　好吃的東西，亦即「零食」之意。
hot and spicy　食物「辛辣」之意。 一般的「熱」或「燙」英文稱為 hot，而食物剛煮好很燙，當然亦叫 hot，但如果是味道很辛辣，也許是放太多辣椒，英文則稱之為 hot and spicy。
shred　成細條狀之意，shredded pork 肉脯
shredded cuttlefish　魷魚絲。

TIP 小博士

吃零食

　　國人很多在出國時，有吃零食的習慣，所以常會帶一些像話梅、瓜子、餅乾、肉乾、魷魚絲，甚至於人參片、醬瓜等物品出國。特別是在約六、七小時的長程巴士（long distance coach）上，就有很多人會吃些零食，佛教界人士則會拿出一整包零食與全車團員、司機、導遊等共享，稱之為「結緣」。

入境食品限制

　　入境國家之不同，對零食限制也不同。如英國，規定只有未拆封的真空包裝零食才可以帶進去，而美國則規定不管是什麼零食，只要是肉類一律不准攜帶入境。澳洲則規定帶進去的零食一律先申報，再由海關人員核定可否帶入境，沒申報被查到的話，會被沒收，但不會被處罰款。

臺灣檳榔 🎧
TAIWAN BEETLE-NUTS

P： Excuse me. Can I bring in these nuts?

客：抱歉，我可以帶這些入境嗎？

O： What are they?

員：那些是什麼？

P： We call them beetle-nut.

客：我們把它叫做檳榔。

" A lot of people in Taiwan enjoy chewing them.

" 臺灣有很多人喜歡吃檳榔。

O： Are you sure it is okay for your health?

員：那對人體健康無害嗎？

P： I don't know about that, why?

客：不清楚，為什麼這樣問？

O： If it is okay for your health,

員：如果對身體健康無害，

" why are you spitting the blood out?

" 那您為什麼吐血呢？

P： No, it isn't the blood.

客：那不是血。

" It's the red paste that comes with the beetle nuts.

" 那是包檳榔的紅石膏。

O： I don't care what they are.

員：我不管那是什麼膏。

" I am going to take away these beetle nuts.

" 我要將這些檳榔沒收。

" You are not supposed to bring in any seeds or plants to begin with.

" 您本來就不應該帶任何種子植物入境的。

" Besides, it will be a terrible thing to pollute the city.

P：Whatever you say, you are the boss.

" 況且，它也會污染大小街道。

客：無論你說什麼，一切由你作主。

 關鍵字詞

beetle-nut	檳榔，beetles 是一種紅色小甲蟲，檳榔外形似小甲蟲，因而得名。
beetle-car	德國最有名之金龜車，亦是外形像 beetle 甲蟲而得名。
spit the blood out	把血吐出來，亦即「吐血」之意。
your are the boss	字面上「你是老闆」，亦即是「一切由你作主」之意。你如果同意某人之建議等，就可以對他說： 例：Whatever you say, you're the boss. 不論你說什麼，一切由你作主就是了。

 TIP 小博士

當街吐血嗎？

　　在臺灣，吃檳榔的人越來越多，也常見到有些開車或騎車的人，隨地吐掉檳榔紅汁，因顏色像血，所以被外籍人士誤會臺灣得肺病的人怎麼那麼多，都在當街吐血。

有應稅品嗎？🎧
ANY DUTIABLE ITEMS?

O：Sir, do you have anything to declare?

P：I don't know. It depends.

"　Do I have to pay duty on this radio?

O：Yon don't have to, if that is for your personal use.

P：What about this video cassette?

"　It's for my personal use.

O：In that case, no duties.

P：By the way, I got these two tins of Chinese tea for my friends in Amsterdam.

"　Do I have to pay duty on them?

O：No, you don't pay duty for inexpensive gift either.

P：That's good, so am I free to go now?

員：抱歉，您有什麼要申報的嗎？

客：不一定，要看情形。

"　這個收音機要打稅嗎？

員：如果是您的個人使用物品就不必打稅。

客：那這個錄影帶呢？

"　是我的個人用品。

員：如果那樣的話，免稅。

客：對了，我這兒帶了兩罐茶葉要來送阿姆斯特丹的朋友。

"　這兩罐茶要打稅嗎？

員：不必，低價位的小禮物也不打稅。

客：那好，我可以走了嗎？

O：Yes, please. Enjoy your trip!

P：Yes, I will. Thank you.

員：可以，祝旅程愉快！

客：好，謝謝。

 關鍵字詞 🎧

declare　宣稱；宣佈，在此指應稅物品的申報而言。
it depends　看情形再說 當別人問你 Can you do me a favor?（你可以幫我忙嗎？），但你並不知道他要你幫什麼樣的忙，所以你就可以對他說 It depends.（看情形再說），亦即讓他說出幫什麼樣的忙，再決定你幫不幫他。
in-expensive　價格便宜，亦可說成 less expensive. 或 cheap。但　　　　　　　cheap 亦有行為人格卑劣之意。 例：Can you show me a less expensive pair of shoes? 　　拿一雙便宜一點的鞋子給我看看好嗎？

 TIP 小博士

快速通關臺

　　有越來越多的國際機場，為加速通過，設有綠燈通關臺，（亦稱快速通關臺）僅提手提行李，或沒有應稅品的旅客，可以逕行綠燈通關臺，由於不打稅，所以可以快速通關。

何謂「存關」？

　　一般來說，歐洲國家對日本電器品打稅很重，假如一個旅客帶了超出「私人使用」數量以上的電器要進入境時，這些超出數量的東西非打重稅不可。這時，旅客可以選擇把多出的東西「存關」（in-bond），不要帶入境，等要出境時，要記得帶走，就不必被課重稅了。

　　所謂「存關」，就是在入境時將本來要打稅的物品暫時存放在海關，等到要出境時將該物品領出的意思。因為物品沒有帶入境，就不會發生打稅的情形。

觀光旅遊實用英語

機場外有人接我嗎？ 🎧
ANYONE MEETING ME OUT-SIDE?

P： I've made my hotel reservation at the Amsterdam Hilton.

" And I am just wondering if there is any hotel representative meeting me outside?

O： No, I doubt it.

" What makes you think they might come?

P： I guess you have the different systems here.

" Most of the leading hotels in Taipei

" would provide free pick up services for their arrival guests.

O： That sounds nice. What about the transfer-out services?

P： Transfer-out service is not free. You'll have to pay for it.

O： Did I get it right? They provide free transfer in services,

客：我已經訂好了阿姆斯特丹的希爾頓飯店。

" 不知道飯店代表會不會在外面接我。

員：應該不會。

" 您為什麼認為他們會來？

客：我想你們這裡的做法大概不同。

" 在臺北大部份一流飯店……

" 都提供在機場免費接機的服務。

員：那不錯，那麼送機服務呢？

客：從飯店送去機場的送機服務就不是免費了，你必須付錢。

員：我沒聽錯吧？接機是免費的，

" and make a charge on transfer out service? 　　" 而送機卻要付錢。

P：Yes, that's what they do. 　　客：是呀！他們是這樣做的。

O：That sounds pretty realistic to me. 　　員：聽起來很現實。

P：Yes, they are. 　　客：對，沒錯。

 關鍵字詞

wonder　奇怪；I wonder... 或 I am just wondering... 皆為「我在想某事或某人會不會⋯⋯？」 例：I am wondering if you can lend me ten dollars. 　　我在想你願不願意借我十塊錢？ 例：I wonder if he is telling the truth. 　　我在想他是不是在說實話？
pick up service　指「接人」之服務，一般指用車去載人的一種服務 　　　　　　　　　如派車去接，亦可稱為 transfer-in service（接機服 　　　　　　　　　務）。
transfer out　指旅館派車將住客送往機場搭機的服務。為 transfer-in 　　　　　　　service 之對。
free　自由；免除，有時間等意 free from 為「免除」之意。 例：Tom is free from paying the tax. 　　湯姆可以不必付稅。

 TIP 小博士

接機服務

　　越來越多的觀光旅館，為了加強對住客（hotelguest）的服務，提供專車去機場，接下機的旅客去住該旅館，這種去機場接人的服務，稱為 pick-up service 或 transfer-in service，一般而言，這種服務是免費的，旅客在做訂房手續時，可以要求提供接機服務。

送機服務

　　相反地，住客退房後如要去機場搭機，有些旅館也可安排派車送已退房住客去機場搭機，這種服務叫 transfer-out service（送機服務）。不過，送機服務可是要付費的。

機場銀行在哪裡？🎧
WHERE IS THE AIRPORT BANK?

P：Excuse me, sir. I am new here.

客：抱歉，先生，我是剛到的旅客。

"　Is there any place I can change some money?

"　附近有地方可以換錢嗎？

O：Yes, you'll find a "BANK" or a "MONEY EXCHANGE" sign down stairs.

員：有，樓下就有「銀行」或「換錢所」的招牌。

"　You can change your money there.

"　可以去那裡換錢。

P：What's the difference between the two you just mentioned?

客：你剛剛說的那兩者之間有何區別？

O：Generally speaking, you'll get the better rates at the regular banks.

員：大概來說，在銀行換的錢會多一些。

"　But the exchanges work longer hours and accept more foreign currencies.

"　換錢所的上班時間比銀行長，可接受的外幣也比銀行多。

P：So that's why they give a little lower rate.

客：所以他們兌換的錢就比銀行少一些。

O：Yes, sir. That's right.

員：是的，先生。

觀光旅遊實用英語

關鍵字詞

money change 或 money exchange 都是外幣兌換處之意，俗稱「換錢所」。

TIP 小博士

何處換錢最有利？

在國外，可以兌換旅行支票或將美金現鈔換成當地貨幣（指美國以外的國家、地區）的地方，除了銀行外，在懸掛有 money exchange（換錢）的錢幣交換處，亦即俗稱的「換錢所」或所住的旅館都可以換錢。對換錢的最有利的立場而言，給你匯率最好的是銀行，再來是換錢所，再來是旅館。

舉例來說，如果你到了法國，拿一塊錢美金向當地銀行換到了 0.96 Euro（法國法朗），那麼你在巴黎的換錢所 money exchange 可能只換到 0.92 Euro。匯兌給你最少錢的是旅館，可能只給你 Euro 0.84。

 本篇相關字詞

luggage carrousel	行李轉盤	pollute	污染
monitor	顯示器	declare	申報
flight number	班次號碼	duty	關稅
patient	有耐性	personal item	個人用品
push-cart	手推車	business sample	商用樣本
suitcase	行李箱	business invoice	商用發票
dry eating seeds	食用瓜子	present	禮物
goodies	零食	representative	代表
turnip	蘿蔔	bank	銀行
spicy	辛辣味	money exchange	錢幣兌換

congee	稀飯	exchange rate	兌換率
shred	細條狀	franc	法朗
cuttlefish	魷魚	transportation	運輸
squid	墨魚	taxi	計程車
octopus	章魚	cab	計程車
beetle nuts	檳榔	subway	地下鐵
spitting the blood	吐血	subway map	地下鐵線路圖
paste	膏狀物	customs declaration form	海關申報單

第⑤篇 🎧

搭計程車

CHAPTER 5
IN THE TAXI

P：Passenger
客：旅客
D：Taxi Driver
員：司機員

載你去哪裡？🎧
WHERE TO GO?

D：Good morning, sir. Welcome to Paris.　　員：您早，先生，歡迎到巴黎來。

P：Thank you. I am so glad you speak English.　　客：謝謝，你會說英語實在太好了。

"　Yes, but I don't speak much English.　　"　但我的英語講得不多。

"　That's okay, neither do I.　　"　沒關係，我也不大會講。

D：Where would you like to go, sir?　　員：先生，您要去哪裡？

P：I've made my reservations for the Paris Hilton.　　客：我已訂妥巴黎希爾頓的房間。

"　Can you take me there?　　"　可以帶我去那裡嗎？

D：Yes, sir. No problem.　　員：好的，先生，沒有問題。

P：How long does it take to go to the hotel from here?　　客：從這裡到飯店要多久？

D：It takes about 40 minutes to ride.　　員：大概要 40 分鐘的車程。

P：I see, that's quite a distance away, isn't it?　　客：明白了，那算滿遠的，對不對？

D：Yes, it is.　　員：是的。

車資怎麼算？🎧
HOW YOU CHARGE?

P： Excuse me. How do you charge the fares in Paris?

客：抱歉，巴黎的車資怎麼算？

D： It is calculated by the meter just like anywhere else in the world.

員：就像世界其他地方一樣是以跳錶計費。

" It costs you 6 Euro for the first kilometer.

" 啓程第一公里 6 歐元。

" And it will be 2 Euro more on every additional kilometer.

" 以後每一公里跳 2 歐元。

" As to the time base,

" 以計時來說，

" you will have to pay 2 Euro on every accumulated 5-minute stop.

" 每一累積五分鐘的停車要多付 2 歐元。

P： That is really expensive.

客：那太貴了。

D： I am not through yet, there is a 20 percent surcharge on night rides.

員：還有，夜間搭乘要加兩成。

P： What do you mean by night rides?

客：什麼意思是夜間搭乘？

D： That's the ride from 10:00 p.m. until 06:00 a.m. in the morning.

員：那是指從晚上十點至凌晨六點之間的搭車而言。

P： How many passengers do you take in a taxi?

客：一部計程車可以載幾個乘客？

D：Three, in the back seat only. 　員：三個，而只能坐後座。

P：What about the front seat? 　客：那前座呢？

D：The front seat is only for either light bags or pets, 　員：前座只放小型提袋或寵物，

" 　not for passengers. 　" 　不可以載人。

P：That's very thoughtful. 　客：設想倒很周到。

關鍵字詞

night ride　夜間搭乘之意
thoughtful　設想周到
例：Thank you. You are thoughtful. 　　謝謝，你設想很周到。

TIP 小博士

安全搭乘計程車

　　英美等先進國家，多年前即已實施計程車的「計程」並「計時」制度，且在尖峰時段或午夜時段，也有加成收費的做法。臺灣近年來也採同樣的做法，另外，甲、乙兩地之「去程」和「回程」車資並不是絕對一樣的，因為「計程」部份的距離雖然一樣，但「計時」部份，交通擁擠與否，產生的時間長短不同，所以才會發生，去程和回程計費不同。在國外搭計程車，有時候當然也會遇到，不誠實的計程車司機，向乘客多收車資，如故意繞遠路等，在此建議一個最安全的做法：在國外搭計程車，最好是請你所住旅館的服務人員（如櫃臺人員），用他們的當地文字，寫一張給計程司機看的字條，上面寫明你要去的目的，大約車資多少錢等。司機看到這張字條，知道這是當地人所寫的字條，就比較不敢亂加車資了。

搭車進城
Taking cabs to town

A：Good morning, sir. I've made my hotel reservation for Raddison Blu Hotel.

先生，早安。我已經預訂好今晚住 Raddison Blu 酒店。

A：Is there any city bus or Metro I can take?

這附近有沒有市公車或地鐵去酒店？

B：Yes. You are now at the Terminal A, but Metro station is at Terminal B.

有的。你目前是在 A 航站，但地鐵是在 B 航站。

B：First, you take the escalator to Basement 1 level.

首先，你搭電扶梯到地下一樓。

B：Turn to the right. You'll see a large sign written "Terminal B".

然後往右走，你會看到一個寫著「B 航廈」的大型指示牌。

B：Just follow the sign. It'll take you to the Metro Station.

只要依「B 航站」的方向走，就可以走到地鐵站。

A：What color of the Metro line will take me to Raddison Blu Hotel?

什麼顏色的地鐵線，有到 Raddison Blu 酒店？

B：I am not quite sure about that. You'd better check with the Metro staff when you get there.

我不太確定。到了車站你最好問問地鐵的員工。

A：By the way, is there any city buses available, to stop somewhere nearby the hotel?

除了地鐵外，有沒有公車可以到 Raddison Blu 酒店附近？

B：Yes, there's a bus line that stop at somewhere near the hotel.

有，有一條公車線在 Raddison Blu 附近有站牌。

B：For any further information, please ask the ticket counter at the bus station.

詳細情形你到了公車站再問售票櫃臺好了。

A：Appreciated for your useful information.

謝謝你提供這些有用資訊。

B：Don't worry about it. Enjoy your trip.

沒事，祝旅途愉快。

搭計程車刷卡付費開收據
Taxi fare by cards and receipt

A：Good morning. This is where I am going, to Raddison Blu. Can you take me there?

早安，這是我要去的地方，Raddison Blu 酒店，你可以載我去嗎？

B：Yes, sir. Let me put you bags in the trunk.

好的。我來把你的行李放入後行李箱吧。

A：Thank you. How long does it normally take to get there by taxi?

謝謝你。通常從這裡開到酒店需要多久？

B：Normally it takes about 40 minutes to go downtown from here. It all depends on the traffic of course.

到市內通常要 40 分鐘，當然要看當時的交通狀況而定。

A：Yes. And tell me how you charge the fare? You go by meter or by a fixed rate?

請問你車資怎麼算，是照錶收費還是固定車資收費？

B：Taxi fares are always charge by the meter, aren't they?

計程車都是照錶收費，不是嗎？

B：I've never heard such a thing "to charge by a fixed rate"?

我從沒聽說過用「固定車資收費」的。

A：You see, in some suburb towns in my country.

是這樣的，在我們國家的一些小鄉鎮。

A：Cab drivers would charge 100 NTD or more for a single ride.

計程車司機單趟車資會定額收取臺幣 100 元或更多。

B：What if I don't accept his offer?

如果我不接受呢？

A：Just get out the cab, and try another cab.

下車，再換另一部車。

B：That's interesting.

那真有意思。

自駕租車櫃臺
Car-rental counter

A：Hi, is there any Car Rental counter nearby?

請問這附近有自己駕駛的租車櫃臺嗎？

B：No, not in this building. You'll see one at the next building.

這棟大樓裡沒有，另外一棟大樓有一家。

A：Can you tell me how to get there?

可以告訴我該怎麼走過去嗎？

B：Yes. You go straight down for about 100 meters, then you'll see Avis Car Rental Counter there. You'll see it !

你往前直走大約 100 公尺，就會看到 Avis 租車櫃臺在那邊。

A：Hi, I have a Taiwan driver's license, but I don't have a German one. Can I rent a car?

嗨，我只有臺灣駕照沒有德國駕照，我可以租你們的車嗎？

B：Yes, please show me your driver's license. Can I make a copy of it?

請讓我看看你的駕照。我可以影印你的駕照嗎？

A：By all means. Tell me how this "rent a car" deal work.

那當然。請告訴我你們的租車費用怎麼算？

B：Yes, the daily rental is 25 Euro, and I'm afraid you'll have to pay 10 Euro to cover the insured amount of 50,000 Euro.

每日租金 25 歐元，另加保險額 5 萬歐元的保費 10 歐元。

A：Is there any mileage limit?

有沒有里程限制？

B：Yes, it is. It will be limit to 100 miles per day.

有的。每日不能超過 100 英里。

A：Do you require any mortgage fund?

你們會收押金嗎？

B：Yes, we do. It will be 200 Euro.

是的，會收 200 歐元當押金。

你是哪裡人？
WHERE ARE YOU FROM?

D：Where do you come from, sir?

P：I am Taiwanese from Taiwan.

"　　Do you know where Taiwan is?

D：No, I've never heard of Taiwan.

"　　Where is it?

P：Let me put it this way.

"　　Have you heard of "Formosa"?

D：Yes, I've heard of "Formosa".

P：Good, Taiwan is the modern name for Formosa.

"　　We haven't used the name "Formosa" for a long time.

D：No wonder you can hardly see the word "Formosa" these years.

P：You are absolutely right.

員：先生，您是哪裡人？

客：我是臺灣人，臺灣來的。

"　　你知道臺灣在哪裡嗎？

員：不，沒聽說過臺灣這個名字

"　　它在哪裡？

客：我這麼說好了。

"　　你聽說「福爾摩沙」嗎？

員：這我聽過。

客：好，臺灣就是福爾摩沙的現代名字。

"　　我們已經很久不用福爾摩沙這個名字了。

員：難怪這些年來已經很難看到福爾摩沙這個名字了。

客：說得很對。

本篇相關字詞

communicate	通訊、溝通	calculate	計算
taxi driver	計程車司機	additional	額外

sense of humor	幽默感	accumulated	累積
traffic	交通	pay a visit	拜訪
trunk	後行李箱	Formosa	福爾摩沙
franc	法朗	can hardly	難得
fare	費用	generous	慷慨
night rides	夜間搭乘		

 自由行實務及緊急事件處理

購買當地SIM卡
Buying SIM cards

A：Hi, can you tell me where I can buy a local SIM Card for my cell-phone?

你好。請問哪裡有賣本地的手機 Sim 卡？

B：There used to be a counter here selling phone card, but they are not here any more.

以前這裡有一家賣手機電話卡的店，不過已經搬走了。

A：What do you suggest I do?

您建議我應怎麼做？

B：You'll find the SIM Card at any convenience store, bus or train station.

在任何便利商店、公車站或火車站都有賣。

A：I guess I'll try my luck tomorrow.

那我明天就去找找看。

B：Good luck!

祝好運

A：Thank you. I need it.

謝謝，我需要好運。

B：Wait, there is one phone-card shop two blocks away from here.

等一下，兩條街外，有一家專賣手機 Sim 卡的店。

" Do you want to try? I'll write you the address of that shop.

要不要去試試看？我寫店家的地址給你。

A：Why not? I got nothing to lose to browse around.

為什麼不去，去逛逛無妨。

" What about the security in this city?

你們這裡治安好嗎？

B：It's okay I guess.

我想還好吧。

" No matter where you are, especially in a foreign city,

不管你人在哪裡，特別是在外國地方，

" be careful with your passport and handbag.

要小心你的護照和手提包。

" Don't ever shows a lot of money in public.

絕對不要公開秀出很多現金。
（財不露白）

背包遺忘計程車裡
Left my bag in the taxi

A：I am here to report for missing backpack.

我的背包遺失了，我來報案。

B：Yes. Can you show me your passport?

好的。我可看看你的護照嗎？

A：Here you are, sir.

B：Tell me how it happens.

A：My wife and I were sitting there by "Information" desk.
Suddenly I found my backpack was gone.

B：You mean you had left the backpack unattended?

A：I am afraid so. I was busy talking with my daughter at home.

B：Okay, please fill in this "Lost & Found" Form, and sign it right here.
What's the brand, color, size of your backpack?

A：It's "Addida" backpack, navy blue color, and it's a normal backpack size.

B：This is your receipt with our phone number below.
Why don't you call us back about this time tomorrow, we'll let you know.

在這裡。

說明一下怎麼弄丟的。

我太太和我兩人，就坐在服務台那邊。
忽然間我發現背包不見了。

你是說，你把背包放在一旁你看不到的地方？

是這樣，我當時忙著跟我在家裡的女兒講電話。

好吧，請填好這張失物報案表，並在這裡簽名。

你背包的品牌、顏色、及尺寸呢？

它是 Addida 牌背包，藍色，跟一般的背包大小差不多。

這是您的收據，底端有我們的聯絡電話。
請你明天這個時候打電話給我們，我們會告訴你查詢結果。

住飯店

CHAPTER 6
AT THE HOTEL

G：Hotel Guest

客：旅客

S：Hotel Staff

員：服務員

有訂房嗎？🎧
HAS MADE RESERVATION?

G：Excuse me. My name is Tom Lee.

"　We've made a reservation for a room with a bath.

"　My wife and I would like to have a double room

"　if that is available.

S：Just a second, sir.

"　Let me see if I can find your names in our check-in list.

"　Yes, here you are.

"　The reservation card says you are staying with us for three nights.

G：Yes, we are.

S：It also says here

"　your reservation has been made by Global Travel in Taipei.

G：Yes, that's correct.

客：抱歉，我是湯姆‧李。

"　我們已經訂好附有浴室的房間。

"　我太太和我要一個雙人房……

"　如果有的話。

員：稍等一下，先生。

"　我來看看名單上有沒有你們的名字。

"　有了，你們的名字在這裡。

"　訂房卡登記的是你們要住三晚。

客：對，沒錯。

員：另外這也寫著……

"　是臺北的全世通行社幫你們訂的房。

客：是，說得對。

S：You must have a hotel voucher for us?

員：您應該有訂房憑單給我們。

G：As a matter of fact, yes. This is the voucher for you.

客：確實有，這憑單給你。

S：How many pieces of luggage do you have?

員：您有幾件行李？

G：Three pieces, and two carry-ons.

客：三件，另有二件手提的。

關鍵字詞

---

have made a reservation

「已訂了某種訂位」之意不論訂房、訂餐、訂機位、訂車票等等，皆為 make a reservation。

例：Have you made the reservation for two tickets tomorrow?

你訂了明天的兩張票了嗎？

例：She has made the room reservation.

她已經訂了房間。

---

that's correct

「那很正確」之意，同意別人的說法，你可以回答 Yes, sir（或 Ma'am），That's right, that correct 等用法。

---

double-room

房內為一張供兩人睡大床的雙人房，如果房內有二張單人床的雙人房則稱為 twin room

---

hotel voucher

指已經訂了房的單據憑證。

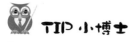

旅館客房的說法

　　SINGLE ROOM：單人房

　　TWIN ROOM：雙人房（房內有兩張單人床者）

　　DOUBLE ROOM：雙人房（房內有一張雙人床者）

　　TRIPLE ROOM：三人房（於雙人房內加一床，房內睡三人者）

以住房人數計費

　　由於大部份旅館的雙人房比單人房多出很多，在沒有客滿的情況下，有時旅館會讓單身旅客住空出的雙人房，雖然住的是雙人房，但是仍以單人房（稍便宜些）計費，叫做 single occupancy（單人使用計費），即使兩人住單人房的話，亦是以雙人房來計價，換句話說，是以住的人數多寡來計價，而不是以單人或雙人房來計價。

索取訂房憑證

　　向訂房單位（如國內的旅行社、航空公司等）訂妥國外的某旅館後，代訂單位在收了你預付的局部或全部的房間費用後，必須開立一張確認憑證（即 hotel voucher）給你，上面寫明旅館名稱、旅客名稱、房間種類、數量、住宿天數、預計抵達及離去日期、班機號碼、旅客已付清之全部房價或訂金等資料。你到達目的地時，即可憑此張旅館確認憑證，住進所訂旅館。

扣好門內小鍊

　　為了安全起見，當你住進旅館房間後，應立即將門內小鐵鏈扣上，有人敲門時不能隨便關門，應從門上小孔看清楚來人，確定沒問題才可以開門。

已無空房 🎧
ROOMS SOLD OUT

G：Good afternoon, we haven't made any reservation for the room,

"　but we would like to have a double room with bath.

S：I am sorry sir. All rooms are sold out.

"　We are fully booked for the next couple of days.

G：Why is that? This is only April.

"　It's not the peak season for traveling.

S：No, it isn't. But Lion's Convention is to be held in this city for 3 days.

"　They blocked nearly every available room in the city, including civilian houses.

G：That's tough. Can you take us in for just one night?

客：午安，我們沒有事先訂房，

"　但我們想要一間有浴室的客房。

員：抱歉先生，房間都租出去了。

"　明後天也都客滿。

客：為什麼會這樣？現在只是四月份。

"　又不是旅遊旺季。

員：雖不是旺季，但獅子會要在這裡開三天的年會。

"　他們都包了市內每一個可用的客房，甚至包括一些民房。

客：糟糕，設法讓我們擠一晚好嗎？

" 　My wife and I will take any room available.

S：Let me see. There is a single room I can probably squeeze out for one night.

G：Like I said, we take any thing.

　" 　任何房間我們都可以。

員：我看看，我也許可以擠出一個房間給你們住一晚。

客：就像我剛剛說的，只要有房間就好。

 關鍵字詞

sold out　貨品已賣完 在旅館而言，房間就是他們的商品，全部客滿就表示售完。 例：We sold out all the rooms this week. 　　我們已經把這個禮拜的房間賣完了。
fully booked　全被訂滿。 所有之訂位（訂席、訂房等）全被訂滿之意。 例：We are fully booked next week. 　　我們下週全被訂滿了。
meeting 會議，亦可說成 conference 或 convention 等，如 Lion's convention 獅子會議。
civilian houses　民房 此指在國際大型會開會期間，當地所有旅館房子仍不夠用，必須借用民間的客房。
that's tough 「那很糟」之意，tough 亦有粗魯、粗糙強壯等意。 例：He is a tough guy. 　　他是一個強壯的人。

take us in

接納我們，等於讓我們住進來之意。

squeeze out

擠出，如 squeeze out the milk.（把牛奶擠出）此指旅館人員經過進一步統計，而設法把僅有的空房挪出來之意。

懼高者住低樓
LOWER-FLOOR ROOMS

G：Excuse me. I like to have a room, but on the lower floors,

客：抱歉，請給我一個房間，但要低樓的，

" because I am afraid of height.

" 我有懼高症。

S：How many nights are you staying with us?

員：您要住幾晚？

G：For three nights, please.

客：要住三晚。

S：The last vacant room is on the third floor,

員：最後一個空房是在三樓，

" but it's noisier than higher floor rooms.

" 可是比其他高樓的房間吵一點。

G：I don't mind at all taking the noisy room

客：我不介意吵的房間……

" as long as I don't go to higher floors.

" 只要不必上高樓就好了。

S：Okay, please fill out this registration form.

員：好，請填住宿登記表。

G：Gee, thank you for everything.

客：哇，太謝謝啦！

S：Don't mention it. We are glad to have you here.

員：不客氣，我們也希望您能光臨。

G：By the way, is service charge and tax included in the room rates?

S：No. Service charge and tax will be extra.

G：In that case, what's the percentage rate on them?

S：Ten percent each.

客：還有，你們房價含服務費嗎？

員：沒有，服務費及稅金不在內。

客：那樣的話，要加多少？

員：各加百分之十。

 關鍵字詞

vacant room　空房，相反的已經有人住的，稱為 occupied room.
as long as　只要……   例：He will go as long as you ask.   　　只要你跟他說，他就會去。
register   登記：註冊 registration form 登記表格，亦即旅客住進旅館時，所填之登記表。
by the way　順便提出；順便說出。   例：By the way, are you going to Tom's party tomorrow?   　　順便問一下，你明天會去湯姆的派對嗎？

 TIP 小博士

預訂低樓客房   　　對某些較有懼高症的旅客，在訂房時可以事先聲明要住較低樓層的客房，旅館會盡量配合住客的要求。

免費飲料 🎧
FREE DRINKS

S： Sir, this is the key card with your name and room number on it.

員：先生，這是您的鑰匙卡，上面有您名字及房號。

" This card entitles you to a free drink at the bar.

" 憑此卡可去酒吧間要一份免費飲料。

" The free drink is the compliment of the hotel.

" 免費飲料是本飯店提供的。

" It means that the drink is on the house.

" 意思是本飯店請客。

G： I like this idea, thank you.

客：這主意我喜歡，謝謝。

S： Please hang on to your key card all the time,

員：請隨時保管好您的鑰匙卡，

" because you need this key card for exchanging the room key.

" 您需要出示這張鑰匙卡來拿房間鑰匙。

" That is to say, we only recognize key cards.

" 那是說，我們只認鑰匙卡。

" Anyone could ask for a room key as long as he has a key card.

" 任何人只要有鑰匙卡就可以來拿房間鑰匙。

" It would be terrible if you lose the key card.

" 如果您的鑰匙卡丟了就麻煩了。

" So please be very careful with it.

" 所以要小心保管。

G： Yes, I will.

客：好，我會的。

觀光旅遊實用英語

關鍵字詞 🎧

key card 鑰匙卡，此指辦理住宿手續後，旅館櫃臺人員所發給住客，以後可持卡向櫃臺人員拿所住房間鑰匙的卡片。
be entitled to 有權享有某事之意。 例：You are entitled to have one meal free. 　　你有權享用一頓免費的餐點。
compliment of 由……即「他人請客」之意。另一說法為 on the house. 亦即他人請客。 例：This trip is provided by the compliment of IBM. 　　這趟旅行是由 IBM 公司所招待的。 例：The dinner is on the house. 　　晚餐是他人招待的。
hang on 拿好、握住。 例：Hang on this book, don't drop it. 　　拿好這本書，不要掉在地上。

TIP 小博士

飲料招待卡 　　很多高級觀光旅館，在旅客辦完住宿手續後會贈送房客一張飲料招待卡，以表歡迎。房客可以持卡向該旅館酒吧要免費飲料，但僅限一杯，多出的仍須付費。

房內咖啡茶包收費嗎
Are coffee and tea free?

A：Hello Reception, I've noticed that there are some tea bags, and the coffee bags and biscuits on my desk, are they free?

櫃臺你好，我的房內桌上有茶包、咖啡包及餅乾，是免費的嗎？

B：Yes, they are free of charge.

是，那些是免費的。

A：What about the small bottle of wine, are they free as well?

還有一小瓶的酒，也是免費的？

B：No, the drinks are not free. They are 3 Euro a bottle.

不是，酒品不是免費的，每瓶 3 歐元。

A：By the way, do you have an iron and iron board in the room?

房間內有熨斗、燙衣板嗎？

B：Yes, you will find them in the closet.

有，這些東西放在衣櫃裡。

A：There are two small bottles of mineral water here, are they free?

櫃上還有兩小瓶礦泉水，是免費的嗎？

B：Yes, they are.

是的，是免費的。

The drinks in the small fridge?

小冰箱內飲料呢？

I'm afraid you'll have to pay all drinks in the fridge.

小冰箱內的所有飲料都需付費。

A：What about watching TV?

那麼，看電視要付費嗎？

B：All TV programs are free except "Pay TV Channel."

除了收費頻道外，看電視當然不用錢。

交回房鑰 🎧
TURN-IN THE KEY

S：Excuse me, Mr. Lee.

"　We appreciate if you can leave your key here every time you go out.

G：I think I will.

"　This key is much too heavy to carry in my pocket.

"　Why do you make such a heavy key handle?

S：Well, most hotels would purposely design heavy or clumsy key handles.

"　So it makes it very inconvenient to carry in the pockets.

G：So what?

S：The whole idea is

"　we want our guests to leave the keys at the front desk.

"　Whenever they leave the hotel,

員：抱歉，李先生。

"　您每次離開房間時把鑰匙放回櫃臺好嗎？

客：我會的。

"　這鑰匙放在褲袋裡太重了。

"　你們爲什麼把鑰匙柄做得那麼大？

員：大部份飯店都故意把鑰匙柄設計得又笨又重。

"　所以放在衣服口袋或手提皮內都會太笨重。

客：那會怎樣呢？

員：這種設計的主要用意是……

"　我們希望房客會把房鑰放回櫃臺。

"　當房客出去的時候，

<table>
<tr><td>"   we don't want the hotel guest to lose the keys outside the hotel.</td><td>"   我們不希望房客將鑰匙遺失在外。</td></tr>
</table>

 關鍵字詞

heavy and clumsy   又笨又重之意。
whole idea   整個想法，即「主要用意」之意。
front desk   旅館的接待櫃臺。

 TIP 小博士

客房鑰匙

大多旅館會故意將客房鑰匙之把手，設計得又大又笨重，很不好放進衣褲口袋或小皮包之內。主要的用意就是要房客每次暫離旅館時，不要把房鑰一齊帶出門，以免遺失。

客房物品可以購買

如果房客有收藏各地旅館房間鑰匙（或旅館其他物品，如浴巾，煙灰缸……等）的嗜好的話，可向旅館人員接洽購買，不可私下帶走，以免發生誤會。

鑰匙憑證卡

所謂 key card，正確中文說法應為鑰匙憑證卡，是旅館櫃臺人員幫房客辦完住宿手續後，發給房客的一張卡片，上面寫有房客姓名，預定住幾晚等資料，讓房客在住宿期間，持卡向櫃臺人員索取房間鑰匙的一種憑證卡。

磁卡鑰匙

另外有一種，叫 card key，中文稱為卡片式鑰匙，模樣類似一般信用卡，是用來開啟房門之用的磁卡鑰匙。

各樓的「服務櫃臺」

絕大多數的國際觀光旅館，是向接待櫃臺拿房間鑰匙的，但是在莫斯科等俄羅斯旅館，卻是由設於每一層樓的「服務櫃臺」SERVICE DESK 保管房間鑰匙；房客進、出都需向他們索取或繳回鑰匙。

再給一張房卡
One more room-card

A：Hello, I have some problems with this Card Key.

這張房卡有點問題。

A：It doesn't work properly. Sometimes it works, sometimes it doesn't.

它的功能失常，有時可以開房門，有時開不了。

A：Can I have a new room-card? I don't want to use the card I couldn't rely on.

是否可以給我一張新房卡？我不要用時好時壞的房卡。

B：Certainly I'll give you another one. But be sure not to put it together with your credit cards or phone cards, which might interfere with your card Key.

我給您換一張房卡。但要確定不能將房卡跟信用卡或電話卡放一起，這樣會干擾的。

A：Are you sure this one works properly? My room is located at the end of the hallway. It's quite a walking distance from the elevator.

你確定這張卡沒有問題了嗎？我的房間是走道的最後一間，出電梯後要走很遠的。

B：It should be okay now, but I can't guarantee anything.

應該沒有問題了，但我也不能保證。

A：Okay, we'll see.

好吧，再說囉。

B：Wish you good luck this time.

希望您這次好運。

A：Certainly hope so.

當然希望這樣。

B：In case this key doesn't work properly again, I can give you another
room instead.

如果這個新房卡還是不好用的
話，我就給你換個房間給你。

A：That sounds brilliant.

那就太好了。

房卡遺忘房內
I locked myself out

A：Hello, I am staying at room 629.
I've just lock myself out. I left the
room key in my room.

您好，我是住 629 房的房客，我
剛剛把自己鎖在房門外，房卡沒
帶出來。

B：What's your name, sir?

您的大名是……？

A：My name is C.K.Lee.

我是 C.K.Lee。

B：I can replace you another room
key, but I need your photo-ID just
to make sure your are the right person.

我可以給您另一張房卡，但我必
須看您的有照片身份證明文件，
以確定您是本人。

A：Here is my passport.

這是我的護照。

B：Thank you. And here is your new
card-key.

謝謝。這是您的新房卡。

A：Sorry for the trouble.

不好意思給您添麻煩。

B：That's nothing.

沒事。

A：Do I have to turn-in the room card
when I check out in the morning?

明天早上退房時，房卡要繳回嗎？

B：Yes, we must collect all the room cards for re-use purpose.
We can input new data, so a room-card can be used by the next guest.

要的。我們必須收回房卡、再用電腦輸入新資料給下一個房客使用。

A：Can I keep this card as a souvenir? Collecting hotel key is one of my hobbies.

我可以保有我的房卡當紀念品嗎？收集房卡是我的嗜好之一。

B：No. I don't think so.

抱歉不行。

A：Okay, where can I buy one instead.

那我可以買一張吧？

B：The Card Key is not for sale.

房卡是非賣品。

"　Alright! You can keep that one then, since you so persistent. But don't tell anyone I say "OK".

好了你那麼堅持，那一張就給你。不能說是我給的喔。

A：No. I won't.

不會，我不會講出去。

客房內保險箱操作
Using the safe in the room

A：Hello, Reception. I've noticed that there is a small safe in my room. But I don't know how to set up the combination lock. Can you send someone up to show me how it works?

櫃臺你好，我注意到我的房內有一個小型保險箱，但我不會設定號碼鎖，可以請人上來教我操作嗎？

B：Certainly. What's your room number, sir?

當然可以。您的房號幾號？

A：My room No. is 629.

我住 629 號房。

B：I'll sent someone up right away.

我馬上請人上去幫你。

B：Hi, I am Joe, from House-keeping.

我是維修部的 Joe。

A：Please come in. Can you show me how this combination lock works?

請進。你可以教我設定保險箱的號碼鎖嗎？

B：You'll just follow the instruction printed here.

你只要依照這邊的使用說明就可以了。

A：So the first step is, make it 000 to clear the previous combination.

第一步，把號碼鎖全部歸成三個 0。

B：Then set the number you want, take 333 for instance.

然後，轉到你想要的號碼，像是 333。

B：And close the safe, and to spin the combination lock.

然後把門關上，再將號碼鎖轉幾圈。

B：Now, why don't you try to set the combination to 333.
And see what happens?

現在，讓你動手把它轉到 333，看看有什麼反應？

A：It works. It's easy, isn't it?

可以了，很容易操作，對不對？

B：You can say that again.

你說得太對了。

客房沒有冷氣
On air-condition in the room

A：Hello, Reception. I am C.K.Lee of Room 629.

B：Yes, Mr. Lee. Can I help you?

A：Yes, you can. It's very hot in the room, don't you have any air-conditioning in the hotel room?

B：I am afraid we don't. It might help if you open the window.

A：No, I don't want to open the window to get the mosquitoes.

B：I can send some to bring a fan to your room if you want.

A：Why didn't you say so in the first place?

B：Do you need a fan or not?

A：Yes, of course. Is it free to use the fan?

B：Yes, it is free.

櫃臺你好，我是 629 房的 C.K. Lee 先生。

是，李先生，我可以為您服務嗎？

可以的。房間內很熱，你們酒店的客房沒有冷氣設備嗎？

抱歉，沒有。打開窗戶可能會好一點。

不，我不想打開窗戶讓蚊子跑進來。

你要的話，我可以請人送電風扇去你房間。

你一開始應該早點說？

電風扇你需要嗎？

當然要。使用電風扇是免費的嗎？

是免費的。

保管箱 🎧
SAFETY DEPOSIT

G：Excuse me. Where can I get a safety deposit box? 　客：抱歉，請問保管箱在哪裡租？

S：Yes. The cashier over there will help you. 　員：那邊的出納會幫您辦。

G：Hi, I am Mr. Lee at room 511. 　客：嗨！我是 511 房的李先生。

"　I would like to have a safety box. 　"　我要借用一個保管箱。

"　Do I pay for a safety box? 　"　借用保管箱要付錢嗎？

S：No, you don't. Just fill out this card 　員：不必，請將這卡填好，

"　and sign your name and room number on it. 　"　並簽好您的名字和房號。

G：Here you are. 　客：簽好了。

"　Can I have a larger envelope 　"　給我一個大一點的信封好嗎？

"　to put my valuable things in it? 　"　我要把貴重物品放入。

S：Yes, will this do? 　員：好，這個應該可以了。

G：Yes, it's perfect. 　客：可以，這剛好。

"　There, I am through with this. 　"　好了，通通放進去了。

S： Wait a second. Okay, this is your safety-box key, don't lose it.

" You'll have to pay 100 Euro if you lose the key.

G： I will be very careful.

員：請等一下，好了這是您的鑰匙，別弄丟了。

" 遺失鑰匙要賠償 100 歐元。

客：我會非常小心的。

 關鍵字詞

safety box 銀行或旅館所設之保管箱。

 TIP 小博士

旅館保管箱

　　所有旅館都有提供房客保管貴重財物的服務，樣子就像郵局的出租信箱一樣，是一種分成很多格的鐵櫃。旅館裡，使用保管箱是免費的，一般做法是每保管箱有兩個鑰匙孔，必須用兩把鑰匙去開，所以旅客把貴重物品放入鎖上保管箱後，由旅館和房客各保管一支鑰匙，以策安全。貴重物品如果是在房間遺失，旅館當局是不負賠償責任的。

早餐
BREAKFAST

G：Hi, what are your breakfast hours?

客：嗨！你們的早餐時間是什麼時候？

S：I think they serve breakfast from 6:30 to 10:00 a.m.

員：應該是上午六點至十點。

"　Hold on, let me check with the restaurant.

"　稍等一下，我問問餐廳。

G：Just tell me where the restaurant is.

客：你只要告訴我餐廳在哪裡。

"　I would like to find it out myself.

"　我想親自去問清楚。

S：Yes, go straight in, you'll see it.

員：好，往前直走您就會看到。

G：Thank you.

客：謝謝。

"　Good evening, I am the hotel guest.

"　你好，我是旅館房客。

"　Can you tell me how many kinds of breakfast do you serve?

"　可以告訴我你們的早餐有幾種嗎？

S：There are European, American, and Japanese breakfast available.

員：有歐式、美式及日式早餐。

G：What about their prices?

客：各種的價錢呢？

S：European breakfast is 6 Euro, American is 8 Euro and Japanese is 9 Euro.

員：歐式是 6 歐元、美式 8 歐元而日式 9 歐元。

G：Don't you serve any buffet on breakfast?

S：Yes, we do. But we serve them on Saturday and Sunday only.

客：你們的早餐，難道沒有自助式的嗎？

客：有，但只週六和週日才有。

 關鍵字詞

serve 「服務」之動詞用法。 通常是問對方有無賣吃或喝的東西。 例：Do you serve coffee here? 　　（你們這裡賣咖啡嗎？）
hotel guest 住宿旅館的客人。

 TIP 小博士

旅館早餐

　　很多國際級觀光旅館，都把他們的早餐，包括在「房價」裡面，也就是說，你住進後吃早餐不用再付錢，特別歐洲地區的旅館都是如此。另外，早餐也大致可分為美式早餐（American breakfast）和歐式早餐（European breakfast 或稱 Continental breakfast）。前者有肉有蛋等，後者則無，僅有法式麵包、果醬、牛奶等。近年來，也有越來越多旅館的歐式早餐也有少量的火腿及水煮蛋了，另外有些旅館，乾脆提供西餐自助餐式的早餐，什麼都有。這種早餐，最受歡迎。

有早午餐嗎？ 🎧
SERVING BRUNCH?

G：Hello, do you serve any brunch in this hotel?

客：哈囉！你們飯店提供早午餐嗎？

S：No, we don't.

員：沒有。

G：What is "BRUNCH" anyway?

客：到底什麼是早午餐？

S：Well, the word "BRUNCH" actually is the blended word for "breakfast" and "lunch".

員：「BRUNCH」這個字其實是早餐和午餐的合併字。

〃　It is the type of meal being served between breakfast hour and lunch hour.

〃　是一種在早餐時間和午餐時間之間所提供的餐食。

〃　Most likely, "BRUNCH" is being served for the convenience of the hotel guests.......

〃　最可能的情況是，早午餐是為了方便房客而提供的……

〃　Hotel guests stay up late at casinos, for example.

〃　比如說為晚上上賭場而晚睡的人。

〃　You can hardly find any hotel without casino serving brunch.

〃　不過沒有附設賭場的旅館就不太會提供早午餐。

〃　Only hotels in Las Vegas with casinos serving "BRUNCH".

〃　只有拉斯維加斯設有賭場的旅館才有早午餐。

G：What about the hotel in Monte Carlo?

客：那麼蒙地卡羅的旅館呢？

" Do they serve "BRUNCH"?

S： I have no idea about that.

" 他們有早午餐嗎？

員：那我就不太清楚了。

 關鍵字詞

brunch 早午兩餐併為一餐，此字是 breakfast 和 lunch 二字之混合字（blend word）。
most likely 「最可能……」。 例：He will be here most likely tomorrow. 他最可能明天會來。
stay up late 晚睡。 例：Don't stay up too late. 不要太晚睡覺。
casino 供應娛樂或賭博之場所，一般指賭場而言。

 TIP 小博士

早午餐

　　美國最有名賭場，當屬內華達州的拉斯維加斯（las vegas），於此大多數旅館皆附設有賭場（casino），旅館的重要收入，是靠附設賭場的收入，而非旅館住宿收入，所以旅館本身之吃、住費用都很低。因為，賭場是 24 小時開放的，他們更鼓勵房客最好不睡覺，通霄的賭。既然晚睡，當然晚起床，所以他們才想出一個提供早午餐（brunch）的點子，讓晚起的賭客，早午兩餐併成一餐吃，吃完趕快再賭。沒有附設賭場的旅館通常是不會提供早午餐的。

附近有賭場嗎？
ANY CASINO AROUND?

G：Is there any hotel with casino around?

客：請問附近有附設賭場的旅館嗎？

S：I doubt it. I've never heard one before.

員：應該沒有，從沒聽說過。

G：That's strange. I was told there is one nearby.

客：那奇怪了，別人告訴我這附近有一家。

S：Well, come to think of it,

員：噢，想起來了，

"　there used to be a casino in the hotel next block.

"　隔壁那條街，以前是有一家旅館附設有賭場……

"　But they closed down two years ago.

"　但兩年前他們就關門了。

G：Why is that?

客：為什麼關門？

S：Business were not good enough, I think!

員：我想是生意不好吧！

"　But I am not sure.

"　但我不能確定。

G：Well, whatever it is.

客：好吧，無論他什麼原因。

關鍵字詞

> I doubt it 「我想不會」之口語說法。
>
> doubt 指「懷疑」，為否定用法，對別人的說法、看法你不以為然，可用此句。

例：I think it'll rain tomorrow.

　　甲說：我想明天會下雨。

你不以為會如此，你可以說：

I doubt it = I doubt that it'll rain tomorrow.

（我想不會）等於「我想明天不會下雨」。

---

used to　　兩種不同用法，說明如下：

a> 當動詞片語用，後接動詞，表示「以前的習慣或動作」。

例：I used to come here everyday.

　　我以前每天來這裡，但現在不天天來。

b> 亦當形容詞片語用，後接名詞，表示已經習慣現在所做之事。

例：You must get used to your new job.

　　你必須要習慣你的工作。

例：I am already used to dangerous work.

　　我已經習慣於危險性工作。

旅館內有中式餐廳嗎？🎧
CHINESE RESTAURANT IN THE HOTEL?

G： Excuse me, sir. How many restaurants are there in this hotel?

客：抱歉，先生，這個旅館內有中式餐廳嗎？

S： There are three restaurants here.

員：本旅館內有三家餐廳。

" "Ming Garden" is the Chinese one, located on the second floor.

" 中國餐廳「明園」在二樓。

" "Old Pine" the Japanese one, located on the 11th floor.

" 日本餐廳「老松」在十一樓。

" And "Royal Palace" the steak house, is on the ground floor.

" 而牛排餐廳「皇宮」在地下樓。

G： I am interested in this Chinese restaurant.

客：我對這家中國餐廳滿感興趣。

" How is their food? Do you know?

" 他們的菜怎麼樣，你知道嗎？

S： Yes, I had been there a couple of times.

員：是，我去吃過幾次。

" They serve good food.

" 菜還不錯。

" But since you are Chinese yourself,

" 由於您是中國人，

" I am sure you know more than I do about your own food.

" 您一定比我更了解中國菜。

G：Yes, I agree with you on that part.

"　I am goint to try their food this evening.

客：是，你說得沒錯。

"　我今天晚餐就去那兒吃吃看。

關鍵字詞

the Chinese one　此「one」為不定代名詞，指餐廳而言，以避免前面已經提過 restaurant 一字之重複。	
a couple of　一些。 例：I want a couple of canned beer. 　我要買一些罐裝啤酒。	

第六篇　住飯店

樓層說法 🎧
SAYING FLOOR LEVELS

G：Excuse me, I am always confused with European way of saying floor levels.

客：抱歉，我對歐式各樓層的說法常常弄不清楚。

S：Do you find it difficult?

員：您認為那很難嗎？

G：I don't know, but I am confused sometimes.

客：我不知道，但有時候滿困擾的。

S：I see. I'll be glad to help you if you want me to.

員：您要的話我很願意幫您忙。

G：Yes. Let me ask you this first.

客：好的，讓我先這麼問你好了。

"　What floor are we on now?

"　我們現在在幾樓？

S：This front desk floor, we call it ground floor or lobby floor.

員：櫃臺的這層樓我們叫它地面樓或大廳樓。

"　But they call it the first floor in America.

"　但在美國則稱為一樓。

G：Yes, in Taiwan we go by American way, too.

客：是，在臺灣我們採美國說法。

S：Let's take our coffee shop for example.

員：讓我們以咖啡廳作例子。

觀光旅遊實用英語

＂　It is located on the first floor of this hotel.

＂　If you come down by the elevator,

＂　you depress the "1" button for the coffee shop.

＂　But if you walk up from the lobby floor,

＂　it is then on your so called the second floor.

＂　But it won't be so much confused on higher floors.

G：Why is that?

S：People would normally take elevator to go to any higher floors.

＂　They could just simply depress the desired floor-button.

＂　Who cares what that floor really is!

G：Yes, I guess you are right.

＂　它位於本旅館的一樓。

＂　如果您搭電梯下來，

＂　您按 1 號鈕才能到咖啡廳。

＂　假如您是從地面樓走上去的話。

＂　它就變成在你們所謂的二樓。

＂　但是高一點的樓層就不會有這樣的困擾。

客：為什麼？

員：人們到高樓大都會搭電梯。

＂　只要按所需的樓層鍵。

＂　不會有人在意是哪一層樓！

客：我想你說得對。

 關鍵字詞

be confused　混淆不清的。

例：I am confused with your report.
　　我被你的報告弄糊塗了。

go by　根據；依照。

例：We go by metric system in Taiwan.

　　在臺灣我們採用公制十進位作法。

in order to　為了要……

例：He studies hard in order to pass the exam.

　　他用功是為了要通過考試。

 TIP 小博士

歐式樓層說法

　　歐洲人對樓層的說法少我們一樓，換句話說，我們稱一樓的，他們叫地面樓；我們稱二樓的，他們叫一樓；我們稱三樓的，他們叫二樓；……。舉例來說，歐洲某旅館的咖啡廳（coffee shop）位於櫃臺上面那一樓（我們稱二樓，他們叫一樓），你如果要搭電梯上去的話，要按的數目字是一號鈕而不是二號鈕。順便一提，如果要從樓上，下電梯到櫃臺那一樓，則要按 G 鈕（ground floor）或 L 鈕（lobby floor）不過，當你拿到的房號如是 366，即為他們的三樓，按 3 號鈕，如是 566 即為他們的五樓，電梯內按 5 號鈕，以此類推。

要求住同樓客房

　　對有些三、四人以上家族，如果參加旅行團出國的話，也可以要求旅行社轉要求國外旅館讓你們家族成員住相鄰近的房間，至少要求在同一層樓。否則，國外旅館對團體旅客房間之安排，多數也是根據姓氏英字母順序，難免會有將家族成員分配不同樓層。不過有很多旅行社的領隊，都會自行重新安排團員的房間。上面問題可找隨團領隊解決。

客房 / 市内通話
ROOM/CITY CALLS

G： Excuse me. How do I dial for room to room?

S： Yes, there are two ways of making room to room calls.

〃 If you want to call a 3-digit room number,

〃 dail "8" first, and then the 3-digit number.

〃 For any of 4-digit room number you wish to call,

〃 you just simply dial the 4-digit number.

G： Do I do the same thing on the local calls?

S： No. You dial "0" for the city line first,

〃 then dial the local number.

〃 That's not difficult, is it?

G： No, not at all.

客：請問客房之間電話怎麼打？

員：是，客房間的電話有兩種打法。

〃 如果您要打給三碼房號的客房，

〃 先撥「8」，再撥該客房房號。

〃 如果要打給任何四碼房號的客房，

〃 你只要照撥該四碼號碼就好了。

客：打市內電話也這樣撥嗎？

員：不，打市區電話要先撥「0」，

〃 再撥當地電話號碼。

〃 並不難，是不是？

客：一點也不難。

關鍵字詞

dial　電話撥號。 例：How do I dial city calls? 　　市內電話怎麼撥號？
3-digit　三碼；市內電話如果是七碼，則叫 7-digit number。 例：Is your office phone number 6-digit or 7-digit? 　　你們辦公室電話是六碼還是七碼？
local call　本地電話，即當地電話，亦可稱為 city call（市內電話）。

 TIP 小博士

客房通話 　　各地觀光旅館，幾乎都是讓房客可在房內直撥「客房通話」、「市內通話」、「越洋電話」等，省去人工轉接，但各地區區域代碼不同，且各旅館內線客房通話之方式也不盡相同。所以，最好的作法是住進旅館後，請問工作人員正確的撥號方法。

越洋電話 🎧
OVERSEAS CALLS

G：Excuse me, operator, I would like to make an overseas call in my room.

" Can I dial directly?

S：Yes, you can dial the overseas number directly in your room.

" You simply dial "0" for available tone first,

" and then dial "01" for overseas line.

" Then you dial the country code.

" Then followed by the city code.

" Skipping the first "0" if there is one in the city code,

" then dial the local number to end up dialing.

G：It sounds complicate. Can you give me an example of it?

S：Yes, say if I want to make a call from your room to Taiwan.

客：接線生，我想在房內打越洋電話。

" 我房內電話可以直撥嗎？

員：可以，您可在房間裡直撥。

" 您只要先撥「0」聽到外線已通的聲音，

" 再撥「01」接越洋電話線。

" 再撥對方的國碼。

" 再撥當地的都市代碼。

" 都市代碼如前面有「0」的話，這個「0」不要撥。

" 最後撥您要的當地號碼。

客：聽起來滿複雜的，你能舉例說明嗎？

員：好，假設我要在你房內打電話回臺灣。

" I'll dial "0" to get outside line first.	" 我會先撥「0」接外線。
" Then I'll dial "01" for the international lines.	" 再撥「01」接國際線路。
" Then I'll dial "886" the country code for Taiwan.	" 再撥臺灣的國碼「886」。
" Then I'll dial "2" instead of "02" the city code for Taipei.	" 再撥臺北的市碼「2」，不是「02」。
" Then I'll dial "555-6789" the local number I want in Taipei.	" 再撥我要的臺北號碼 555-6789。
" So the whole dialing sequence is 001-886-2-567-6789.	" 所以整個撥號順序是 001-886-2-567-6789。
G : Please tell me why you dial only "2" instead of "02" the city code for Taipei?	客：請告訴我爲什麼臺北的市碼只撥「2」而不是「02」。
S : Yes, any city codes starting with "0" is only good for domestic dialing.	員：好，任何市碼如以「0」開頭，只適用於國內的長途電話。
" You just don't dial that "0" on overseas calls.	" 不適用於國際的越洋電話。

 關鍵字詞

---

overseas call　越洋電話，亦可稱之爲 international call（國際電話）
　　　　　　　或 long distance call（長途電話）。
國內長途電話叫做 domestic long distance call。

國外長途電話叫做 overseas long distance call。

available tone　指電話可以使用、可隨時撥號之有效「嗡……」聲。
反之如果有人在你的線上佔線，或你的線路故障，則會出現「嘟‧嘟‧嘟」聲。

country code　撥號之國家代碼。
從國外打電話回臺灣，臺灣的國碼是 886，如從臺灣打出去，首先所須撥的
「002」，不叫國碼，那只是打出去國際線路的「進入碼」（access code）。

dialing sequence　撥號順序。

其他通話

OTHER TYPES OF CALLS

G： Excuse me, are there any other types of calls?

客：抱歉，有其他種類的通話嗎？

S： Yes, you can place either "person to person" calls or "station to station" calls,

員：有，您還可以打「叫人電話」或「叫號電話」，

" but they cost you more than dialing directly.

" 但費用比直撥貴。

G： I see. What is a collect call?

客：我明白了，什麼是對方付費通話？

S： That is the type of call for the receiving party to pay the phone bill.

員：那是一種由受話人付費的通話。

G： That means I don't have to pay any money?

客：意思是我就不必付任何一毛錢？

S： No, you don't have to pay the phone bill.

員：你是不必付電話費。

" But I am afraid you'll have to pay 5 francs for the sur-charge.

" 但您需付5法朗的附加費用。

G： What is the sur-charge?

客：什麼是附加費用？

S： That is something like service charge.

員：意思和服務費差不多。

G： That's alright. I don't mind paying the small money.

客：那沒關係，我付小錢沒問題。

關鍵字詞

person to person call　叫人電話。
station to station call　叫號電話。
collect call　對方付費電話。
surcharge　附加費用；即服務費之意。

TIP 小博士

國際通話種類

　　國人出國，常會打電話回臺灣，茲介紹通話種類及方式如下：

1. 人工轉接：

　⑴ 叫人電話（person to person call）：經由所住旅館話務員之人工轉接，費用最高。但如果沒找到你要通話的對象時，就不必繳交任何電話費（但有些旅館會向你收取小額的所謂「服務費」）

　⑵ 叫號電話（station to station call）：亦是經由人工轉接，只幫你接通你要的號碼，不負責找你要通話的特定的人，費用較低些。

　⑶ 對方付費電話（collect call）：由話務員轉接你要的號碼，經徵求對方同意支付此次通話費用後，才讓雙方通話。

2. 直接撥號（direct dialing）：

　⑴ 使用所住客房內之話機，直接撥號通話，但需先查明撥號代號順序，省時省力，但費用稍高。

　⑵ 使用公共電話話機撥號，需準備足夠硬幣。費用最低便宜。

國際通話不撥「0」

　　都市代碼很多在前面都有個「0」，如臺北是「02」，高雄是「07」，這種有「0」的代碼是設計來給「國內長途電話」所用，不是給國際長途電話所用。所以在國外直撥長途電話回臺北時，是 886 國碼之後撥「2」（不能撥 02）再接當地號碼，如 555-6666 等。

使用公共電話 🎧
USING THE PUBLIC PHONE

G：Excuse me, I've been told

   " that it costs less to call home through the public phone outside the hotel.

S：Yes, it is. But it takes up a lot of coins,

   " and the charge is not that much different on short conversation.

   " For the time and comfort,

   " I would rather call home from my room if I were you.

   " So I could lie down while talking.

   " I could wear something very casually, even a pajama.

   " I could do almost anything I want while talking in my room.

   " But I just can't do that while using the public phone, can't I?

客：抱歉，有人告訴我。

   " 用旅館外公共電話打長途電話會便宜一些。

員：沒錯，但要用很多銅板。

   " 如果通話時間不長時，兩者費用相差不是很大。

   " 如以時間和舒適來考慮。

   " 如我是您的話，我寧願在房間打。

   " 所以通話時我甚至可以躺著。

   " 也可以穿得很隨便，穿睡衣也可以。

   " 在房間內打，要怎麼做都可以。

   " 但使用公共電話通話時，就不能這麼自由，對不對？

G：I guess you are right.

"　Thank you for your thoroughful explanation.

S：Don't mention it. The pleasure is mine.

客：你說得沒錯。

"　謝謝你的詳細解釋。

員：不用客氣。

 關鍵字詞

take up　佔用；用到。
casually　很隨意的；不正式的。

兌換旅行支票 🎧
CASHING CHEQUES

G：Good morning, sir. Where can I cash traveler's cheques?

客：你早，先生我要在哪裡兌換支票？

S：The cashier counter could cash them for you.

員：出納櫃臺可以幫您兌換。

G：Yes, thank you.

客：好，謝謝你。

"　Can I cash the cheques here, miss?

"　小姐，妳這裡可以兌換支票嗎？

S：Certainly, how much do you want to cash?

員：可以，您要換多少？

G：I would like to cash two hundred dollars worth of traveler's cheques.

客：我要換 200 元的旅行支票。

S：Yes. How do you want them in euro?

員：好，您要怎麼換？

G：I would like five in hundreds, and the rest in smaller bills.

客：我要 100 元的五張，其他的小鈔好了。

S：May I see your passport?

員：您的護照我看看好嗎？

G：Yes. Here it is.

客：好，護照在這裡。

S：Thank you, sir.

員：謝謝你，先生。

觀光旅遊實用英語

旅行支票沒簽名
NO SIGNATURE ON CHEQUES

S：Excuse me, sir. Are these cheques yours?

員：這些是您的支票嗎？

G：Yes, they are. Why?

客：是的，爲什麼這樣問？

S：There is no signature on the cheques.

員：支票上都沒有簽字。

"　How can you prove these are your cheques?

"　您怎麼證明這些是您的支票？

G：I sure can, because I have a bank receipt.

客：可以，我有銀行開的收據。

S：Show it to me, please.

員：請給我看看。

G：This is it. It indicates the cheques I bought in different amount.

客：就是這張，上面寫明我所買的不同面額的支票。

S：Yes, I guess these are your cheques alright,

員：這些應該是您的支票沒錯，

"　but why didn't you sign them?

"　但您爲什麼沒在上面簽名？

"　You are supposed to sign your name on your cheques when you buy them at the bank,

"　當您向銀行買支票時，您應該在上面簽名，

" and counter-sign them upon the presence of the cashier who accepts the cheques.

G：I didn't know that. No one told me to sign my cheques at the bank.

S：That's odd.

" 而在用支票付款時，必須在受款人面前，在支票上再簽第二次。

客：我當時並不知道，銀行的人也並沒有告訴我要這麼做。

員：那很奇怪！

 關鍵字詞 🎧

cheque　支票。美式用法是「check」。
旅行支票（traveller's cheque）
私人支票（personal cheque）
counter-sign　副署簽名；或稱「對簽」，亦即旅行支票上的第二次簽名，以示與第一次簽名相符。
that's odd　「那就奇怪了」之意。美式用法。

 TIP 小博士

旅行支票簽名

　　國內某些銀行賣旅行支票給客戶時，並不要求支票持有人，當場簽下第一次簽字。所以持有人的支票是空白的。這是非常危險的作法，因為旅行支票可當現金使用，萬一遺失被他人檢去，隨便簽下他人的名字，就可使用，較會有被他人冒用的可能。再者，銀行如果發現，你的旅行支票是完全空白，沒有簽第一次簽字的情況下遺失的話，他們可以不負賠償責任。

不兌他人支票

CAN'T CASH OTHER'S CHEQUES

G：Good morning. Do you cash cheques?

客：早安，你兌換支票嗎？

Yes, except personal cheques.

員：有的，但不包括私人支票。

G：Here are some traveler's cheques I want to cash.

客：我要兌換這些旅行支票。

S：I am sorry, Mr. Lee. But some of these traveler's cheques are not yours.

員：抱歉，李先生，但這裡有幾張不是您的支票。

G：No. Those are my wife's cheques.

客：不是，那些是我太太的旅行支票。

"　Those are the cheques left from her last trip to New York.

"　那些支票是她上次去紐約用剩的。

S：I am sorry, but I can't accept her cheques.

員：抱歉，她的支票我不能收。

"　It's against the rules.

"　這樣是不符規定的。

G：But I am her husband.

客：但是我是她的丈夫呀！

"　In fact, it was my money to pay for her cheques.

"　事實上，她買支票的錢還不是我給她的。

S：I am sorry, but the rule is rule.

員：抱歉，規定就是規定。

" It's not our concern whose money she bought the cheques with.

" Any person who wishes to cash traveler's cheques must be the person who owns the cheques.

" Legally she is the owner of these cheques, not you.

G : That's all right. Give me back those cheques.

" What about this personal cheque? It is under my name.

S : We don't cash any personal cheques.

" The only way for you to cash this cheque is........CHECK

" to deposit the cheque with a local banking account,

" may be through your local friend banking account for instance.

" And when the cheque is verified and the money is transfered to his account,

" they will notify your friend.

" And you can get the money from him then.

" 我們不管她買支票的錢是誰給的。

" 任何人要兌換支票,只能兌屬於他自己的支票。

" 依法而言,她才是這支票的所有人,不是你。

客:沒關係,把支票還給我就好。

" 那這張私人支票呢?上面是我的名字。

員:我們不兌現私人支票。

" 要兌這種支票的唯一方法是……

" 存入本地的某銀行帳戶裡,

" 比如說你本地的朋友的帳戶裡。

" 當這張支票被認可了,錢也轉入你朋友的帳戶裡時,

" 他們會通知您的朋友。

" 您就可委託他把錢領出來給您。

against the rules　違反規定。
owner　所有權人。
personal cheques　私人支票。
deposit　此指將款存入銀行。
for instance　舉例來說。
be verified　被證實無誤。

 TIP 小博士

旅行支票使用須知

　　國人對旅行支票購買，使用等情況並不是很了解，所以常有在國外不能兌現支票的麻煩。茲介紹如下：

1. 出國前向國內銀行單位購得旅行支票時，需當場在銀行櫃臺把購得之所有支票，簽完第一次簽名（一般叫做上聯簽字）。

2. 清點手上旅行支票的序號，是否和銀行給你的收據上序號相符合？符合後，應將支票和收據分開存放，不應該放一起，以免遺失時一起遺失。

3. 在國外旅行時，一定要養成將每次用掉的旅行支票序號記下。萬一支票遺失欲向銀行掛失時，才知道已用的幾張，未用的幾張。

4. 在國外使用旅行支票時，需出示護照，並當著銀行或商店、旅館等出納人員面前，簽下第二次簽名，叫對簽（counter sign），以示符合第一次簽名。

5. 旅行支票如同現金，需妥存保存，萬一遺失，可就近向所屬銀行申請補發。補發手續在本書第八篇第六單元有詳細介紹。

6. 不能使用他人支票，包括夫妻、父母、子女的旅行支票在內，即使你太太的購買旅行支票的錢是你出的，你也不能兌換寫她名字的旅行支票。

7. 近年國人使用信用卡的情形越來越普遍，可能比較少人使用旅行支票，但相關常識不可不知。

以什麼匯率算？🎧
WHAT RATES YOU GO BY?

G：Excuse me. What's the exchange rates you go by today?

客：抱歉，你今天以什麼匯率算？

S：We go by 0.88 Euro to 1.00 USD dollar.

員：我們以 0.88 歐元兌一美元算。

G：How come hotels only go by lower rates?

客：為什麼旅館都給較差的匯率算？

S：The banks here go by flexible rates.......0.88

員：我們這邊採用的是浮動匯率……0.88

"　and we have to protect ourselves

"　而我們旅館必須保護我們自己……

"　while exchanging money for the hotel guests.

"　當我們在換錢給房客時。

G：I don't get it, can you give me an example?

客：我不明白，可以舉例說明嗎？

S：Sure. Take today's selling rate at the bank 0.88 Euro to a dollar for example.

員：可以，以今天銀行賣出匯率 0.88 一美元為例，

"　If I go by the bank rate

"　假使我們也依銀行匯率算。

"　and I pay you 0.88 Euro for your "one dollar" this morning,

"　而如果今早您以一美元來換，我兌給您 0.88 歐元，

〃 so I go to the bank in the afternoon.

〃 Try to sell your "one dollar" to them.

〃 But to stand in their position,

〃 they are buying "one dollar" from me,

〃 and the buying rate is always less than the selling rate at the bank.

〃 So the bank will buy this "one dollar" from me at their buying rate 0.68 to a US dollar.

〃 That is to say, if I go by the bank rate at the hotel,

〃 I will lose twenty cents on each dollar I buy from our hotel guest.

G：I think I understand now.

〃 So the hotels would offer only lower rates

〃 in order to avoid your losses on exchange rates.

S：That's right. But we provide "convenience".

〃 而下午我去銀行。

〃 準備把您兌的那一美元賣給銀行。

〃 但以銀行的立場而言，

〃 他們是向我「買入」我的一美元，

〃 而銀行的「買入」價一定比「售出」價要低。

〃 所以這時銀行會以他們的買入價 0.68 Euro 比一美元來買我的一塊錢美金。

〃 那就是說，如果我的酒店以銀行匯率來算給房客，

〃 那我每向房客收一美元，酒店就虧 2 角。

客：哦！我明白了。

〃 所以旅館只有給房客較少的兌換率……

〃 才能減少匯率上的損失。

員：沒錯。但我們提供了「方便」。

G：Yes, there is no doubt about that. 客：這是不用懷疑的。

" I appreciate for this good example. " 謝謝你這個好例子。

S：You are welcome. 員：不客氣，我願意這麼做。

 關鍵字詞

exchange rate　外幣兌換率。	
flexible rate　機動匯率。	
I don't get it　我不明白。	
selling rate　售出匯率。	
buying rate　買入匯率。	

 TIP 小博士

匯率差別

　　我們在第四篇第六單元，曾介紹過在國外換錢，依匯率的高低分為銀行（bank）、匯兌處（money exchange office）及酒店、百貨公司等。在酒店換最方便，但換到的錢最少。銀行則太遠不方便，雖換到多一些錢，但扣除車資、時間等，也就變成差不了太多。

銀行匯差

　　各銀行貨幣的買賣，都有向客人「買進」和「賣出」給客人的買進匯率（buying rate），和賣出匯率（selling rate）。請記住，銀行的賣出匯率一定要比買進匯率高一些，這樣銀行才有匯率上的價差可賺。

兌換當地貨幣
Currency exchange

A：Excuse me. Is there any bank somewhere around here?

請問，這附近有銀行嗎？

B：Yes, there is one down stairs. Take the escalator down. You'll see the bank to your right.

樓下有一家，你搭電扶梯下去，在你的右手邊就是。

A：Good morning. I'd like to cash some traveler's checks.

早安，我要兌換幾張旅行支票。

B：Yes, please counter-sign it here. And your passport, please. How do you want them?

好的，請副簽在這裡。還要您的護照。您要哪些面額與張數？

A：I want 2 in hundred notes, 4 in fifty, 10 in twenty and the rest in five.

我要兩張百元鈔、四張五十元鈔、十張 20 元鈔，其餘的都換五元鈔。

B：Here's your passport and the local money.

好了，這是您的護照及本地貨幣。

A：Can I have an envelop to put the money in?

可以給我一個信封裝這些錢嗎？

B：Yes, here you are.

好的，這個信封給您。

" Is there anything else I can do for you?

還有什麼是我可以幫忙的？

A：No. Not really. But I assume much appreciated by your friendly service.

沒有。我對你的友善服務非常感激。

B：Oh that's very nice of to say that.

你這樣說太好了。

A：Bye now, hope to see you again.

再見了，希望能再看到你。

傳真信函 🎧
TRANSMITTING A LETTER

G：Good morning, miss. Can you fax this letter to Taipei for me?

客：小姐早，幫我把這封信傳真回臺北好嗎？

S：Yes, sir. Where do I send this fax to?

員：好，要傳到那個號碼？

G：To the fax number written on this letter sheet.

客：傳到信紙上的那個傳真號碼去。

S：Please wait a while. I will send it right away.

員：請稍等一下，馬上就傳好。

G：Yes, please. I'll wait.

客：好，我在這裡等。

S：I think something is wrong, sir.

員：好像有點問題。

"　I've tried many times but it just wouldn't go through.

"　撥了幾次但傳不出去。

"　Are you sure you have the right number, sir?

"　您的號碼對嗎？

G：Let me see. What I wrote here is 886-02-555-6789.

客：我看看紙上我寫的號碼是 886-02-555-6789

S：Mr. Lee. Is "02" the city code for Taipei?

員：李先生，「02」是臺北的市碼嗎？

G：Yes, it is.

客：是的。

S：I think I got it now.

" On overseas calls, you don't dial the first "0" of any city code.

G：Yes, I think you are right.

員：啊，我弄明白啦，

" 撥國際電話時，您不可以撥市碼的第一個「0」，

客：我想妳說對了。

 關鍵字詞 🎧

fax 「傳真」簡稱；正式用字是 facsimile。

 TIP 小博士

傳真機

　　傳真機上市十餘年，通訊上做了一個很大的改變，不像以前只能傳送文字的商用電報機（telex）只能傳送文字而已，傳真機亦可傳送圖案，方便太多了。

 自由行實務及緊急事件處理

免費WiFi與帳密
Free wifi account & code

A：Is there any free wifi in the hotel?

你們酒店有提供免費 wifi 嗎？

B：Yes, there is. The wifi account is the name of the hotel and the code is 12345678.

有的 wifi 帳號就是酒店名稱。密碼是 12345678。

A：Can you show me how to connect to wifi on my cell phone?

您可否用我的手機，告訴我怎麼連上酒店的 wifi？

B：Yes, first to search Raddison from "TOOL" or "GEAR" logo on your cell phone.

首先你在你手機內的「TOOL」或「GEAR」的地方點進去，搜尋本酒店名稱「Raddison Blu」。

A：Yes, I've found it. Then what?

有搜尋到了，然後呢？

B：Then you open an Internet Browser on your mobile phone.

然後，點開你手機上的網際網路。

A：Yes, I got that, too.

有了，網際網路也點開了。

B：Now scroll downward slowly your screen, until you see a blank asking you to key in wifi code, which is the hotel phone No. 12345678.

現在將畫面慢慢往下捲，直到你看到一個長形框，要你填入密碼，也就是酒店的電話號碼12345678。

A：Yes, it work perfectly on my cell phone. Much appreciated.

好了，我可以用我的手機正常上網了，謝謝你。

B：It's a piece of cake. Don't mention it.

舉手之勞，不用客氣。

市街圖 🎧
CITY MAPS

G：Excuse me, sir. Do you have any city map in this hotel?

客：抱歉，先生，你們旅館內有市街圖嗎？

S：I am sorry, sir. We don't provide free city maps,

員：抱歉，我們不送免費市街圖。

"　but you are able to buy one at the souvenir shop.

"　但您可以去紀念品店買一份。

G：Yes. I'll get one later.

客：好，我等一下去買。

"　Can you show me with this city map

"　您能以這張圖來告訴我……

"　how to go to this address shown on the name card?

"　我名片上的這個地址該怎麼走。

S：The address you want is on Duncan street.

員：您要的地址在鄧肯街。

"　It is two blocks down from our hotel.

"　在離旅館的兩條街之外。

"　Ask someone else when you get to that area.

"　到了那裡之後，再問一下別人。

G：Yes, I'll do that. Thank you!

客：我會的，謝謝！

觀光旅遊實用英語

關鍵字詞

| city map | 市街道圖。 |
| name card | 上有書寫名字的卡片，此指私人名片而言。 |

TIP 小博士

觀光地圖

　　世界各觀光都市幾乎都有兩種地圖，一種是給當地人看的，密密麻麻的本地地圖。另外一種是給外來觀光客所看的觀光市街圖，僅將重要觀光點和大條市街列出，易於找尋。

地下鐵路線圖 🎧
SUBWAY MAPS

G：Hello, is there any subway station nearby?

客：請問，附近有地下鐵站嗎？

S：Yes, you'll find a subway station by the "M" sign throughout the city.

員：全市有「M」招牌的就是地下鐵站。

"　And the nearest one is called "Farmer's Station". It's about one block away.

"　距離最近的一個叫「農民」站，就在下條街。

G：If I want to go to the airport tomorrow,

客：如果我明天要去機場。

"　which line should I take?

"　我應該搭哪一線？

S：Let me see. The blue line should take you there.

員：我看看，搭藍線應該可以到。

G：What stop do I get off for the airport?

客：在哪一站下車可到機場？

S：You should get off at Garden Square for the airport.

員：在「花園廣場」站下車就可到機場。

G：Thank you for your information.

客：謝謝你的資訊。

S：You are welcome, sir.

員：不用客氣，先生。

G：Is there any subway I can get?

客：你們有地下鐵路線圖嗎？

S：No, we don't. You can get then at the station.

員：沒有，地鐵站才有。

G：Do you know what they do in Japan about the subway maps?

客：你知道日本怎麼處理地下鐵圖嗎？

S：No, I don't.

員：不知道。

G：Well, most hotels in Tokyo provide the free subway maps.

客：東京的大部份旅館都免費送地下鐵路線圖。

"　They even do that at their visa office in Taipei.

"　甚至他們派駐臺北的簽證辦事處都送。

S：How thoughtful they are.

員：他們真周到。

 關鍵字詞

---

subway　地下鐵。

像臺北的捷運系統，正確稱呼是 Municipal Rapid Transport 不叫 subway。

 TIP 小博士

地下鐵路線圖

　　很多大都市都有非常便捷的地下鐵（subway）且各種鐵線路圖都以各類色來表示不同的路線。各地下鐵站也都會提供免費路線圖給旅客。

地下鐵指標

　　世界各地有地下鐵的都市，都會看到地下道出入口的「M」標誌（代表metro）或「U」標誌（代表 unde ground），不管那一個，都是代表旁邊就是地鐵站。

租車 🎧
CAR RENTAL

G：Good evening, is this a car rental desk?

客：晚安，這裡是租車櫃臺嗎？

S：Yes, this is it. Can I help you?

員：是的，可以爲您效勞嗎？

G：Yes, I need a car tomorrow, and I want to know about your charges first.

客：是，我明天要一部車，我想先知道車租怎麼算。

S：Yes. We charge 50 Euros per day, free mileage.

員：是的，每天 50 歐元，哩程沒有限制。

G：How do you figure as "per day".

客：你們的「每天」是什麼意思？

S：That is eight hours a day.

員：那是以每天八小時計算。

G：Do I turn in the car to wherever I got the car from?

客：還車需要還到原來租的地方嗎？

S：Not necessary, you can turn the car in, to any of our offices.

員：不必，您可將車交還給我們任何一個營業處。

G：That's good. How do I pay?

客：很好，怎麼付錢？

S：You can pay tomorrow when you get the car,

員：明天拿車時才付錢，

"　but we need to see your passport and driver's license.

"　但我們要看看您的護照和駕照。

觀光旅遊實用英語

G：Sure, I will bring them over in the morning.

客：好，我明天一起帶過來。

"　What model of the cars do you rent out here?

"　你們出租的有哪些車型？

S：Mostly European cars, and some Japanese ones.

員：多數是歐洲車，也有一些日本車。

G：I see. I'll probably take BMW.

客：好，我可能會要 BMW 車。

S：Whatever, see you tomorrow.

員：都沒問題，明天見。

 關鍵字詞 🎧

desk　桌；指辦公之櫃臺而言。亦稱 counter。
例：Do you have any tour-desk in the hotel? 　　你們旅館內有旅遊櫃臺嗎？
charge　收費。
turn-in　交出，交回。
例：Did you turn in the purse you found yesterday? 　　你昨天撿到的錢包交出了嗎？

 TIP 小博士

國外租車

　　在歐美先進國家，租車來開的風氣很盛行。國內很多自助旅行的人，三五成群，如果租個車，大家輪流開，分擔費用，也不失為個好辦法。最好讓有在國外都市開車經驗的人先開，先做路況、標誌等的示範，才讓沒國外開車經驗的人，選擇在次要道路輪流開，才比較不會危險。

要旅館卡 🎧
ASKING FOR HOTEL CARDS

G：Excuse me. Do you have any hotel cards

客：抱歉，你有旅館卡嗎？

"　or anything with the hotel name on it?

"　或是有旅館名字的任何東西。

S：Yes. Here is the card.

員：有，卡片在這裡。

G：That's my habit to ask for a hotel card at any hotel I stay.

客：我住旅館都有要旅館卡的習慣。

S：What do you need the hotel card for?

員：您要旅館卡做什麼呢？

G：Mainly for language problems.

客：主要是語言問題。

S：I don't see it, why is that?

員：我不明白，話怎麼說。

G：You see, if I lost my direction in a strange city,

客：你看看，如果我在陌生城市迷了路，

"　I might not be able to speak the local language.

"　可能我不會說當地的話。

"　I can always show my hotel card to the local people.

"　我就可以拿旅館卡給當地人看。

"　And I am sure they understand the hotel name on the card,

"　他們當地人一定看懂卡片上旅館的名字，

" because the hotel name would always being written in their own language.

" So I will never have any problem to find my way back to the hotel.

S： That is a nice habit indeed,

" but what if you don't find a hotel card available?

G： That's okay. Anything with hotel name on it will serve the same purpose,

" such as napkins, match boxes, letter sheets of the hotel.

S： That sure is a good thing to do when you travel.

G： Yes, it is. Isn't it?

因為旅館卡上的名字一定也是用他們的文字寫的。

所以回去旅館是沒有問題的。

員：那的確是個好習慣。

如果找不到旅館卡呢？

客：也沒關係，任何有旅館名字的東西，也有相同的效果。

比如說旅館的餐紙、火柴盒、信紙等。

員：旅行時能這麼做是很好的。

客：是的，不是嗎？

 關鍵字詞 🎧

hotel card	以英文及當地文字寫有旅館名稱的卡片。
lost one's direction	迷路。
local language	當地語言。
local people	當地人。
indeed	確實是；加強語氣說法。
serve the same purpose	有相同作用。

TIP 小博士

隨身攜帶旅館卡

　　到國外旅行，如果養成向每一家所住旅館索取旅館卡的習慣，的確是一個解決迷路的好方法。因為旅館卡都是以英文和當地文字（如在日本當然會寫日文）將旅館名字印於卡片上。你將卡片隨時放在身上，絕對有利無害，萬一迷路了，也可以請當地人、警察人員等協助，安全送回旅館。

 自由行實務及緊急事件處理

櫃臺的分機號碼
Phone extension to Reception

A：Excuse me, what's the extension number for Reception?

打擾了，請問櫃臺的電話分機是幾號？

B：You dial "11" for Reception, "12" for Coffee Shop in the lobby, "13" for House-keeping, "0" for Phone Operator, "14" for Bell Captain.

櫃臺的分機是 11，樓下咖啡廳分機是 12，客房維修分機是 13，總機的分機是 0，行李員櫃臺分機是 14。

B：To cut it short, there is a "Phone Directory" in the room, right next to the phone set. You'll find most extensions are listed on the directory.

簡單說，在你們房內的電話機旁，有一個電話分機表，列有酒店內大部份部門的分機號碼。

A：Is there any ATM machine in the hotel by any chance?

在酒店大廳，會不會碰巧也有銀行的 ATM 提款機呢？

B：No, I'm afraid we don't.

沒有，我們沒有提款機。

觀光旅遊實用英語

A： What about hotel facilities? And their working hours?

那麼酒店設施呢？各項設施的使用時間為何？

B： You'll find them listed in the phone directory as well.

房內的電話分機表上，也有這些資料。

B： As for the facilities opening hours and charges,

至於有關設施的開放時間與費用，

B： please call the Reception ext.#11

請你打櫃臺的分機 #11

B： You'll get more information there.

那裡有更多的資訊。

客房餐飲服務 🎧
ROOM SERVICE

198

G：Excuse me, operator. How late is room service available?

客：抱歉，接線生客房餐飲服務幾點打烊？

S：It doesn't close until 11:30 p.m.

員：11 點半才打烊。

G：What number do I dial from my room, for room service?

客：要點客房餐飲，用我房間的電話怎麼打？

S：There is an extension chart next to your phone.

員：您電話旁邊有個分機表。

"　It shows the number to dial for front desk, bell captain,

"　上面有櫃臺，行李領班、

"　house keeping, room service phone operator and so on.

"　客房管理、客房餐飲、電話接線生等的分機號碼。

"　You just dial the extensions.

"　你照分機號碼撥號就行。

G：Another thing, do I leave them a tip when they bring anything here?

客：他們拿食物來時，我要不要給小費？

S：It depends on their service.

員：那以他們的服務好壞而定。

"　You can give them something if the service is good.

"　如果服務好，可以給一些小費。

G：I see, thank you.

客：我明白了，謝謝您。

room service	各旅館提供將簡單餐飲送至客人房間的一種服務，至於服務時間也各有不同，應向工作人員詢問。
extension chart	分機號碼表。
so on	「等等」之意。等於 etc. 用法。
tip	為感謝服務所給的小費。

TIP 小博士

客房餐飲服務

　　「room service」字面上是「房間服務」。事實上它所指的是「旅館客房之簡單餐飲服務」，可不是拿毛巾、修理水龍頭之類的房間服務。觀光旅館多數全由旅館內的咖啡廳，所提供給房客的簡便餐飲，如蛋糕、三明治、啤酒、果汁、茶、咖啡等。但服務時間通常是只到午夜為止，並不是 24 小時服務。

叫醒服務 🎧
WAKE UP CALLS

G： Whom do I make my request to,
　　 for wake-up calls?

客：需要「叫醒服務」該跟誰說
　　 呢？

S： You can either contact with recep-
　　 tionist or the phone operator.

員：跟櫃臺接待員或電話接線生
　　 說都可以。

"　 Either one can arrange wake-up
　　 call for you.

"　 他們任何一方都可以幫您。

G： Good. Thank you.

客：好，謝謝。

"　 Hello, is this reception?

"　 喂，請問是櫃臺嗎？

S： Yes, This is Helen at the reception,
　　 can I help you?

員：是的，我是櫃臺的海倫，我
　　 可以幫您忙嗎？

G： Yes, Helen. This is Mr. Tom Lee at
　　 room 511.

客：是，海倫，我是 511 房的李
　　 先生。

"　 I would like to have a wake-up call
　　 at 6:30 in the morning.

"　 請於明天早上六點半叫醒我。

S： Yes, your request has already been
　　 accepted by the computer,

員：好，您的叫醒要求已輸入電
　　 腦了，

"　 and you will be awakened accord-
　　 ingly tomorrow.

"　 到時會叫醒您。

"　 Is there anything else, sir?

"　 還有其他事嗎，先生？

G：No, that's all for now. Good-bye.

S： Good-bye.

客：沒有，就這樣了。

員：好，再見。

 關鍵字詞

wake-up call	呼叫起床的服務。
be awakened	被叫醒。

 TIP 小博士

叫醒服務

　　旅館提供把房客叫醒的服務叫 wake-up call service。一般多是於早上叫醒，所以可稱之為 mornini call。如果是想睡個午覺之後，請人幫你叫醒，則叫做 afternoon call。不過，最不受時間限制的說法，以 wake-up call 最正確。

床頭鬧鈴

　　很多高級旅館床頭也有鬧鈴的裝置，讓房客自行設定起床時間，房客如果看不懂英文說明，不知道怎麼調時間，或是怕鬧鈴的聲音不夠大，叫不醒人，還是可以請旅館用人工叫醒，比較保險些。

酒店特約醫生
HOUSE DOCTOR

G：Hello, operator. I've got a diarrhea for two days.

　客：哈囉，接線生，我拉肚子拉兩天了。

"　Can you get me the house-doctor?

　"　幫我請旅館醫生來好嗎？

S：What is your room number, sir?

　員：先生，您房號幾號？

G：511, tell the doctor I am in bad shape, and he had better hurry up.

　客：511，告訴醫生說我情況很糟，請他盡快過來。

S：Okay, Mr. Lee, but it is "she". She is a lady doctor.

　員：好，李先生，但醫生是女的，她是一位女醫生。

"　I'll ask her to come here right away.

　"　請她盡快來。

G：Yes, please.

　客：拜託啦。

S：Hello, Mr. Lee. Doctor Smith is called away somewhere else,

　員：李先生，史密斯醫生現在在外應診，

"　and she isn't expected to get back till 5 this afternoon.

　"　要到下午五點才會回來。

"　Will that be all right with you?

　"　這樣可以嗎？

G：It's not all right, can you get me someone else?

　客：不可以，麻煩找別位醫生好嗎？

S：Yes. I can get someone from private clinic for you.

　員：好，我可以找別診所的醫生來。

"	But that'll cost you 20 Euro extra.	" 但您要多付 20 歐元。
G :	I don't like that idea of paying extra,	客：我不想多付，
"	but I don't have much choice, do I?	" 但我根本沒有太多選擇。
S :	No. I am sorry about that.	員：沒有，很抱歉。

 關鍵字詞

diarrhea 　拉肚子。
house-doctor 　旅館醫生通常指旅館所聘之特約醫師。
in bad shape 　身體健康不好之意。反之則說 in good shape。
had better 　「最好要……」意。 例：You had better come here now. 　　你最好現在就來。
hurry up 　快一點。 例：Hurry up, we are late. 　　快一點，我們已經遲到了。
lady doctor 　女醫師。 某些行業，如要強調是女性工作人員，可加 lady、woman、female 等字稱呼， 如 lady doctor、woman doctor 或 female doctor 等。
called away 　醫生在外出診。 例：Is doctor Brown there? No, he was called away to the Smith's. 　　布朗醫師在嗎？ 　　不在，他去史密斯家出診了。
private clinic 　私人診所。

TIP 小博士

旅館特約醫師

　　旅館之特約醫師，一般多是在旅館附近之診所醫師，在旅館房客身體狀況
有問題時，可以就近趕往處理。當然出診、醫療等費用，都是要旅館房客負擔
的。

電視頻道 TV CHANNELS

G：Hello, miss. How many TV stations are there in Paris?

客：小姐，巴黎有幾個電視臺？

S：About six of them.

員：大概有六個電視臺。

G：Is there any English program?

客：有英語的節目嗎？

S：Yes. There are quite a few in English,

員：有，有好幾個。

"　but most of them are in French.

"　但，大部份是法文的。

G：Any programs in other languages at all?

客：有其他語言的節目嗎？

S：Yes. There are some programs in other languages, but I am not sure.

員：是有些外語節目，但我不是很清楚。

G：No Chinese programs?

客：沒有華語的？

S：I am afraid not, sir.

員：恐怕沒有。

G：That's not fair.

客：那不公平。

S：I don't know about that.

員：這我就不知道了。

 關鍵字詞

TV station　電視臺。
在問本市有多少家電視臺時，可有下列兩種說法：

How many TV stations are there in this city?

本市有多少家電視臺？

How many TV channels are there in this city?

本市有多少個電視頻道？

有線電視
CABLE TV

G : Excuse me, is there any cable TV in my room?

客：抱歉，我的房內有有線電視嗎？

S : Yes, there is one.

員：有的。

G : What about video tape programs?

客：那麼錄影帶節目呢？

" I mean do I pay anything to watch video tapes?

" 我是說看閉路節目要付錢嗎？

S : Yes. You have to pay 6 Euro to watch video program or cable TV like CNN.

員：要，看閉路節目或有線電視要付 6 歐元。

" And you pay nothing on regular TV programs.

" 普通節目不需付錢。

G : Why is that?

客：為什麼？

S : We are paying a lot money a year to the cable-TV company in Paris,

員：我們旅館每年要付很多錢給巴黎的有線電視公司，

" and we must collect something from the users before we broke.

" 所以我們必須向使用者收一些費用。

" This is something they called "Users pay the fee"

" 就是所謂的使用者付費。

G : That's fair enough.

客：那很公平。

關鍵字詞 🎧

video tape　錄影帶。
CNN　美國最有名氣的有線電視系統。 全名是 Cable News Network（有線新聞網路）。
users　使用者。
users pay the fees　使用者付費。

 TIP 小博士

旅館電視節目

　　在國外高級旅館在客房提供的電視節目有下列三類：

1. 當地電臺的一般節目：就像臺灣的臺視、中視、華視節目，一般家庭都可以收看，不用付費。
2. 有線電視節目：像美國有名的 CNN 新聞專業電臺，旅館須付費給 CNN 當局，才有權播放 CNN 的節目，所以基於使用者付費原則，旅館房客戶也須付費給旅館解除鎖碼，才可以收看這類節目。
3. 錄影帶（VIDEO TAPE）節目：此為旅館本身自選錄影帶，常為限制級錄影帶，房客亦需付費透過解碼才有辦法收看此類節目。

計費頻道控制盒

　　多數旅館的做法是在客房內電視機上，安裝一電視頻道控制盒，旁邊附有簡單英文使用說明，告訴你按那些按鈕，可以看免費之普通電視節目，或須付費的有線鎖碼節目等方法，由於英文說明有很多人看不懂，不小心按錯的話，收看費用會自動由電腦計費算在你的房帳上，多冤枉！

如何避免按錯收費電視節目之控制鈕

　　在此告訴各位一個不會按錯控制鈕而冤枉付費的作法：前面說過，頻道控制盒是安放在室內電視機上的一個控制盒，盒子上面的按鍵是用來選看付費節目的，所以，假設你只是想觀賞一下當地的電視節目有那些的話，就像在家看電視一樣，只需操作電視機本身的開關（power 是電源、channel 是頻道、volume 是音量等），不要去動到控制盒的任一按鍵，就不會有按錯鈕的情形發生。

反鎖於門外
LOCKED ONESELF OUT

G：Hello, bell captain. This is Tom Lee at room number 511.

客：哈囉，行李領班，我是 511 房的李先生。

〞 I just locked myself out.

〞 我剛剛把自己反鎖於房門外。

〞 I left the key in my room.

〞 我把房鑰留在房內。

〞 Can you send someone up here to open the door for me?

〞 請派人來幫我開門好嗎？

S：Yes. Please wait at outside the door.

員：好，請在門外等一下。

〞 Someone will be there soon, with master keys.

〞 有人會馬上帶鑰匙去。

〞 Sorry, sir, what did you say your room number was?

〞 抱歉，先生，您說您房號幾號？

G：My room number is 511. Let me repeat : 511.

客：我房號 511，我重覆一次 511。

S：Okay, don't go away now.

員：好，請不要走開。

G：No, I won't. I'll wait here.

客：不會，我會在這裡等。

 關鍵字詞

locked myself out 　把自己反鎖於門外。

master key	旅館用來可以打開任何房間的鑰匙。
go away	離去；離開。

 TIP 小博士

反鎖門外

　　出國在外，常會有旅客忘了帶房間鑰匙而把自己反鎖在門外的情形。參加旅行團的旅客更常常因站在房門口與住對面房間的團員聊天，因聊得太起勁，而可能稍稍離開自己的房門口，此時自己的房門會因房門有自動關門裝置，或甚至是由於窗外吹進來的風太大，而把房門關上，就這樣把自己鎖於門外。

請服務生開門

　　當你房間鑰匙遺忘在房門內而進不去時，請不用驚慌，你可以通知樓下櫃臺，請派人拿他們旅館的主鑰匙 MASTER KEY 來幫你打開，這個時候你可以給來開房門的服務人員一些小費，表示謝意。

客房維修
HOUSE-KEEPING

G：Excuse me, operator. Can you give me the House-Keeping department?

客：抱歉，接線生，幫我接客房管理部好嗎？

S：Yes, I will connect it for you now.

員：好，我現在幫您接過去。

" But next time you want the House-Keeping,

" 下次您要客房管理部的話，

" you can dial directly, their extension is "5".

" 您可直撥他們的分機「5」號。

G：Yes, thank you.

客：好，謝謝。

S：Good evening, This is House-Keeping. May I help you?

員：午安，這裡是客房管理部，有什麼需要我幫忙嗎？

G：Yes. This is room 511.
There isn't any hot water in my bath room.

客：可以，我是 511 號房，我的浴室沒有水。

" Can you send somebody here, and do something about it?

" 請派人上來檢查一下好嗎？

S：Yes, sir. We'll be there shortly.

員：好，先生，我們馬上去。

" I am Jerry, from House-keeping.

" 我是傑瑞，維修部派我來的。

G：Yes, I am so glad you are here.

客：你能來太好了。

" See if you can find the problem.

S：Sir, everything is okay now.

G：Thank you for reparing the faucet, how much do I owe you?

S：Oh no, please don't pay me any-thing.

" It's our job to keep things run smoothly.

G：Thank you. I might as well as ask you to check while you are here.

" I don't think the air conditioner is working properly.

S：What makes you say that?

G：It makes a lot of noise, and I can hardly feel any cool air.

S：As a matter of fact, it is warm here.

G：And I couldn't find any button or switch to turn it up.

S：The air conditioning in this hotel is operated by a central-controlled system.

" And there is nothing in yourroom

" 看看你可否找出問題。

員：先生，沒問題了

客：謝謝你修好水龍頭，要多少錢？

員：不用，請不用付錢。

" 那是我們的工作，把事情管理好。

客：謝謝，既然你人在這裡，我順便問你一下。

" 我想冷氣機有點問題。

員：您爲什麼這麼說呢？

客：聲音很大，而冷氣一點也不涼。

員：事實上，這裡滿熱的。

客：也找不到什麼大小開關來把冷氣開大一點。

員：本旅館的冷氣是採中央系統。

" 您的房內並沒有任何開關。

| for you to adjust the volume or temperature of the air. | 能讓您調整風量或溫度之高低。 |

G：So, what do you want me to do?　客：那麼，我怎麼辦？

S：Nothing, just be patient and wait.　員：不用怎麼辦，只要耐心等待。

" I am going to fix the central system right away.　　我馬上去修中央系統。

" And you will have a nice and cool air in no time.　　您很快就會有又涼又舒服的冷氣。

G：I certainly hope so.　客：希望如此。

關鍵字詞

house-keeping　旅館之客房維修部門
extension　電話分機
do something about　設法解決某些問題 例：My car has broken down, can you do something about it? 　　我的車子拋錨了，你可以設法修理嗎？
keep things run smoothly　使各事都很順利
can hardly　幾乎不能 例：I can hardly hear you. 　　我幾乎聽不到你講的話。 例：She can hardly type. 　　她根本不會打字。
warm　溫暖 形容天氣熱，歐美人士常用 warm 而不是用 hot 來說。

turn up　把音量；出氣量等轉大一些之意。
central controlled system　中央控制系統。
in no time　極短時間內。

 TIP 小博士

客房維修

　　國際旅館的部門分成很多個，其中的客房維修（house-keeping）部門，卻是一個非常重要的部門，凡是有關客房大如門窗、地毯、冷氣的修理、維護、保養等，小至浴巾、肥皂、信封、信紙等的供應都是 house-keeping 部門的事。

枕頭小費

　　參加旅行團的人，都會被導遊告知，每天出門前最好能在枕頭上放一些小費給清理你房間的清潔人員，這是一個很好的作法，放一些小錢，以示感激與尊重，值得鼓勵。

有我的留言嗎？
ANY MESSAGE FOR ME?

G：Good afternoon, ma'am. Is there any message for me?

客：午安小姐，有我的留言嗎？

S：Yes. There are quite a few calls for you.

員：有的，有不少的電話找您。

"　You must be very busy while you are here.

"　您在這裡一定很忙。

G：Yes. I am in import business.

客：是，我做進口生意。

"　I've been buying a great deal from Europe.

"　我從歐洲進口很多東西。

S：What do you buy from France?

員：您在歐洲買什麼呢？

G：Mostly liquor, and some ladies' perfume.

客：大部份是酒類，也有些女人的香水。

S：That's a good business.

員：那種生意不錯。

G：I agree with you 100 percent.

客：我完全同意。

"　Anything related with ladies are considered good business.

"　任何跟女人有關的生意都是不錯的。

S：I think that's the same all over the world.

員：我想全世界都是這樣。

G：Yes. That's true.

客：是的。

觀光旅遊實用英語

關鍵字詞 🎧

message　留言
例：Is there any message for me?
有人留言找我嗎？
a great deal　很多
liquor　酒類
perfume　香水
be considered　被認為
例：Tom is considered good person
湯姆被認為是好人。

 TIP 小博士

房客留言

　　旅館在處理房客的留言，一般來說有以下方式：

1. 將他人要找房客的留言，用書寫方式寫於留言條上，上面註明留話的人姓名、電話號碼及留言時間，以及需不需要該房客回電話等，然後將此留言條放在房客的鑰匙格子裡，所以房客回來，要拿鑰匙時一定會看到有人留言要找他（她）。

2. 另外一種作法，假如有人留言要找某房客，那麼，房內床櫃邊電話機的紅色留言燈會亮著，當房客回到房間看到留言燈亮著時，表示有人找他，他可以和電話總機或樓下接待櫃臺連絡，看看是誰在找他。

退房 🎧
CHECK-OUT FROM HOTEL

G：Hello sir, this is room 511.　　　　客：哈囉，這是 511 房。

"　I am about to check out.　　　　　"　我馬上要退房了。

"　Can you send the bell-boy up for my luggage?　　　　　　　"　請派人來拿行李好嗎？

S：I am sorry, sir, but this is the front desk.　　　　　　員：抱歉，但我這裡是櫃臺。

"　Please call the bell-captain for your luggage.　　　"　請打行李領班分機找人拿行李。

"　His extension is "6".　　　　　"　他的分機號碼是「6」。

G：Can't you switch this call to the bell-captain?　　　　客：妳難道不能把這個電話轉接給他嗎？

S：Yes, I could, but it will be much easier for you to call him directly.　　員：可以是可以，但您直接打給他會更容易。

G：Okay, if you say so.　　　　　客：好吧。

S：Hello. This is the bell-captain, how can I help you?　　員：喂，我是行李領班，我可以為您效勞嗎？

G：Yes. This is room 511. Please send someone up for my luggage. I am leaving soon.　　客：可以，我是 511 房，我要退房了，請派人來幫我拿行李。

S：Yes, sir. Right away.　　　　　員：馬上就去，先生。

關鍵字詞 🎧

check-out　辦理旅館退房之意。
bell boy　旅館內搬運行李人員。
bell captain　旅館內行李部門領班。

 TIP 小博士

簽賬付費

　　旅客在住進旅館後的一切電話餐飲等消費都可以先簽名，將費用算在房帳上，等要退房時，當然要到樓下出納櫃臺，把所有的房帳結清，除了使用現金、支票等支付外，最方便的法是用信用卡支付房帳，省時、省力又安全。

提早結帳

　　建議各位在退房當天，記得要早一點辦理退房結帳手續，免得臨時要退房時，卻已經有太多的人在排隊等著結帳（特別是上午八、九點的時候）你一方面趕著要搭飛機，一方面又不能插隊結帳，真是急死人，所以還是提早結帳才好。

退房時間

　　一般旅館的住房 CHECK-IN 或退房 CHECK-OUT 大都是在中午 12 點至 1 點之間，如果某一天你要退房的話，應在 12 點半之前退掉，否則，如晚退一、二個小時，也許又要付一整天的房租，實在不划算。不過，在旅遊淡季，客房沒住滿時，通常可以和旅館商量遲一、二個小時退房，不另加費用。

付房帳 🎧
PAYING THE BILL

G：Hi, my room number is 502, the room-bill please.

　　客：嗨，我的房號是 502，我要結帳。

S：Yes, sir. Just a moment.

　　員：好，請等一下。

"　This is your bill, sir.
　A total of 1000 Euro.

　　"　您的帳單在這裡，總共 1000 歐元。

G：Can I pay by credit cards or traveler's cheques?

　　客：我可以用信用卡或旅行支票嗎？

S：Sure. We accept most credit cards and traveler's cheques.

　　員：當然可以，我們接受各信用卡和旅行支票。

G：By the way, I would like to have the change in U.S. dollars if that's available.

　　客：如果你有美金，請找我美金好了。

S：Sorry, sir. I don't have enough U.S.dollars at the moment.

　　員：抱歉，我現在沒有那麼多美金。

"　You can always reconvert it back to US dollars at the airport.

　　"　您可以在機場兌換回美金。

G：That's good.

　　客：那很好。

"　Here is my name card. Write to me if you are coming to Taiwan some day.

　　"　這是我的名片，哪一天如果要來臺灣的話，寫信給我。

S： Thank you, I will. Have a nice trip home.

員：謝謝，我會的，祝返家平安。

 關鍵字詞

room bill　客房帳單
credit cards　信用卡
traveler's cheques　旅行支票
re-convert　再兌換；兌換回某種貨幣之意

 TIP 小博士

付帳仔細查對

　　旅客在支付房帳時，應該仔細看清楚，帳上所列每一項目是否都是自己的消費，會不會有帳目算錯的地方？若有不清楚之處，應客氣向旅館出納人員指出，問清楚，正確之後才付款結帳。

冰箱的機關
TRICKY ICE BOX

G : Excuse me, it shows a 11 Euro beer charge on my bill.

客：抱歉小姐，這賬單上面有一筆我在房間喝啤酒的 11 歐元。

S : Yes, what about it?

員：是，有什麼問題嗎？

G : I didn't take that beer.

客：我並沒喝那罐啤酒。

" As a matter of fact, I don't drink.

" 事實上我根本不會喝酒。

S : That's unusual.

員：那奇怪啦。

" Beverage bottles in your ice box are detected by a sensor.

" 你房間冰箱內的飲料都由感應器感應。

" And it will automatically put the beverage charge to your room bill

" 它會自動將費用加到您的房帳上，

" if any bottle is being moved.

" 如果有瓶子被動過的話。

G : I don't know about that.

客：那我可不知道。

" But I didn't take the beer from the ice box.

" 但我根本沒喝冰箱內的啤酒。

" Out of curiosity, I did pick up the beer bottle and read the label.

" 只是為了好奇，我曾經把啤酒瓶子拿起來，看了上面的標籤說明。

S : That explains everything.

員：這就說明了一切。

觀光旅遊實用英語

G：What is it?

S：Like I just said, the sensor will detect any movement of the bottle.

"　The moment you picked up the beer bottle,

"　the sensor had already sensed the movement,

"　and automatically charge the beer to your account.

G：But I had put that bottle back to where it belongs.

S：Yes, I understand that,

"　but the sensor doesn't understand that.

"　The sensor is not designed for detecting for two ways,

"　so it is not able to detect the returning movement of that bottle.

G：I shouldn't have touched the bottle in the first place.

S：Just like the old saying: "Curiosity could kill a cat".

客：為什麼？

員：我剛剛說過，感應器會感應到瓶子的移動。

"　當您把瓶子拿起來的時候，

"　感應器已經感應到這個動作，

"　就自動把啤酒的價錢加到您的房賬。

客：但後來我把啤酒瓶又放回原位。

員：是，這點我了解，

"　但感應器無法偵測到這一點。

"　那感應器沒有設計來偵測雙向的，

"　所以它無法偵測瓶子放回的動作。

客：我根本就不應該去動那個啤酒瓶的。

員：就像一句老話說：好奇心可害死一隻貓。

	But that's okay now, just don't do the same thing again.		現在已經沒關係了，以後不要再這樣就好。

| | I am going to deduct that 11 Euro from your total bill. | | 我這就把那11歐元扣除掉。 |

G：I appreciate it.　　　　　　　　　　客：非常謝謝。

關鍵字詞 🎧

as a matter of fact 「事實上」之意，亦可說成 in fact beverage 飲料之總稱，含有酒精性或無酒精性之飲料。
detect　偵查、偵測。
sensor　感應器。
out of curiosity　「出於好奇心」之意。
label　標籤。
in the first place 「首先就……」；「根本就……」之意。 例：If I knew you hate me so much, I shouldn't have come to see you in the first place. 　　如果我早知道你這麼恨我，我首先就（根本就）不應該來看你。
deduct　減去；扣減。

TIP 小博士

冰箱的機關

　　高級旅館房間內，多放有一個小冰箱，內有各式飲料及零食，如巧克力，餅乾等，供房客取用，這些都不是免費供應的。像本單元對話所舉的例子，有些冰箱內部是暗藏開關的，對每一個瓶子的移動，都會被感應器（sensor）感應到，而將該飲料費用，算在房客的房賬上，即使你沒有喝，只是將瓶子拿起來看看而已，之後又將瓶子，原封不動放回原位，但這樣已經太遲了，因為冰箱內感應器，只會感應你拿瓶離瓶做的動作，而不會感應你放瓶回瓶座的動作，建議最好是看清楚決定要了再拿。

送機 🎧
TRANSFER-OUT SERVICE

觀光旅遊實用英語

226

G：Excuse me, I am leaving for London on flight AF-124 this afternoon.

客：抱歉，我下午搭 AF-124 班機去倫敦。

" My departure time is 4:40 p.m.

" 我的起飛時間是下午 4 點 40 分。

" Can you get me a car to the airport?

" 幫我叫部車送我去機場好嗎？

S：Sure. Do you want a large limousine or just a taxi?

員：沒問題，您要大轎車或計程車呢？

G：How much do they charge?

客：價錢怎麼算？

S：A limousine will cost you 80 Euro and 50 Euro for taxi.

員：大轎車要 80 歐元，計程車只要 50 歐元。

G：I'll take limousine.

客：我要大轎車好了。

" Do I pay you now?

" 現在付車資嗎？

S：No. Please pay the driver directly this afternoon.

員：不，您下午直接付給司機好了。

" He will write you a receipt if you ask for one.

" 如果您要收據他也可以開一張給您。

" What time do you need the car?

" 您幾點鐘要搭車？

G : I don't know how long it takes from here to the airport.

" What time do you suggest I go to the airport?

S : Don't leave here later than 1:00 p.m.,

" because it takes about forty-five minutes to get there.

" And you should be at the airport at two hours before the departure time.

" That's what all international flights request.

G : Good, so you want me to come back here by 1:00 p.m., right?

S : Yes, sir.

客：我不知道從這裡到機場要多久。

" 你建議我幾點去機場好呢？

員：最好在下午1點以前就出發，

" 因為這裡到機場車程要 45 分鐘。

" 而您應該在起飛之前兩個小時到達機場。

" 那是所有國際班機都這麼要求的。

客：好，所以你要我1點鐘來這裡搭車對不對？

員：對的，先生。

 關鍵字詞 🎧

limousine　大型房車，亦指接送旅客於機場和市區之間的巴士。
請參考本書第四篇第五單元〈機場外有人接我嗎？〉有關接機和送機的介紹。

 本篇相關字詞 🎧

single room	單人房	message	留言
twin room	雙人房	visitor	來訪者

twin beds	雙人床	check-in	辦理住房
double room	雙人房	check-out	辦理退房
double bed	雙人床	television	電視
triple room	三人房	issue paper	衛生紙
with bath	附有浴室	soap	肥皂
reception	接櫃檯臺	towel	浴巾
front desk	接櫃檯臺	shampoo	洗髮精
cashier	出納員	shaver	刮鬍刀
information desk	服務臺	air conditioner	空氣調節機
tour desk	旅遊櫃臺	heating	暖氣機
airlines desk	航空公司櫃臺	fire exit	逃生門
duty manager	值班經理	room service	客房餐飲服務
bell captain	行李領班	laundry service	洗衣服務
bell boy	行李員	wake up call	叫醒電話
meal coupon	餐券	morning call	叫醒電話
registration form	登記表	room rate	房價
safety box	保險箱	hotel card	旅館卡
telephone	電話	envelope	信封
extension	分機	letter sheet	信紙
overseas call	國際電話	stamps	郵票
local call	本地電話	address	地址
collect call	對方付費電話	air mail	航空信函
hold on the line	電話不要掛斷	switch board	交換總機
hang up the line	掛斷電話	phone operator	電話總機
line is busy	忙線中	waiter	男服務員

line is occupied	忙線中	waitress	女服務員
area code	區域號碼	city code	都市代碼
country code	國家代碼		

再確認機位

CHAPTER 7
RECONFIRMING THE FLIGHT

G：Hotel Guest

客：旅客

S ：Staff

員：服務員

再確認機位 🎧
RECONFIRMING THE FLIGHT

G：Hello, is this Air France?

客：喂，您那裡是法航嗎？

S：Yes, it is. Can I help you sir?

員：是的，我可以為您服務嗎？

G：This is Mr. & Mrs. Tom Lee at the Paris Hilton.

客：我們是住希爾頓的李先生和李太太。

"　I would like to reconfirm our flight AF-322 to London on Friday.

"　我要確認週五 AF-322 去倫敦的機位。

S：Yes. Please hold on a second.

員：請稍等一下。

"　I've got your names on my screen,

"　我們的記錄裡有你們的名字。

"　and you are leaving on AF-322 for London, Friday.

"　你們是週五搭 AF-322 班機去倫敦。

G：Yes, we are.

客：是的，沒錯。

S：Sir, is there any phone number we can reach you in Paris?

員：先生，你們有本地的聯絡電話嗎？

G：Yes. We are staying at the Paris Hilton, room number 511.

客：有，我們住巴黎希爾頓，房號 511。

"　I don't have the number of the hotel on hand,

"　我手邊沒有希爾頓的電話，

"	but I am sure you are able to find that out.	"	我相信妳可以查得到。
S：	That's no problem.	員：	那沒問題。
"	Okay, Mr. Lee, your flight has been confirmed.	"	好了，李先生，你們的機位確認好了。
"	And please be at the airport two hours before the departure time.	"	請在起飛前兩個小時去機場。
G：	Yes. We will be there on timer.	客：	好的，我們會準時去。
"	We can't afford to miss that flight.	"	我們負擔不起錯過那班機。
S：	No. Have a nice trip.	員：	祝旅程愉快。
G：	Thank you. Good bye.	客：	謝謝，再見。

 關鍵字詞

reconfirm　再確認 例：Can you reconfirm my flight? 　　你可幫我再確認我的機位嗎？
hold on　握住；「等一下」等意
screen　此指電腦螢幕而言。
on hand　手邊；手頭上之意。
on time　準時。in time 是指「及時」。
can't afford　負擔不起，或辦不到某事之意。 例：I can't afford to fail the exam. 　　我考試失敗不起，即不能不及格之意。

例：I can't afford to buy that car.

我買不起那部車子。

 TIP 小博士

訂位、買票及確認

　　國人出國機位，旅館的預訂，大都是由旅行社代為服務，團體的訂位更是非旅行社莫屬。機位的預訂，雖是旅行社代辦，但旅客身為當事人，也不可不知一些機位預訂的相關知識，在此我們特為介紹如下：

1. 訂機位（make reservation）：向航空公司訂位組，預訂某特定日期某特定班次之機位，如臺北／東京，東京／洛杉磯等。

2. 候補（request）：如果旅客所想預定之特定班次暫無空位，訂位人員會將所訂之機位列為候補機位，英位字母代號是 WL（waiting-list）或 RQ（request）等，以後旅客的機位有了，經確認後才改成 kk 或 ok。

3. 確認（confirm）：如果因旅客要訂的某段或數段機位已有，也都確認了，那麼這位旅客的訂位記錄上顯示的就是 kk 或 ok。

4. 開票（issuing tickets）：出國前，可憑已確認過之機位，到航空公司票務櫃臺付錢購票，稱為開票。票上主要寫明下列各項：

旅客姓名	name of passenger	稱謂	title
啓程地	from(origin)	目的地	to(destination)
開票日	date of issue	機票號碼	ticket number
班機號碼	flight number	起飛時間	departure time
票價	fare	訂位情形	booking status
艙等	class		

5. 再確認（reconfirm）：在國外向有關航空公司用電話做機位之再確認手續，是保有原已確認之機位的唯一方法，各航空公司都有規定，各段機位，啓程前雖都全部確認了，但在旅行途中之每一旅行航段搭機前的 72 小時內，須向當地的航空公司再次確認一遍，表示說你這是按照原訂航班旅行，這種再確認一遍的作法，就叫做「再確認」。

名、姓說法 🎧
WAYS OF SAYING NAMES

S：Excuse me, sir. Can you tell me what your name is?

員：抱歉，先生，您叫什麼名字？

G：Yes, we are Mr. & Mrs. Tom Lee staying at the Paris Hilton Hotel.

客：我們是住巴黎希爾頓飯店的李先生和李太太。

S：What is your Chinese name?

員：您的中文名字是什麼？

G：My Chinese name is Lee, Chai-yi.

客：我的中文名字是李甲乙。

S：Please tell me which is the last name and which is the first name.

員：麻煩告訴我哪一個是姓？哪一個是名？

G：Yes, my last name is Lee L-E-E and the first name is Chai-yi C-H-A-I- and Y-I-

客：好，我姓李，名字叫甲乙。

"　and my English name is Tom Lee.

"　我的英文名字叫湯姆李。

S：Thank you, and what is your wife's full name?

員：謝謝，您太太的全名叫什麼？

G：Her first name is Mei-hua and maiden name Chen, last name now is Lee,

客：她的名字叫美華，婚前姓陳，現在姓李陳，

"　so her full name is Lee Chen, Mei-hua.

"　所以她的全名叫李陳美華。

S：Very good, this is all I need for now, thank you.

G：You are welcome, bye now.

S：Good bye.

員：很好，我就需要這些資料而已，謝謝。

客：不客氣，再見。

員：再見。

 關鍵字詞 🎧

last name	姓氏
first name	名字

 TIP 小博士

姓名拼音

中國姓氏有很多發音都相當接近（如 Chang、Cheng、Ching、Chong、Chung 就是張、鄭、程、鍾、叢等姓的拼法，其發音都頗接近）所以最好的辦法是除了念出來，也把它拼出來，就不會有錯，特別是在電話中，要報名字的時候。

報出姓、名的方法

華人在姓名時，都會用耳東「陳」、弓長「張」、木子「李」等來說明姓名、英文也有一套類似的說法，以 Huang 這個字的拼法為例：你可向對方說 H for Helen，U for USA，A for America，N for Nancy，G for George，以表示 Helen 的 H. USA 的 U，America 的 A.Nancy 的 N. George 的 G，都是用相關的字的第一個字母去形容，習慣上，盡量以人名或地名來做相關字的說明。也有其他字，雖不是人名、地名，但聽起來，不會讓人家混淆的字如 B for boy，K for king，Q for queen 等。

訂位電腦代號
RESERVATION CODE No.

S：Mr. Lee, like I said your flight has been confirmed,

員：李先生，就像我說的，您的機位已確認好了。

" but do you know your reservation PNR code?

" 您知道您的訂位 PNR 代號嗎？

G：What is PNR number?

客：什麼是 PNR 代號？

S：It stands for Passenger's Name Record.

員：PNR代表「旅客姓名記錄」。

G：No, I don't. Can you tell me about it?

客：不知道，你告訴我好嗎？

S：Yes, I am going to. That helps, you know!

員：是，我會的，那會有幫助的。

" It's a computer code number given for any booking record.

" 那是給予每個訂位記錄的旅客姓名記錄。

G：Good, what is my PNR number?

客：好，那我的 PNR 幾號？

S：Yes, your code number is ZM-R340C.

員：好，你的電腦代號是 ZMR-340C。

G：I am sorry. I don't catch you.

客：抱歉，我沒聽清楚。

" Do you mind repeating it once more, but slowly?

" 你介意重複一遍嗎？慢慢的。

S：No, I don't mind at all.

"　Z as Zebra, M as Mary, R as Roger, the number 3.4. zero. and the last letter C as Canada.

G：Good. I got it this time. Thank you.

S：You are welcome.

員：我不會介意。

"　ZEBRA 的 Z，MARY 的 M，ROGER 的 R，數字 3.4.0 最後字母是 CANADA 的 C。

客：好，這次我聽清楚了，謝謝。

員：不客氣。

 關鍵字詞

PNR number
是航空公司訂位組給予訂位旅客（或團體）的一個訂位編號，正式稱呼是學乘客姓名記錄（passenger's name record）簡稱訂位代號或稱訂位的電腦代號通常是由英文字母和阿拉伯數字組成的一組字串，如 kj36a 等。
booking record　訂位記錄。
catch　捕捉；此指「明白」之意。

 TIP 小博士

電腦代號

　　要出國旅行的人，應該主動向所訂機位的航空公司，要你的機位訂位代號（或稱電腦代號）。如前所述，這是航空公司訂位人員，所給予訂位旅客的一個訂位識別代號，只要你行程還持續進行中，你的這個電腦代號就仍存在著。當你在國外各站，向有關航空公司，確認機位或甚至機位行程有所更改時，只要將你的電腦代號事先報出來，他們就可以很快的找到你的訂位記錄。即使你的行程改變了，但你的電腦代號是還原先那一個，不會改變。除非你行程中斷，之後又重新訂位，航空公司才會再給你一個新的電腦代號。

訂位記錄人數

　　一個電腦代號，也就是一個訂位記錄所包含的人數不一，換句話說，一個人旅行，那訂位記錄就是指他一人而言，如十個人，甚至二十人同時旅行，同時訂位，那這個訂位記錄就是這十人或二十人共用的。

寫下全名 🎧
WRITING DOWN THE FULL NAME

G：Excuse me, miss. Did you say my reservation has been confirmed?

S：Yes, I did, why?

G：In that case, I would like to have your full name.

S：Any particular reason for that?

G：Yes, with the full name of the person reconfirming my flight,

" no one at the airport could deny my confirmed reservation.

" Unpleasant experience happened to me once last summer.

" I had reconfirmed my flight by the phone,

" just like what I am doing now.

" But I didn't ask the name of the girl confirmed my flight.

" When I was at the airport the next day,

客：抱歉小姐，妳剛剛說我的機位已再確認沒有問題了。

員：我是說過，有什麼問題嗎？

客：那樣的話，我需要知道妳的姓和名。

員：有特別理由要這麼做嗎？

客：有，有了再確認我機位人的名字後，

" 在機場你們航空公司的人就不會否認我的機位。

" 去年夏天，我就有一件不愉快的經驗。

" 那時候我用電話確認了我的機位，

" 就像我現在做的一樣。

" 但我沒有問那位幫我確認訂位小姐的姓名。

" 當我第二天去機場搭機時，

" the airlines staff at the counter said he couldn't find my name on the passenger's list.

" And I got nothing to prove

" that my flight was confirmed at the previous day.

S： So you didn't catch the flight?

G： No. But I've learned my lesson since.

" That's why I pretty much insist having your full name.

" Just to play safe, that's all.

S： Okay, my name is Mary Simpson.

G： Thank you, Miss Simpson.

" 機場航空公司櫃臺的職員說旅客名單上沒有我的名字。

" 而我也沒什麼可以證明。

" 說我的機位在前一天已確認過了。

員：所以您沒搭上那一班機囉？

客：沒有，但我學乖了。

" 所以我相當堅持要知道妳的全名。

" 這樣做比較保險。

員：好，我的姓名是瑪莉‧辛浦森。

客：謝謝，辛浦森小姐。

 關鍵字詞

reservation　訂機位；訂房等。	
has been confirmed　已經確認好了。	
particular reason　特別的理由。	
unpleasant experience　不愉快經驗。	
airlines staff　航空公司職員。	
have learned one's lesson　學乖。	

TIP 小博士

寫下確認者姓名

　　本單元所舉的例子，是非常少有的例子，大部份的航空公司訂位組人員不至於那麼惡劣，故意否認旅客的再確認，但也的確發生過，所以最保險的作法是，在電話中再確認完畢你的機位時，務必很客氣的向對方請教他（她）的姓名，並且記下再確認的日期、地點、時間等，盡量以很多的資料來證明你的確已再確認過你的機位了。

冠夫姓 🎧
CARRYING HUSBAND'S LAST NAME

S：Can I ask you something, sir?

員：我可以問您一些事情嗎，先生？

G：Sure, what is it?

客：當然可以，什麼事？

S：Do most Chinese women take husband's name as their last name?

員：大部份中國婦女會冠夫姓嗎？

G：Yes. Most of married women do.

客：大多數婚後婦女是如此。

"　What about your married women in France?

"　那麼你們法國的已婚婦女是怎麼做的？

S：We do about the same thing.

員：我們也一樣。

"　I guess I always have the problem pronouncing Chinese names.

"　我時常說不好中國名字的發音。

G：Why is that?

客：為什麼？

S：Chang, Cheng, Ching, Chong, all sound like Chinese music to me.

員：張、鄭、程、鍾這些發音聽起來都像中國音樂。

G：Well, it's not really that difficult if you get used to it.

客：妳習慣後就不會覺得那麼難了。

S：Maybe you are right.

員：也許您說得對。

關鍵字詞

get used to it 習慣了某事

 TIP 小博士

冠夫姓

　　大多數華人婦女，婚後都有冠夫姓的做法，婚後就成為複姓，如「陳林美麗」、「張李美華」等，有複姓的人，在國外旅行時各種表格上（如入境卡、退稅單等）必須填複姓，要跟妳護照上的英文姓氏一樣。

 本篇相關字詞

reconfirm	再確認	full name	全名
last name	姓氏	surname	姓氏
family name	姓氏	maiden name	女子婚前姓氏
first name	名字	given name	名字
nick name	小名	reservation	訂位
particular	特別的		

第八篇 🎧

當地旅遊節目

CHAPTER 8
THE LOCAL TOURS

G：Hotel Guest
客：旅客
S：Hotel Staff
員：服務員

有當地旅遊嗎？🎧
LOCAL TOURS AVAILABLE?

G：Good evening, miss. Do you have any bus tour service at this hotel?

客：小姐，晚安，你們旅館有安排觀光旅遊節目嗎？

S：Yes, we do. Where would you like to go?

員：有，您想去哪裡？

G：Why don't I go through the tour brochure first?

客：讓我先看看觀光簡介好了。

S：Here is an English brochure for you.

員：這裡有一本英文版的簡介給您看看。

G：Which tour would you recommend?

客：妳推薦哪一個節目呢？

S：They are all good,

員：這些節目都不錯，

"　but I highly recommend tour No. I the city tour.

"　但我鄭重推薦第一種的市區觀光。

G：Why is that?

客：爲什麼？

S：The city tour will at least give you an idea about what we have in this city

員：市區觀光至少會告訴您本市有哪些可以看。

"　and it covers most of points of interest in town.

"　且包括大部份的名勝地區。

G：Yes. That's nice.

客：那很好。

觀光旅遊實用英語

" What about famous museums or cathedrals in Paris?

S： The Olsen Museum is worth visiting.

G： That's good. What about night clubs and strip-tease shows?

S： Lido is a famous night club for topless and variety show,

" and you'll find strip-tease shows in Piquile.

G： How far is Piquile from here?

S： It's not within a walking distance.

" You had better take a cab.

" 那麼巴黎有哪些著名的博物館或大教堂呢？

員：奧森博物館值得去參觀。

客：很好，那麼夜總會和脫衣舞節目呢？

員：麗都是有名的夜總會，有上空及各種表演節目，

" 而匹給區則有脫衣舞。

客：匹給區有多遠？

員：走路去太遠了。

" 最好搭計程車去。

 關鍵字詞

bus-tour service　用巴士到各大旅館接載觀光客至某定點旅遊的服務。	
tour-brochure　旅遊小冊子說明書等。	
recommend　推薦	
city tour　市區觀光	
points of intrest　觀光重點	
cathedral　大型教堂	
ninght club　夜總會；俱樂部等	

topless show	上空表演
variety show	綜藝表演
walking distance	走路可到的距離

 TIP 小博士

國外旅遊節目

出國在外，有空時免不了會想參加當地有哪些值得去看的地方。各大都市的觀光節目、行程不只一個，有半天行程的，有一天行程或兩天以上的等等，依觀光客興趣的不同，可參加不同的節目。

市區觀光

各大都市觀光行程雖然有很多種，但我們都建議參加其中的一種叫 CITY TOUR（市區觀光）的行程，因為這種行程最具代表性，它雖然是一種走馬看花的行程，但至少會約略介紹市內各有名的觀光據點。如果有更多時間，再考慮參加其他行程。

麗都夜總會 🎧
ABOUT LIDO SHOW

G：Excuse me, do you know anything about Lido show?

S：Yes, what do you like to know?

G：How is their show these days?

S：It has always been a good show there.

"　In fact, you are not really visiting Paris without seeing the Lido show.

"　There are quite a few good shows in Paris,

"　but the Lido is the best as far as I am concerned.

G：Yes. I've heard so much about the Lido in Paris.

"　I just can't afford missing the Lido show this time.

"　I saw the Lido show in Las Vegas two years ago.

客：抱歉，你熟悉麗都的節目嗎？

員：熟，您想知道什麼？

客：最近他們的節目怎麼樣？

員：他們的節目一直都不錯。

"　事實上，您不去看麗都的節目就等於沒來巴黎。

"　巴黎有些好的表演，

"　但我個人以為麗都是最好的。

客：是，我早就聽過有關麗都的種種。

"　這一次絕不能錯過去麗都看看。

"　兩年前我看過拉斯維加斯的麗都表演。

" Is the Lido show here about the same with that of Las Vegas?

S：Well, they are more or less the same,

" because they are from the same group.

" I am sure you will find something different in the Paris Lido.

G：I certainly hope so. Do they require coat and tie?

S：Yes, they do.

G：Thank you.

" 這邊的麗都和拉斯維加斯的麗都表演相同嗎？

員：大致上是差不多，

" 因為他們是屬於同集團。

" 我確信這邊巴黎的麗都還是有它的特色的。

客：很希望如此，他們要求正式穿著入場嗎？

員：是的。

客：謝謝。

 關鍵字詞

these days 「這些日子以來」；「最近的情況」等意思。
例：How is your business these days?
你最近的生意好嗎？
Lido show 巴黎有名的夜總會之一
as far as I am concerned 「以我的想法」之意。
例：As far as I am concerned, Tom is the best singer.
以我來看，湯姆是最好的歌手。
more or less 「多多少少」；「差不多」之意
coat & tie 字面上是西裝領帶，即「正式服裝」之意

TIP 小博士

夜總會

　　在花都巴黎，比較有規模的夜總會，就屬麗都夜總會、紅磨坊夜總會及瘋馬夜總會三處，國人到巴黎觀光，特別是團體旅行，也大部份會把巴黎有名的上空夜總會的表演排進必看的行程。類似的表演在美國賭城拉斯維加斯，大西洋城等地也有。

治安好嗎？
HOW IS THE SECURITY?

G： Excuse me, sir. Am I safe to go to a strip-tease show alone?

客：抱歉，我一個人去看脫衣舞安全嗎？

S： Not really. I wouldn't do that if I were you.

員：不見得，如果我是您，我就不會這麼做。

" I have been living here all my life.

" 我一輩子住這裡。

" I don't even want to go any dark street at night in Paris.

" 我晚上就不敢一個人出去走暗路。

" Security is terrible here.

" 這裡治安很糟。

G： Doesn't your government do something about it?

客：你們政府不想想辦法嗎？

" Bad security will eventually jeopardize your tourist industry.

" 不好的治安會傷害你們的觀光事業的。

" Don't you realize that?

" 你們難道不明白這一點嗎？

S： Yes, I do, but the lousy police-men don't.

員：我明白，但差勁的警察不明白。

" And there is nothing I can do about it.

" 而且我也無能為力。

G： I guess not.

客：我想也是。

觀光旅遊實用英語

關鍵字詞

alone　單獨
例：Are you alone?
你現在是單獨一個人嗎？
if I were you　如果我是你的話
例：I will buy that hat if I were you.
如果我是你的話，我會買下那頂帽子。
security　治安狀況
例：How is your security in the city?
你們城內的治安好嗎？
jeopardize　使之頻於險境；冒……
tourist industry　觀光事業
lousy　不好的

 TIP 小博士

當地治安

　　一個都市如果治安不好，那麼不管他的其他方面有多好，都無法吸引外來觀光客的，更進一步說，連本地人都會留不住，變成所謂的產業外流，所以世界各主要觀光地區，莫不以保持良好治安為要務，才更能夠發展觀光事業。

在郵局 🎧
AT THE POST OFFICE

G：Excuse me. Can I buy some stamps here?

客：抱歉，這裡賣郵票嗎？

S：Yes. How do you want them?

員：有，您要怎麼買？

G：Please tell me first.

客：請先告訴我。

"　How much would it cost for air-mail letters and postcards to Taiwan?

"　寄到臺灣去，航空信多少錢？明信片多少錢？

S：It is 3 Euro for letters

員：信函要 3 歐元。

"　and postcards 1.80 Euro only.

"　明信片只要 1.8 歐元。

G：Does it cost more if I want to make it register?

客：如果要掛號，要加錢嗎？

S：Yes. It will be 1 Euro extra.

員：要，要加 1 歐元。

G：What about parcels?

客：那包裹呢？

S：We charge parcels by weight.

員：包裹以重量計費。

G：How do you charge them?

客：怎麼計？

S：The starting kilogram is 10 Euro.

員：第一公斤是 10 歐元。

"　Any additional half kilo is 4 Euro, up to 20 kilos only.

"　以後的每半公斤 4 歐元到 20 公斤為止。

" Any thing less than a kilo, will be charged as one kilo.

" 少於一公斤皆以一公斤計算。

" This chart would give you an idea about the charges.

" 這張計費表可以給您，一些有關收費的參考。

" The rule is, the heavier the parcel, the more you pay.

" 規定上來說，重量越重收費越高。

G：It's the same all over, and that's only fair, isn't it?

客：世界各地都是如此，那也很公平，不是嗎？

" How long does this airmail take to get to Taiwan?

" 寄這個包裹到臺灣要多久？

S：It normally takes about five days to a week.

員：通常是 5 天至一個禮拜。

G：The last time I mailed my wife a letter from London two years ago.

客：兩年前我從倫敦寄一封信回臺灣給我太太。

" She didn't get the letter until a month later.

" 她一個月以後才收到信。

S：I am sorry about that, but it happens sometimes.

員：很抱歉，但有時的確如此。

G：That's alright. You can't win them all.

客：沒關係，人生沒有永遠是順遂的。

 關鍵字詞

airmail letter	航空信函
postcards	明信片

第八篇　當地旅遊節目

255

register　登記；註冊
parcel　郵寄小包
additional　加添的；補充的
You can't win them all　字面上「你不能全贏」意指「人生總有逆境」

 TIP 小博士

購買郵票
國人出國觀光，去當地的外國郵局的機會不多，除非是去寄包裹。平常要寄信或明信片回臺灣所需的郵票，可以向旅館櫃臺或大廳的郵票販賣機購買。

報護照遺失 🎧
REPORTING LOST PASSPORT

G： Excuse me, sir. I think I am in trouble.

客：抱歉先生，我有麻煩了。

S： What kind of trouble?

員：什麼樣的麻煩？

G： I think I've lost my passport.

客：我的護照遺失了。

S： Oh oh, that's really a trouble alright.

員：噢！那真的是麻煩。

G： What do I do?

客：我該怎麼辦？

S： Okay Mr. Lee, Don't panic. I'll handle this.

員：好了，李先生，不要驚慌，我來處理。

" First, you'll have to report this to the police.

" 首先，您必須向警方報案。

" Let me get you the police station on the phone

" 我來幫您接警局的電話。

" and you talk to them yourself.

" 由您自己跟他們講。

G： Thank you, I will.

客：謝謝，我來說。

" Hello, police? This is Tom Lee from Taiwan.

" 哈囉，警局嗎？我是臺灣來的湯姆李。

O： Yes, what can I do for you?

員：是，我可以為您效勞嗎？

G：I am reporting on lost passport.　　客：我要報護照遺失。

"　　I think I lost the passport this after-　　"　　我今天下午遺失了護照。
noon.

O：When did you see your passport　　員：你最後一次見到你的護照，
the last time?　　　　　　　　　　　是什麼時候？

G：It was only this morning when I　　客：今天早上在旅館的藝品店
used my passport in the hotel sou-　　　裡，我還用到護照。
venir shop.

O：What is your name, sir?　　　　　員：先生，你的大名是什麼？

G：My last name is L-E-E, first name　　客：我的名字是李甲乙。
is C-H-A-I Y-I

O：Good, do you have any other iden-　　員：好，你有沒有其他的身份證
tification?　　　　　　　　　　　　明？

G：Yes, I have the copy of my pass-　　客：有，我身邊帶有護照的影
port with me　　　　　　　　　　本。

"　　if that helps.　　　　　　　　　"　　如果這有用的話。

O：That sure does. Please come to our　　員：當然有用。請你明天來局裡
department tomorrow morning.　　　一趟。

"　　And bring any of your identifica-　　"　　把你貼有照片的身份證明也
tion with your photo on it.　　　　　帶來。

"　　Your driver's license, for example.　　"　　比如說，你的駕駛執照也可
以。

"　　Come to see me in the morning. I　　"　　明天來找我，我是披薩羅警
am Sergeant Pissarro.　　　　　　官。

G：Yes, sergeant. I'll bring them over in the morning.

客：是，警官。我明早帶過來。

O：Good, see you tomorrow.

員：好，明天見。

 關鍵字詞

panic　驚慌	
first thing in the morning　明早第一件要辦的事	

 TIP 小博士

使用護照常識

　　護照是旅客的身份證明，護照遺失是一件非常嚴重的事，因為在補領到新護照之前，該旅客就是一個無國籍、身份不明的人，不能離境，當然也回不了國。所以護照的保管一定要非常小心。有關護照保管，請參考下列說明：

1. 領到新護照後，應先將護照內頁有關資料如持有人姓名、年齡、護照號碼、發照日、效期截止日等影印一份或數份，與護照分開保管，將一份留家裡，一份帶在身邊（帶在身邊的這一份，不可以和護照正本放一起，以免護照正本遺失時，其影印本也一併遺失，留有這些影印本的作用是，萬一護照正本遺失時，可暫時證明你的身份，並作為充份的資料，提出補發新護照之申請。

2. 出國在外，護照機票等重要旅行文件，最好能夠寄存在所住旅館之保管箱內。但退房離去時，一定記得將保管箱內的物品領回。將護照等文件隨身時帶身邊並不是最安全的作法。很多國人有將護照等重要文件，放在腰間霹靂包的習慣，所以聽說國外某些歹徒，專搶旅客的霹靂包，請大家小心。

3. 萬一在國外發現護照遺失，不必驚慌，再仔細找一遍，如果實在找不到，就應趕快採取下列步驟：

　(1) 請當地人（如所住旅館工作人員等）協助連絡當地警察機關，先用電話報案護照遺失，再設法親自去補辦遺失證明。

⑵ 向最近之我國駐外使、領館單位，文化中心、商務中心等，申請補發臨時護照。

⑶ 辦完護照補發手續後，靜待回音，同時立即通知臺灣的家人做必要之安排。

⑷ 回國之後，再向外交部補辦新護照。

報支票遺失 🎧
REPORTING: LOST CHEQUES

G：Hello, is this the Paris office for Citibank?

客：哈囉，你們是花旗銀行巴黎辦公室嗎？

S：Yes, it is. What can I do for you?

員：是的，我可以為您效勞嗎？

G：Yes, I am reporting on the lost traveler's cheques.

客：是，我是用電話來報旅行支票遺失的。

"　I think I lost my traveler's cheques this morning.

"　我今天上午把旅行支票遺失了。

"　It was only yesterday when I paid by cheques the last time at the department store.

"　昨天我還用支票在百貨公司付帳的。

S：Yes, can you come to our office to fill out the applications?

員：是，你可以來我們辦公室填表嗎？

G：Yes, I will. But I want to report the lost cheques by phone first.

客：我會去，但我要先用電話報案。

S：Alright, what is your full name sir?

員：好。你的大名是什麼？

G：My name is Lee, C-h-a-i Y-i.

客：我名字是李甲乙。

S：Where did you purchase the cheques?

員：你的支票在哪裡買的？

G：I bought them from Citibank in Taipei.

客：在臺北的花旗銀行買的。

S：You mean Taipei, Taiwan?

員：你是說臺灣臺北嗎？

G：That's right, Taipei.

客：對的，是臺北。

S：Do you still have the cheque receipt with you?

員：你身邊還有購買支票的收據嗎？

G：Yes, I do have the bank receipt for the cheques I bought a week ago.

客：是，我有上週買的這些支票的收據。

"　It says here, my cheque numbers is begin from 002-003-004-051 in sequence.

"　這上面寫著，我的票號從002-003-004-051號開始，連號的。

"　For a total of 50 cheques,

"　總共五十張。

"　all are in USD100 face value,

"　全部是一百美金面額的。

"　but I had used 7 cheques already.

"　但我已經用了七張了。

"　So the correct number for un-used cheques are 43 cheques.

"　所以正確未用支票還有 43 張。

S：Are those used cheques numbers in sequence?

員：已用的那些支票都連號嗎？

G：Yes, the 7 cheques I used are in sequence. They are from 051 to 057.

客：是，用掉的七張都依順序開出，051 到 057 號。

S：That's good, but we still need you here to fill out the forms.

員：好，但我們仍需你來填表格。

觀光旅遊實用英語

G：Alright, I'll come to your office as soon as I can.

S：Okay, see you soon.

客：好，我盡快趕來。

員：好，一會兒見。

 關鍵字詞

face value	鈔票或支票面值。
in sequence	按順序
application form	申請表格

 TIP 小博士

遺失旅行支票

旅行支票的正確用法，我們在本書第六篇第十七、十八兩單元已有詳細介紹。在此我們僅補充說明，旅行支票遺失時之處理程序，以供參考。

當你發現旅行支票遺失時，如果不是當地銀行的上班時間，可先以長途電話向臺北你當時購買該旅行支票的銀行報案。第二天上午就必須向就近當地的出售該旅行支票的分支銀行，填表申請補發未用的旅行支票部份（舉例來說，你當時購買了 100 張支票，遺失前已用了 20 張，你僅能申請補發 80 張，因為前 20 張已用掉不可能補發。這個時候就看出來將支用的旅行支票號碼記下來的重要性，如果不記下已用支票的號碼，要報遺失時怎知已用了幾張？未用的幾張？）有些銀行甚至可以在 24 小時之內將新旅行支票補發給客戶。有些銀行，可能要你出示當地的警察單位證明。所以，最好先問清楚。

信用卡之使用

俗稱的塑膠貨幣——信用卡 credit card 這幾年來在臺灣正以驚人的速度在成長，所謂「一卡在身，萬事 OK」特別是出國旅行時，可以免去攜帶許多現金和支票的麻煩。

國內發卡單位皆由銀行來擔任，也就是說，信用卡公司都是授權由銀行來作發卡單位，由銀行直接對其顧客（持卡人）負責，除非重大情事又基於尊重銀行，信用卡公司是比較不會直接去服務持卡人的。各發卡單位服務持卡人的範圍各有不同，茲以一般性的狀況，說明如何使用信用卡，以及應注意事項：

1. 出國前先和你的發卡銀行溝通好你出國期間所需要之額度，免得到了國外才發現你簽帳額度太少而懊惱。

2. 在國外旅行簽帳購物餐飲等消費，就像國內一樣，頗為方便，只是消費單位給你的收據是以當地幣值計算，到時候在匯率的換算上是會有一些差距。請好好保存每一張消費的簽帳收據，以便日後與信用卡銀行要你繳錢的對帳單（statement）核對。

3. 使用信用卡，也可以在國外的提款機，提領每日若干額度的當地貨幣，以供零用。

4. 信用卡也可以當做國際電話卡來用，只要按照發卡銀行給你的指示，依你的電話密碼等資料（請注意一般信用卡的密碼有兩組，一組是信用卡本身的密碼，一組是「用信用卡來打電話」的專用密碼），利用國外，特別是在機場，貼有信用卡標誌的國際通話電話機，打國際電話。

5. 在國外住宿旅館、餐飲、租車等，也常會對持卡人消費有優待。各信用卡公司不管定期或不定期，一般都會和其特約商店、消費單位等設有對持卡人消費的優惠計畫。所以，在此建議持卡人在出國前向你的發卡銀行洽詢持卡消費情報，以得到更多的優惠。

6. 某些五星級觀光旅館已大力推行並鼓勵房客盡量用信用卡簽帳消費，如果你check-in 旅館時，就告訴旅館人員說你 check-out 退房時是要用信用卡簽帳，那麼在你數天後退房時，就不必與他人大排長龍，可以快速簽帳離去。

7. 另外，如果是信用卡遺失的話，就必須先以長途電話，向臺北發卡銀行報遺失，回臺灣之後，再補辦新卡。

 本篇相關字詞

bus tour service	巴士觀光服務	tour brochure	觀光手冊

recommend	推薦	points of interest	名勝地區
museum	博物館	cathedral	大教堂
church	教堂	chapel	私人教堂
strip-tease	脫衣舞	walking distance	走路距離
dark night	黑夜	jeopardize	傷害
tour industry	觀光工業	damage	損失
coat & tie	正式穿著	itinerary	旅程表
lobby	大廳	badge	胸章

 自由行實務及緊急事件處理

抱歉我迷路了
I lost my direction

A：Excuse me, Ma'am. I think I am lost.

打擾了女士，我想我是迷路了。

B：You look like you are a tourist visiting this city.

你看起來像是來本市造訪的觀光客。

A：Yes, I am.

是的，我是。

B：Which hotel do you stay?

你住哪一家酒店？

A：I stay at Raddison Blu Hotel.

我住 Raddison Blu 酒店。

B：That's good. It's not too far from here.

那好，離這裡不遠。

B：You'll just go straight on this street, and make a right turn at the second traffic light. You'll see the hotel there.

你沿著這條路直走下去，在第二個紅綠燈路口右轉，你就會看到你的酒店。

B：Your hotel is not a walking distance from here.

從這裡走去你的酒店太遠了。

B：For safety reason, you'd better get
a taxi to take you back.

為安全起見，你最好搭計程車回
去。

Do you have a hotel card with you?
Show it to the taxi driver.
He knows where your hotel is.

你有沒有帶著酒店卡片？拿給司
機看他就知道酒店在哪裡。

渡輪與遊輪
Ferry & cruising-ship

A：Excuse me. Can you tell me what
the difference is between "Ferry"
and "Cruise "?

請問，您是否可以告訴我「渡
輪」與「遊輪」有什麼不同？

B：Generally speaking, Ferry is refer
to a boat transport from one bank
to opposite bank of the river.

一般來說，渡輪是指從河的一岸
航行到對岸的船隻運輸。

B：But their destinations can be as far
as 10 kilometers or more away.

但是它們的目的地可能是在 10
公里或更遠的地方。

B：It depends on their route.

這要看船班航線而定。

B：Some larger ferry boats are large
enough to load tour buses, trucks,
cars motorbikes and the passengers
of course.

有些大型渡輪，大到可以裝載遊
覽車、卡車、轎車、摩托車。當
然也包括乘客。

B：If you travel with tour bus, you must remain seated in the bus while the bus is being drive to the boat or being drive to leave the boat.

如果你們是搭遊覽車的乘客，當遊覽車開上或開下渡輪時，所有乘客都必須坐在自己座位上。

B：Passengers can not get off the bus until the bus is securely parked.

遊覽車沒有安全停妥之前，乘客不可以下車。

B：After the bus is securely parked at the bottom deck of the boat,

遊覽車安全停妥與底艙後，

B：passengers can leave the coach, and go up or by the elevator or by walking up the staircase to the cabin deck.

乘客可以下車，搭電梯或走室外鐵梯，上去甲板層，進入室內座位區。

B：They can sit back and relax, to enjoy the scenic view alone the way.

他們可以進入乘客休息室欣賞航行兩岸景色。

A：When do passengers get back to the bus again?

乘客什麼時候要下去底艙回到遊覽車內？

B：About 10 minutes before arriving at the destination pier, they will make an announcement informing all passengers to get back to their vehicle at the bottom deck.

抵達目的碼頭的 10 分鐘前，船上會廣播請大家下去底艙上車。

A：After all bus passengers get back to the bus, the driver will then continue the journey afterward.

乘客全部上車後，司機就可以繼續之後的行程。

參加當地旅遊

CHAPTER 9
TAKE LOCAL TOURS

T：Tourist
客：旅客
G：Local Guide
員：導遊員

遊覽時間多久？🎧
HOW LONG THE TOUR LAST?

G：Good morning, sir.　　　　　　　　員：先生，您早。

T：Good morning, is this the bus for the city tour?　　　　客：早，這是去市區遊覽的巴士嗎？

G：Yes, it is. I am Helen, your guide this morning, welcome aboard.　　　員：是的，我叫海倫，是你早上的導遊，歡迎上車。

T：Thank you, Helen. I am Tom from Taiwan.　　　客：謝謝，海倫，我是臺灣來的。

"　Am I the only Chinese in your bus?　　　"　我是本車的唯一華人嗎？

G：Yes, as a matter of fact, you are.　　　員：是，你是的。

"　Is there anything wrong?　　　"　有什麼不對嗎？

T：No, nothing wrong, just ask.　　　客：沒有，只是問問而已。

"　How long does this tour take?　　　"　這個行程要多久時間？

G：It takes about three and half hours.　　　員：大概 3 小時半。

"　We should be back here around twelve thirty.　　　"　大約中午 12 點半我們就會回來。

T：Is lunch included on this city tour?　　　客：這個市區遊覽有包含午餐嗎？

G：No, sir. I don't think so.　　　員：沒有的，先生。

〃 We will bring you back to this hotel after we get through.

T：I don't want to come back here
after the tour.

〃 Drop me off somewhere near the
Opera House if you don't mind.

〃 So I can do some shopping there.

G：No problem, sir. I'll keep that in
mind.

〃 遊覽完畢後我們會帶你回來
這個酒店。

客：遊畢後，我不想回到這裡。

〃 請在歌劇院附近放我下車，
如果你不介意的話。

〃 我要去買些東西。

員：沒問題，先生，我會記得
的。

 關鍵字詞 🎧

welcome aboard	歡迎上車、上機等之意亦有「歡迎加入我們行列」之意
drop me off	放我下車
I'll keep that in mind	我會記住

 TIP 小博士

巴士觀光

　　國人如果是個人而不是參加旅行團出國的話，在國外應該多去參加這種在
大都市為外來觀光客所提供的巴士旅覽（bus tour），車上成員多為外來觀光
客，可以有很多交外國朋友的機會，英文不是很好的人，也可以利用此機會練
習英語會話，一舉兩得。

觀光小冊

　　每個巴士遊覽行程的時間長短不一，在節目簡介（tour brochure）上都會寫
明，如果看不懂，可以問車上的導遊人員，以利你自己的時間安排。

洗手間收費

　　女性同胞上公共廁所必須付費，國內外都是一樣的，唯一的不同是，國內是用人工收費，但國外有人工收費，也有投幣式女廁所。投幣式的較麻煩，因為它只接受某特定當地零錢，太大或太小都投不進去，有時真會急死人。最好是到餐廳去借，就不會有問題。

艾菲爾鐵塔
EIFFEL TOWER

T：Helen, where are we going now?

G：We will make our first stop at the Eiffel Tower.

T：That's good. I've seen plenty of the tower pictures before,

"　but I've never seen the tower itself yet.

G：You will see them soon. We'll be there in about 20 minutes.

T：Yes. When was the tower built?

G：The tower was completed in 1889, designed by Mr. Alexandre Gustave Eiffel.

T：How high is it?

G：It is about 300 meters high.

T：Please tell me more about the tower.

G：Yes, I will. I'll tell you more about it during the tour.

客：海倫，我們現在要去哪裡？

員：我們第一站先停艾菲爾鐵塔。

客：好，我以前看過許多鐵塔的照片，

"　但鐵塔本身還沒看過。

員：你很快就可看到的，大概20分鐘就到鐵塔了。

客：好，鐵塔何時建立的？

員：該塔於 1889 年完成，是由艾菲爾先生設計的。

客：鐵塔有多高？

員：大約 300 呎高。

客：請多講一些關於鐵塔的事。

員：好的，參觀的時候我會多講一些。

T：How much will the taxi fare be if I want to come back here tomorrow?

客：如果我明天還要再來，計程車資大概多少錢？

G：It'll be approximately 5 Euro from your hotel.

員：從你的旅館來大約要5歐元。

T：Helen, have you ever been to Taiwan before?

客：海倫，妳去過臺灣嗎？

G：No. I've never been there, but I would like to go someday.

員：沒去過，有機會想去。

T：You will, if you keep on working hard, and save enough money.

客：可以的，如果妳工作認眞，存夠了錢就行。

G：I certainly hope so.

員：眞希望如此。

 關鍵字詞 🎧

designed by　由某人設計
taxi fare　計程車資
approximately　大約

臺灣特產
SOUVENIR FROM TAIWAN

T：By the way, how would you like to have a souvenir from Taiwan?

客：對了，妳想不想要臺灣的特產？

G：Sure, why not?

員：好呀，當然要啦

T：This is a lucky charm from Taiwan.

客：這是臺灣製的幸運之符。

G：It's cute. What is this made of?

員：很可愛，什麼做的？

T：It's made of Taiwan jade, semi-precious stone.

客：臺灣玉做的，為半寶石類的玉石。

G：Is it very expensive?

員：很貴嗎？

T：No. It is not expensive.

客：不會很貴。

T：But it'll bring good luck to a nice girl like you.

客：它會帶幸運給像妳一樣的好女孩。

T：Oh, I am flattered. Thank you so much.

客：我真是受寵若驚，非常謝謝。

 關鍵字詞

souvenir	紀念品；特產
lucky charm	幸運之符
semi-precious	半寶石類
be flattered	受寵若驚

TIP 小博士

臺灣小禮物

如果出國前能夠購買一些臺灣特產品，如臺灣玉片、大理石手鐲等便宜但實用的小東西，帶到國外做公共關係，交交朋友，相信是會很受歡迎的。

 本篇相關字詞 🎧

tour brochure	觀光小冊	slides	幻燈片
tour itinerary	觀光旅程表	mountain	山脈
tour schedule	觀光行程	river	河流
tour fare	觀光費用	lake	湖泊
tour map	觀光地圖	bridge	橋樑
tour group	觀光團體	subway	地下鐵
bus tour	巴士觀光	memorial hall	紀念館
tour guide	觀光導遊	city hall	市政廳
driver	司機	monument	紀念碑
pick up time	接人時間	tower	高塔
embassy	大使館	park	公園
train station	火車站	statue	銅像
police station	警察局	national park	國家公園
hospital	醫院	boulevard	大道
church	教堂	road	路
museum	博物館	street	街
school	學校	lane	巷
souvenir shop	紀念品店	alley	弄
restaurant	餐廳	address	地址

fast food	速食	under-pass	行人地下道
night club	夜總會	over-pass	行人天橋
strip-tease	脫衣舞	pedestrians only	行人專用
film	底片	vechile only	車輛專用
stamps	郵票		

第十篇

購物

CHAPTER 10
SHOPPING

C：Customer
客：旅客
S：Sales Person
員：售貨員

百貨公司 🎧
DEPARTMENT STORE

C： Excuse me. Can you tell me where the department store is?

客：抱歉，你可以告訴我百貨公司在哪裡嗎？

S： Yes, it is near the train station.

員：可以，它就火車站附近。

C： Do you mind telling me how to get there?

客：你介意告訴我該怎麼走嗎？

S： No. To take a taxi is the best way for you.

員：不介意，您最好搭計程車去。

C： How far is it from here?

客：從這裡去要多遠。

S： It takes about 15 minutes by cab.

員：搭計程車要 15 分鐘。

C： Can you get me a cab?

客：你可以幫我叫部車嗎？

S： There are plenty of them waiting outside the hotel.

員：旅館外面有很多在排班。

C： Good, thank you.

客：好，謝謝。

S： Welcome to Lafayette department store, sir.

員：先生，歡迎來到「拉法葉」百貨公司。

C： Hi, where is the shoes department?

客：嗨！請問鞋子部門在幾樓？

S： It's on the third floor.

員：在三樓。

C： Thank you.

客：謝謝。

關鍵字詞

cab　計程車 taxi 之別稱，亦可連稱為 taxi cab
Lafayette department store　拉法葉百貨公司法國巴黎最有名的百貨公司

TIP 小博士

百貨公司

　　百貨公司，英文稱之為 department store. department 是「部門」，store 是商店，顧名思義就是分成很多部門的大型商店之意。世界各地的大型百貨公司部門分類很多，不勝枚舉，至於百貨公司之各部門中英文名稱，請參閱本篇後部之相關字詞部份。

營業稅外加

　　在臺灣的百貨公司買東西，稅金都是內含。但在美國卻不同，他們是將稅金外加，而且每州所訂的營業稅也不盡相同。所以，在美國購物時，如標價是一百美元，而該州之稅金如為百分之四時，你總共需付一○四元。

財不露白

　　另外，臺灣旅客在國外購物時，常看到的一個現象，那就是常常將大筆美金百元大鈔在大庭廣眾下露了白，真是犯了「財不露白」的大忌。由於國人較喜愛用現鈔，到了國外還是照用現鈔，殊不知先進國家，特別是美國，大都用信用卡，或是小額現鈔，很少人用百元美鈔了。

尺碼大小 🎧
SIZE & MEASUREMENT

C：Excuse me. Can I see that pair of shoes over there?

客：抱歉，那雙鞋讓我看看好嗎？

S：Which one? The brown one or the black one?

員：哪一雙？棕色的還是黑色的？

C：Yes, the black one on the right.

客：右邊那雙黑的。

S：Yes, sir. Here you are.

員：好的先生，這雙就是。

C：How much does it cost?

客：多少錢？

S：120 Euro but you'll get 13 percent discount on duty free.

員：120 歐元，但您可享有百分之十三的免稅。

C：I see, can I try it on?

客：好，我可以穿穿看嗎？

S：Yes, what size do you want?

員：可以，您穿幾號的。

C：I think I wear size 72.

客：我想是 72 號的。

S：No, it can't be.

員：不，那不可能的。

"　You must be using different size numbers in your own country.

"　您們國家可能用的是不同系統的尺碼。

"　We don't use No.72 for men's shoes.

"　很顯然你們的系統和我們的不同。

C：Well, I don't know about that.

客：這我並不知道。

" But to go by your size numbers,

" what size do you think I wear?

S：I think you can wear size 40.

" Do you want to try it on?

C：Why not, I've got nothing to lose.

S：Here you are. Try this brown one.

C：But I don't want the brown one.

S：But this is only for you to try the size.

" If you get the right size, I'll get you the color you want later.

C：I think this pair is a little too loose.

" Can you show me one size or half size smaller? But in black.

S：I'll bring you size 39 and size 39 1/2 , one each.

C：Are there any other colors available?

S：No, sir. They come in black and brown only.

C：Okay, I think I'll take this one.

" 但如果依妳們的尺碼，

" 我應該穿幾號？

員：我想您可以穿 40 號的。

" 您要試穿嗎？

客：好呀！試試無妨。

員：好，請試試這雙棕色的。

客：但我不是要買棕色的。

員：這只是讓您試試尺碼而已。

" 尺碼對了，我再給您拿您要的顏色。

客：我想這雙稍微太鬆了些。

" 可以讓我試試小一號或小半號的，但是要黑色的。

員：我拿來 39 號和 39 1/2 兩雙讓您試試。

客：有其他顏色嗎？

員：沒有，先生，只有黑色和棕色。

客：好吧！我要這雙好了。

" I am going to pay by credit card.
Do you accept cards?

S： Yes, we do.

" 我要用信用卡付錢，妳們收嗎？

員：會，我們會收。

 關鍵字詞

discount 價格上之折扣
duty-free 免稅
must be 「一定是」之意，屬強烈的假設。 例：He must be very rich to own that car. 擁有那部車，他一定是很有錢。 You must be crazy to say that. 你一定是瘋了才那麼說。

 TIP 小博士

尺碼不同

　　人們購買衣服、鞋類等物，都是以自己所穿之尺碼，來做採購的標準，但是，你一旦到了國外，可能會發現，有些地方所採用的尺碼和臺灣不同。這時候你只有請教當地的售貨員，請他們告訴你，以他們的尺寸標準而言，你應該是穿幾號的，然後拿來試穿，就不會有問題了。

退稅 🎧
TAX REFUND

C： Excuse me, miss. Do I get any duty-free on what I just bought?

客：抱歉，小姐，我剛買的東西有免稅嗎？

S： Yes, you do.

員：有的。

" Please go to the "duty free" counter downstairs.

" 請您去樓下的「免稅」櫃臺。

" Show them this receipt I gave you.

" 給他們看我給您的這張收據。

" They will tell you what to do next.

" 他們會告訴您怎麼做。

C： Good, thank you.

客：好，謝謝。

" Hello, is this the "duty free" counter?

" 你好！這裡是免稅櫃臺嗎？

S： Yes, what can I do for you, sir?

員：是，先生，我可以幫您忙嗎？

C： Here is the receipt for what I just bought upstairs.

客：這是我在樓上購物的收據。

" How do I claim that for duty-free?

" 我該如何申請我的免稅。

S： Please fill out this duty-free form.

員：好，請填好這張免稅表格。

" Fill in your full name, passport number, date and place of birth, home address and contact phone number.

" 請填寫您的全名、護照號碼、生日、出生地、住址及聯絡電話。

| " | And I will fill out the rest of it. | " | 其他的我來填。 |

C：What do I fill out this for?　客：我填此表要做什麼用？

S：Anything a foreigner buy in France is duty free.　員：外國人在法國買的任何東西都是免稅的。

" With this form copy and the passport,　" 有了這張表格的影本及護照，

" you are able to get 13 percent tax refund from the bank at the next counter.　" 您就可以向隔壁銀行櫃臺退回 13% 的稅款。

" That means you'll get the tax money back in about 5 minutes.　" 那意思是說您在五分鐘之內就可以領回退稅款。

C：Wow, that's fantastic.　客：哇！那太棒了。

" But how come I got the tax money back at the airport last time, not at the store?　" 但為什麼我上次是在機場辦理退稅？而不是在商店退？

S：Every country has its own way of doing things.　員：每個國家做事方法不同。

" In most European countries.......　" 在歐洲的大部份國家……

" You'll get the refund only from the bank at the airport or border area on your departure day.　" 您只能在出境當天，在機場或邊界的銀行領取退稅款。

" But we are different, we make it even better.　" 但我們不同，我們做得更好。

" We want you to get the money back at the same day you make the purchase.

C：Like I said, that's a bravo idea. I like it !

" The store I bought perfume from 6 years ago, refunded me with a cheque,

" but I didn't get the cheque until two months later.

S：I am sorry about that, but it is more efficient now.

C：That's just marvelous. I wish we could do the same thing in our country.

S：Yes, that will be good. Good bye.

C：Yes, you take care!

" 我們讓您能夠在購物當天就拿到退稅款。

客：就像我說的，這個做法太棒了，我喜歡！

" 六年前我買香水的商店，寄了一張退稅支票給我，

" 但我是在購物的二個月之後才收到該支票。

員：很抱歉，但現在的做法更有效率。

客：那非常好，我希望我們國家也有同樣的做法。

員：對，那會很棒，再見。

客：是的，保重吧！

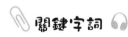 關鍵字詞

duty-free counter　免稅櫃臺	
claim　要求；申請	
contacted phone number　聯絡電話	
foreigner　外國人	
refund　購物之退款	

bravo idea　太好的主意	
efficient　有效率	
marvelous　美妙；神奇	
You take care　你「保重」之口語說法	

 TIP 小博士

購物退稅

　　在國外購物，特別是歐洲地區，很多國家都會退稅給外國人，以鼓勵外國人多購物，然而，每個國退稅百分比之高低，以及退稅的方式都不盡相同，有些國家退百分之十，有些退百分之十七等。有些國家是可以當天退（如法國），有些是外國人離境時在機場或邊界檢查站退。最好向當地售貨員問清楚，以保障你的權益。

　　茲以一般購物之退稅手續說明如下：

1. 填寫店家所提供之退稅表格，你只須填寫你的姓名（中英文皆可，符合護照上之簽名即可）臺灣之居家地址，護照號碼等少數幾項，其餘的售貨員會幫你填）

2. 全部填好之表格，由店家簽署，證明東西的確是他們所賣。

3. 退稅方法：

   (1) 當場退：（以法國巴黎之拉法葉百貨公司為例）購物完畢，售貨員會給你收據（就是一般商店收據，作為辦退稅用的收據）將此收據交給樓下退稅櫃臺，稅款會當場退給你。

   (2) 離境時退：購物完畢，填寫退稅表格，並由店家填寫部份資料，放於書寫有店家名稱，地址之回郵信封，由顧客在離境時，交給機場或邊界退稅櫃臺或相關人員查驗無誤後，蓋上可退款之官章，再持之向旁邊銀行單位領取現金，通常是以當地貨幣退回稅款，如果有美金，他們會折算美金退給你。

(3) 用支票退稅：將上述 (2) 項所述店家回郵信封內那一份退稅表格，交由離境檢查人員查對無誤（有時會抽看所購之免稅品）蓋上官章，你須將蓋好官章之表格，放入回郵信封，封口黏好，投到旁邊他們指定放退稅信的籃子等容器。店家在收到有離境海關所蓋過章之退稅表格後，會辦理你的退稅，然後將退稅款以支票寄至你表格上所寫的地址給你，前後約需一個半月的時間。

4. 不管你是在機場或陸地邊界離境，海關人員有時會抽查，查看你所購之免稅品是否確實攜帶離境。

本篇相關字詞

department store	百貨公司	shoes department	鞋類部
super market	超級市場	toy department	玩具部
drug store	雜貨店	dress	衣服
fish market	魚市場	stationery department	文具部
watch shop	錶店	trousers	西褲
shoes store	鞋店	shirt	襯衣
bakery shop	麵包店	mini skirt	迷你裙
fast food	速食	blouse	女用上衣
souvenir shop	紀念品店	boots	長統鞋
cassette shop	錄音帶店	skirt	裙子
book store	書店	under wear	內衣褲
toy shop	玩具店	socks	短襪
radio shop	收音機店	too tight	太緊
men's department	男裝部	waist belt	腰帶
ladies' department	女裝部	electric-item department	電氣部

自由行實務及緊急事件處理

歐洲購物退稅
Tax-refund in Europe

A：Excuse me, if I buy something, can I get the tax-refund?

請問一下，如果我在德國買東西，可以辦退稅嗎？

B：It depends. A foreigner must buy from "Tax refund" shops, and plus a total purchase must be more than a certain amount of money before he can claim for tax-refund.

那要看情形。外國人必須在「退稅商店」購買某一金額以上的貨品，才可以辦理退稅。

B：Since you are now traveling in Berlin, Germany, here is an example. If you buy something from a tax-refund store with a total purchase over 175 Euro, then you are entitled to get approximate 13% of tax refund.

既然你現在是在德國柏林旅行，我給大家舉例說明，如在你在德國的某一「退稅商品」，一次購買金額在 175 歐元以上，那麼你就有資格申請約 13% 的退稅。

A：As for the minimum purchase and percentage of tax-refund, are they the same every European country?

至於最低購買額與退稅的百分比，是不是每個歐洲國家都相同？

B：No, they are not the same. Every European country has a different refund-policy.

不，每個歐洲國家的退稅政策不同。

A： When and where do I get the re-fund? How does it work?

請問我要在何時、何地辦理退稅？

B： Here are the steps to be followed:

辦理退稅的步驟如下：

B： Step 1　Any thing you buy from a tax refund shop, be sure to get a receipt.

步驟一：任何你從「退稅店」所購買的商品，都要保有收據。

B： Step 2　Some shop would make out a "refund cheque" on your merchandise.

步驟二：有些退稅店，會針對你買的商品，開一張退稅支票給你。

B： Step 3　You can only claim for tax refund at the airport, harbor or border in the last E.U country.

步驟三：你只能在你行程最後一個歐盟國家機場、碼頭、邊界關卡辦理退稅。

B： Step 4　Let's assume that you claim the refund at the internation-al airport. You'll have to check-in at the airlines and get the boarding pass.

步驟四：假設你是經由國際機場離境，你必須先去航空公司櫃台，報到也拿到登機證後，

B： Step 5　Next, you go to a Customs Office Counter.

步驟五：接下來，你要去海關辦公室櫃台。

Show the officer your passport, all your purchase receipts.

將你的護照、所有的購物收據。

And fill in the form with your Eng-lish name shown in the passport, date of birth,

在退稅表上，寫上你護照上的英文名字，出生年月日，

home address, the name of your country,	住家地址，國家名稱，
to be refunded by cash or to remit the refund to your credit card account,	要退回現金、還是要退回到你的信用卡帳戶，
with your signature signed neatly and correctly.	並清楚、正確地簽上你的簽名。
B：Step 6　Sometimes, the officers would require to see the item you purchased.	步驟六：有時候，官員會要求查看你買的商品。
B：Step 7　If every thing goes well, the officer will stamp an official seal on your receipt.	步驟七：如果一切順利，官員會在你的收據上蓋上官章。
B：Step 8　For those wishes to make the refund in cash, will get the money right away at the bank counter nearby.	步驟八：對那些要求退現金的人，立刻可在旁邊的銀行櫃台領到現金。
A：A friend of mine told me that two years ago,	有個朋友說，她兩年前去過挪威，
A：she bought something in Norway,	她在挪威買些東西，
A：and she was asked to claim her tax refund before she left Norway,	但卻被要求在離境挪威之前辦退稅，
A：not the last EU country.	而不是在最後歐盟國家辦退稅。
B：That's possible. Some country has their own tax-refund policy.	那也有可能。有些國家有不同的退稅做法。

在餐廳

CHAPTER 11
AT THE RESTAURANT

G：Guest
客：旅客
W：Waiter
員：服務員

招牌菜
RESTAURANT SPECIALTY

G：Good evening. My wife and I would like to have a table by the window.

客：晚安，我太太和我想要一個靠窗的桌子。

W：Yes, sir. We'll get you one by the window.

員：好的先生，我們會找一個靠窗的桌子給您。

"　Here is the menu. I'll be back in a minute.

"　這是菜單，我等一下再來。

"　Can I take your order now, sir?

"　先生，我可以幫您點菜了嗎？

G：Yes. What's the specialty of this restaurant?

客：是的，你們餐廳的招牌菜是什麼？

W：Kobe beef steak is our specialty,

員：神戶牛排是我們的招牌菜，

"　but if you tell me what your favorite food is,

"　如果您告訴我您最喜歡吃什麼菜，

"　I may be able to help you.

"　我也許可以幫上忙。

G：Yes, I love seafood, and my wife enjoys beef steak.

客：好，我喜歡海鮮，我太太喜歡吃牛排。

W：You sure have come to the right place,

員：你們真是來對了地方，

" because we are good at both beef " 因為這些菜我們都很拿手。
steak and seafood.

 關鍵字詞

take order 接受您點菜
例：Can I take your order?
我可以寫下你的點菜嗎？
No, I am not ready to order yet.
不，我還沒準備好點菜。
specialty　餐廳最拿手的菜
favorite food　最喜歡的食物

 TIP 小博士

待領入座

　　國人上餐廳，比較習慣於隨意入座，但是，國外的高級餐廳可不是這樣。他們的作法是，在入口處，立有一牌子寫 please wait to be seated 意思是說，請等候有人幫你帶位，他們的領檯員會帶你入座。當然你可以告訴領檯員你想要什麼樣的位子。這種領檯入座的作法多年前臺灣也已經有很多高級餐廳跟進了。

用餐禮節

　　國外高級餐廳的用餐禮節（table manner）是告訴人們，在用餐的時候，講話不可以大聲，喝湯嚼食物不可以發出聲音等。在國內用餐如果沒依照上述的約束，旁人不會干涉你，因為中國人一向不管他人瓦上霜。但是，在國外，如果你在餐廳大聲喧嘩的話，是會遭他人白眼，甚至走過來告訴你「Please keep your voice down」意思是說：「講話請小聲一點」。

點菜 🎧
TAKING ORDERS

G：Hello, sir. We are ready to order now.

客：先生，我們要點菜了。

W：Yes, sir. What would you like to have?

員：是，你們想點什麼？

G：I'll take grilled lobster.

客：我要烤龍蝦。

"　Beef steak for my wife, medium rare.

"　我太太點牛排，三分熟。

W：Yes, sir. Would you care for any wine first?

員：好，要不要先來點餐前酒？

G：Yes, that'll be good.

客：那很好。

"　We both would like to have a small glass of red wine.

"　我們都要一小杯紅酒。

W：Anything else, sir?

員：還要點其他東西嗎？先生。

G：No, not at the moment.

客：目前不需要。

"　We'll let you know if we need anything else.

"　如果還需要的話等一下告訴你。

W：Yes, I'll be back with your food shortly.

員：好，你的菜馬上就來。

"　Here comes your delicious food.

"　你們點的餐點來了。

觀光旅遊實用英語

G：It smells good. Hope it tastes just as good.

客：好香，希望也很好吃。

W：Yes, I hope you'll like it.

員：會的，希望你們會喜歡。

G：Yes. The food is so tasty. You sure have a nice cook.

客：菜做得很好吃，你們的廚師手藝真不錯。

W：It's very kind of you to say that.

員：謝謝您這麼說。

"　Enjoy your food, and do let me know if you need anything else.

"　好好享用您們的菜。有事叫我一聲。

G：Don't you worry, I will.

客：好，我會的。

 關鍵字詞 🎧

grilled lobster　烤龍蝦
medium rare　「牛排三分熟」之意 牛排幾分熟之各種說法，請參考本書第一篇第十一單元〈機上用餐〉之說明。
delicious　美味、好吃之意

 TIP 小博士

當地餐食
　　一般說來，國人對西餐食物、酒類等種類名稱等，較不熟悉，所以到了國外，就會盡量上中菜餐廳，吃中國菜，旅行團特別是如此。旅行社幾乎都是訂中菜來滿足臺灣旅客之口味。不過，如果在國外有機會嚐嚐當地食物的話，也可以去試試，不管好不好吃，總是一種不同的經驗。

自己點菜
　　很多國人在西餐廳點菜時，不知道該如何點起，很多西餐的菜餚名稱不是法文就是西班牙文，難怪很多國人在西餐廳點菜時，感到特別麻煩，所以有時候就會以同桌或鄰桌外國人所點的食物向服務生說「我要點和他一樣的菜」，以求省事。事實上，你看不懂菜名沒關係，你可以問服務人員某些菜餚到底是什麼東西，再決定是否要試試看，不一定要點和別人一樣的東西。

 自由行實務及緊急事件處理

Buffet與Cafeteria
Buffet & Cafeteria

G：Good evening, miss. My wife and I would like to have a table away from the piano? It's too noisy to us.

客：午安，小姐，我太太與我想要一個離鋼琴遠些的餐桌。那地方太吵了。

W：Yes, sir. Follow me please.

員：是的，先生。請跟我來。

"　Here you are.

"　就是這裡。

G：Is this a buffet restaurant?

客：妳們這裡是自助餐廳嗎？

W：Yes, it is.

員：是的。

G：This place looks like a very nice restaurant.

客：這個餐廳看起來不錯。

"　How much do you charge per person to have a buffet meal here？

"　請問在這裡用餐，每人的費用多少錢？

W：It is 30 Euro plus a 10 percent service charge per person.

員：每人 30 歐元外加一成的服務費。

G：Do you mind telling me what's the difference between "Buffet" and "cafeteria"?

客：你介意告訴我 Buffet 餐與 Cafeteria 餐有什麼不同？

W：I don't mind at all. A buffet meal means you pay a set price, and you can eat all you can.

" And we will be much appreciated for not wasting good food we have.

G：What do you mean by "not wasting good food"?

W：What I am trying to say is it will be nice if you take a proper portion of the food

" each round you pick up the food.

" In other words, you can fill up your plate as many times you want.

" Just to make sure you are able to finish eating the food you take.

G：It sounds fair.

" What about "cafeteria" meal?

W：Cafeteria is: You pay what you get.

" That is to say, there is not the fixed price like "Buffet".

員：我一點都不介意。它的意思是你付一個固定價錢，就可以吃到飽爲止。

" 我們會非常感激不要浪費我們的好食物。

客：浪費好食物是什麼意思？

員：我想說的是如果你們僅取用適量的食物。

" 每次你去拿菜的時。

" 換句話說，您去拿幾次菜都沒有關係。

" 只要每次拿的菜都能吃完。

客：聽起來很合理。

" 那麼 Cafeteria 餐又是什麼？

員：Cafeteria 餐是你點什麼就付什麼。

" 它意思是說，不像 Buffet 付的是固定價錢。

" You just pay every single item you take.

" 你取用的任一樣東西都要付費。

" The beverage like wine, soft drink, even tea or coffee.

" 飲料類的酒、果汁等，甚至茶或咖啡。

G：We appreciated for all these information. I think we are ready to order something now.

客：謝謝妳提供這麼多訊息，我想我們要點些東西了。

W：Yes, here is the menu, sir.

" 好折，這是菜單，先生。

在餐廳點餐
Ordering food

A：May I have the menu first?

我可以先看看菜單嗎？

B：Yes, here is the menu. Please let me know when you are ready to order.

好的，菜單在這裡。要點菜時叫我一聲。

A：Hello, I am ready to order now.

我要點菜了。

B：What would you like to order?

您想點哪些菜呢？

A：I'd like to have a beef steak.

我要點牛排。

B：How do you want your steak?

您要點怎麼樣的牛排？

A：I'd want it medium well.

我要五分熟。

B：Any sauce with the steak?

你的牛排要配什麼醬料？

A：Regular steak sauce would be just fine.

一般的牛排醬就可以。

B：Anything to drink?　　　　　您要點飲料嗎？

A：Bring me a glass of red wine,　請給我一杯紅酒。
　　please.

咖啡或茶？🎧
COFFEE OR TEA?

W：By the way sir, we have a very special pie at this restaurant.

員：對了，我們有一種很特別的派。

" 　Would you care to try some?

" 　您要嚐嚐嗎？

G：Yes, I think I would, but not too much.

客：是，我要試試，但不要太多。

" 　No pie for my wife, she isn't a pie eater.

" 　不要給我太太，她不吃派。

" 　I am pretty full already,

" 　我已經相當飽了，

" 　but I don't mind to try just a little bit.

" 　但我還可以再吃一點點。

W：Yes sir, not too much.

員：好的，您不要太多。

" 　Which would you prefer to have? Tea or coffee?

" 　您要茶或咖啡？

G：Tea for her, and coffee for me.

客：我太太要茶，我要咖啡。

" 　Please bring the cream, and sugar for her tea.

" 　她的茶要奶精和糖。

" 　And I take my coffee black.

" 　我的咖啡什麼都不加。

W：Yes, I'll keep that in mind.

員：好，我會記住的。

觀光旅遊實用英語

G：That's good. I like your attitude.　　" 　很好，我喜歡你的服務態度。

 關鍵字詞

would you care to. 你可否……之意，等於 do you mind 用法 例：Would you care to see her tomorrow? 　　你可否明天見她？
pie eater 喜歡又很能吃「派」的人。同理，喜歡吃又能吃麵的人也可稱為 noodle eater. 如果你的老爺車吃油很兇，你可說 My car is a gas eater.（我的車耗油很兇）
black coffee　不加奶精或糖等純咖啡
attitude　態度

 TIP 小博士

咖啡或茶須否付費？ 　　國人都習慣的認為，吃西餐之後的附餐咖啡或茶一定是免費的了，在國外，千萬不要這樣認為，一定要問清楚，咖啡或茶要不要錢？如要，要多少錢？甚至於續杯要付錢嗎？多少錢，全部問清楚才點，才不會鬧笑話。

買單 🎧
PAYING: THE MEAL CHECK

G：Excuse me. Let me have the meal cheque, please.　　　客：抱歉，請給我帳單。

W：Yes, sir. To make it in one check?　　　員：是，要一起算嗎？

G：Yes, please.　　　客：是的。

W：Here is the check, sir.　　　員：先生，這是您的帳單。

G：What is the total charge?　　　客：總數是多少？

W：The total charge is 90 Euro including service charge and tax.　　　員：總數是 90 歐元，含服務費和稅捐。

G：Here is 100 Euro. Keep the change.　　　客：這是 100 歐元，不用找錢。

W：Oh, thank you so much.　　　員：哇！非常謝謝您。

G：Don't mention it. You deserve it.　　　客：不客氣，你應得的。

W：Thank you. Shall I get a cab for you, sir?　　　員：謝謝，要我幫您叫部計程車嗎？

G：Yes, please. We are staying at Paris Hilton.　　　客：好的，我們住巴黎希爾頓。

W：Your taxi is here, sir.　　　員：您的車子來了，先生。

G：Thank you, good bye.　　　客：謝謝，再見。

觀光旅遊實用英語

關鍵字詞

meal check　餐費單
You deserve it　「你應得的」之意 好的方面來說：如果你很努力，應得這份報酬，獎賞等。 壞的反面來說：如惡有惡報，你罪有應得之意。

 TIP 小博士

服務費內含

　　在支付餐飲費用（所謂買單）時，如果帳單已加上服務費時，你可以不必再付小費。因為服務費就是小費，不過你如果心甘情願，服務費之外再付小費的話，也沒人說你錯，純粹由你高興。

彈煙灰

　　在國內，常常看到有些飯後抽煙的人，將煙灰彈到使用過的餐具上，他們以為反正盤子已經髒了，放放煙灰有什麼關係？但是，國外高級餐廳服務人員卻不這麼想，他們認為煙灰不應彈到髒盤子上，應彈到煙灰缸裡。

 本篇相關字詞

breakfast	早餐	pepper	胡椒
lunch	午餐	hot sauce	辣淑醬
dinner	晚餐	soy sauce	醬油
snack	點心	spoon	湯匙
drinks	飲料	fork	叉子
soft-drinks	非酒精飲料	knife	刀子
wine	葡萄酒	napkin	餐巾
tea	茶	orange juice	柳丁汁

coffee	咖啡	tomato juice	蕃茄汁
milk	牛奶	lemonade	檸檬汁
hot water	熱水	7-up	七喜
cold water	冷水	coca cola	可口可樂
ice water	冰水	pepsi cola	百事可樂
sugar	糖	salt	鹽

第(十)(二)篇 🎧

在國外機場

CHAPTER 12
PASSPORT CONTROL

P：Passenger

客：旅客

S：Staff

員：服務員

航空公司櫃臺在哪裡？ 🎧
WHERE IS THE AIRLINES COUNTER?

P： Excuse me. Can you tell me where the China Airlines counter is?	客：抱歉，您可以告訴我華航櫃臺在哪裡嗎？
S： You mean departure counter?	員：您是說出境櫃臺嗎？
P： Yes, I am leaving for Taipei today	客：是的，我今天要去臺北。
" and I appreciate if you can tell me where the CI counter is.	" 如果你可以告訴我華航櫃臺在哪裡，我會很感謝。
S： Sir, this floor is only for arrival passengers.	員：先生，這一樓是入境用的。
" The departure area is on the second floor.	" 出境區是在二樓。
" You take that escalator and go straight up to the second floor.	" 你搭電扶梯到二樓。
" You'll see CI counter there.	" 你會看到華航櫃臺在那裡。
P： Thank you, miss. Bye.	客：小姐，謝謝你，再見。
S： Good bye. Have a nice trip.	員：再見，旅途愉快。

觀光旅遊實用英語

308

 關鍵字詞 🎧

departure counter　出境櫃臺
arrival passenger　入境旅客
escalator　電扶梯

TIP 小博士

入、出境區

任一國際機場，一定分成「入境區」和「出境區」兩大部份，有些是入、出境不同建築物，有些是入、出境同建築物，但不同樓層（大部份是出境在樓上，入境在樓下），不過像桃園國際機場的入、出境卻在同建築物的正反兩邊。

同市有兩個以上機場

在國外，有兩個以上機場的城市不少，所以，在搭機 72 小時前再確認機位時，最好問清楚，您所搭班機，是在那個機場起飛，以及機場的正確名稱，這樣才不會在搭機那天跑錯機場，延誤行程。

列舉幾個有兩個以上機場之大都市，及其機場名稱如下：

LONDON：

Heathrow Int'l Airport

Gatwick Int'l Airport

London City Airport

Luton Int'l Airport

Southend Municipal Airport

Stansted Airport

New York：

John K. Kennedy Int'l Airport

Newark Int'l Airport

La Guardia Airport

PARIS：

Charles De Gaulle Airport

Orly Airport

Heliport De Paris Airport

La Defense Hlpt Airport

Le Bourget Airport

CHICAGO：

O'Hare Int'l Airport

Midway Airport

辦理登機手續 🎧
CHECKING-IN AT THE AIRLINES COUNTER

P： Hello, miss. Is this the counter for CI-066 flight to Taipei?

客：小姐，這裡是辦理 CI-066 班機去臺北的櫃臺嗎？

S： Yes, it is. Can I help you?

員：是的，我可以幫你忙嗎？

P： Yes, I am leaving for Taipei on CI-066 today.

客：可以，我今天要搭 CI-066 班機去臺北。

S： Welcome your flying with us.

員：歡迎搭乘我們的班機。

" May I see your passport, and the tickets?

" 我可以看看您的護照及機票嗎？

P： Sure, here you are.

客：當然，都在這裡。

S： Sir, I didn't see your airport tax receipt.

員：先生，沒看到您的機場稅收據。

" Did you buy one yet?

" 您買了機場稅沒？

P： No. I didn't know you collect them.

客：沒有，我不知道要繳機場稅。

" Where can I get one?

" 要去哪裡買？

S： You can pay it to me if you want to.

員：你可以直接付給我就好了。

P： Sure, why not?

客：好呀！當然可以。

TIP 小博士

劃座位

　　搭飛機的第一個步驟是訂位（to make a flight reservation），再來是買機票（to purchase a ticket）至於旅客在機上要坐那一位座位，除了少數航空公司接受在確認訂位時就給座位以外，大多數航空公司機上座位的安排，都是等到登機前，辦理登機手續時，才給旅客劃座位。旅客如果要靠窗、靠走道、吸煙區或非吸煙區等座位的話，這個時候就要講明。當然是先來先服務，遲辦登機手續，比較得不到想要的座位。

改搭他航班機

　　向航空公司買機票如果不是折扣票，或者在機票上沒有特別蓋上「non-endorsable」（不能轉搭他航）或「non-refundable」（不能退費）之類的橡皮章的話，持票人是有權（如臺北／香港等）改搭他家航空公司航班。也就是說，他有權拿著甲家航空公司所開出機票，去搭乘乙家航空公司的班機。其應有步驟如下：

1. 先向乙家航空訂下所欲搭乘之日期、班次等，並獲得機位之確認。
2. 再向原訂出票之甲家航空公司說明欲改搭他家航空公司班機，並己確認好他家航空機位，請甲家同意在機票上簽署同意轉搭。
3. 再赴乙家航空公司，請訂位人員，在你機票上貼上乙家航空的新訂班次貼條（俗稱的 sticker），上面會加註你新訂之乙家航班、號碼、日期等。
4. 記得向原甲家航空公司，取消原訂班次之訂位，免得佔用他人訂位。

如何辦理登機手續？

　　如何辦理國際班機的登機手續，簡單介紹如下：

1. 找到所搭班機之 check-in 櫃臺（辦登機手續之櫃臺），問明班機號碼無誤後，交出下列文件：
   ⑴ 護照 passport
   ⑵ 簽證 visa
   ⑶ 機票 airtiekets

(4) 打預防針證件 vaccination（如需要時）

(5) 託運行李 checked baggage

(6) 機場稅

這時，你可以要求櫃臺人員給你，你所想要的座位，吸煙區或非吸煙區？靠窗座位或走道座位等，如果有的話，他們會盡量配合的。註：絕大多數航空公司的航班，都是禁煙航班。

2. 櫃臺人員辦完手續後，會將下列東西還給你：

(1) 護照 passport

(2) 簽證 visa

(3) 機票 air tickets（僅撕去該用之票段剩下的還給你）

(4) 注射預防針證明 vaccination certificate

(5) 行李託運收據牌。

(6) 登機證，請參考本書第一篇第一單元說明。

機場的登機門，大多會有兩種形式

第一種：就像桃園機場的登機門，是從免稅店區前的那一條長廊，都標有第幾號登機門的指示牌，而且是順著樓梯往下走，位於 B1 層的一個大約有 100 坪的超大空間。裡頭除了座椅特別多以外，洗手間、公共電話、甚至手機充電站、wifi 也有。

第二種：也就是最常見到的登機門，以香港赤鱲角國際機場（Hong Kong Int'l Airport）的登機門為例，這種登機門事實上就是在很長的電扶梯（Escalator）走道兩旁，都會看到標有登機門號碼的指示牌（Gate-number Signs）。當然，每個登機門前，都設有很多長椅的座位區（Seating Zone）。這種登機門都是在電扶梯走道兩旁的開放空間。事實上，全世界機場的所謂登機門，幾乎都是這種開放空間形式的。

在香港的登機門，稱為「閘口」，而不叫登機門，不過其英文用法倒是全世界一致，一律稱之為 Boarding Gate。

里程優惠計劃

　　飛航臺北的國際線航空公司，幾乎都有各種不同的里程優惠計劃；來回饋旅客。不論稱為 mileage plus Awards 也好，或是 Freguent Flyers 也罷，各家航空公司的目的，不外是鼓勵旅客多搭乘他們的飛機旅行，而以飛行里程的累積來做為獎勵旅客的依據，換言之，累積里程越多，所得的回饋就越高。回饋的方式包括贈送免費機票、艙等升級、免費會員服務以及旅館住宿、租車等服務的折扣等。以上所述。僅是一般性的介紹。最好的作法是旅客在購票時先向航空公司問清楚，以維護自己的權益。

 自由行實務及緊急事件處理

機場self-check
Self-checking at the airport

A：Can you show me how to operate this Self Check-in machine?

您可以教我怎麼用這個自辦登機的機器嗎？

B：Yes. First, place your passport facedown onto the screen.

好的，首先將你的護照面朝下放在螢幕上。

B：Then press this KLM logo.

然後按一下這個荷航的標誌，

B：Then select the flight No. KL 422.

然後點選你的航班號碼 KL422，

B：Then key in the PNR code.

然後鍵入您的訂位電腦代碼，

B：Then key-in the passenger name.

然後鍵入乘客姓名，

B：Then select the seat you prefer.

然後點選你想要的座位，

B：Then press "Exit" to leave the system.

再按「退出」離開，完成登機手續。

B：Your "boarding pass" is being printed out now.　你的登機證正在列印中。

You'll need this boarding pass together with your passport, to check your baggage at the checking counter there.　你需要這張登機證與護照，去那邊的櫃台辦行李託運。

And make sure that check your baggage all the way to your destination, Taipei, Taiwan.　並且確定把你的行李掛到你的目的地——台北，台灣。

A：How come I can't find my name here.　為什麼我找不到我的名字？

B：Your name may be listed in a different PNR.　你的名字可能在別組電腦代號裡。

B：One PNR contains numerous names.　每一組 PNR 裡都會有好幾個名字。

B：A tour group normally comes with several PNRs.　每一旅行團通常會有幾組 PNR

行李直掛目的地 🎧
LUGGAGE TO DESTINATION

S： How many pieces of luggage do you have, sir?

員：先生，您有幾件行李？

P： I got two pieces here to be checked-in, and one carry-on.

客：我有兩件要託運，一件手提。

S： Please put your luggage on the scale.

員：請您將行李放於秤上。

P： Sure, no problem.

客：好的，沒問題。

S： Sorry, sir, you have a total weight of 26 kilograms.

員：抱歉，你的行李總重量是 26 公斤。

" I am afraid that you'll have to pay for over-weight charge.

" 你恐怕須付超重費。

P： Wait a minute, on my last trip to New York two months ago.

客：等一下，兩個月前我去紐約時。

" They didn't charge me anything on my 60-kilo luggage.

" 我的行李共 60 公斤，他們都沒有向我收費。

S： You are right, sir. But this is not New York.

員：是的，但是這裡不是紐約。

" The correct baggage allowance is

" 正確的免費行李規定是……

"	on Trans-Pacific flights to the USA or Canada,	"	經太平洋飛往美國或加拿大，
"	your free baggage allowance is a maximum of two checked baggage,	"	你的免費行李最多可以有兩件，
"	not more than 32 kilograms each.	"	每件不要超過 32 公斤。
"	To the areas other than North America,	"	到北美以外的地區，
"	each passenger is only allowed for a total of 20 kilos on Economy, 30 kilos on Business, and 40 kilos on First class.	"	每位經濟艙的旅客，只能帶 20 公斤，商務艙 30 公斤，頭等艙則可帶 40 公斤。
P：	Okay, I'll just do what you say.	客：	好，就這麼辦。
"	By the way, is this a non-stop flight to Taipei?	"	對了，這一班機是直達臺北，中間不停嗎？
S：	No, it isn't.	員：	不是。
"	It will stop at Bangkok before Taipei.	"	到臺北之前會先停曼谷。
P：	Please be sure to check my luggage all the way to Taipei, not to Bangkok.	客：	請一定要把我的行李直掛到臺北，而不是曼谷。
S：	Yes, I will.	員：	好的。

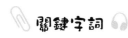

關鍵字詞

carry on	「手提行李」之意，亦可稱 hand-carry bag
over-weight	過重；超重，亦稱為 excess-weight

TIP 小博士

避免行李掛錯目的地

　　搭乘長程班機，且又不是直達航班，最怕在中間短暫停留時，誤下了你的行李，或誤轉至他處。所以，根本之道，應該在起站辦理登機手續時，強調你的行李，要直接掛到你的目的地（假設是該班機的終點站），而不是掛到中途的其他站。所以，當櫃臺人員辦完你的登機手續，而將你的託運行李收據牌（一般稱為行李牌，這是黏貼於你託運行李上，行李標籤的副聯，尺寸約 5.5 公分 ×3 公分，通常櫃臺人員會將它們用釘書機釘於你的機票封面上），你必須看清楚，行李牌上所寫之三碼都市代碼（例如臺北是 TPE，香港是 HKG 等）是否就是你的目的地？如果不是，要請櫃臺人員趕快更正，不然你到目的地時，就會找不到你的託運行李。（直達、中間不停的班次，當然就不會有這種問題）。

行李牌的重要性

　　上述行李牌不要隨便丟棄，它的作用簡述如下：

1. 抵達目的地，行李檢查或打稅完畢後，要從出口 EXIT 處離開行李海關區時，工作人員會核對，你行李上的行李牌號碼，和你手上行李牌的號碼是否相符，才准予放行，（有些機場不嚴格執行，是屬例外）。
2. 抵達目的地，萬一發現你的託運行李遺失，或誤送他站時，只有你手上的行李牌，才可以證明你託運行李有幾件，才可據以辦理理賠或補償。

免費託運行李之限制

　　根據世界航空協會的規定，世界各地航空公司對旅客免費託運行李的限制，一般是維持在頭等艙行李 40 公斤、商務艙 30 公斤、經濟艙 20 公斤的範圍。但是經由太平洋上空飛往美加地區的行李（trans-Pacific）（一般是指從亞洲至美、加兩國）因美、加的移民政策關係，兩國海關同意將免費行李的限制，放寬到不分艙等，一律每人可帶兩件託運行李，每件不可超過 70 磅（約 32 公斤）。

行李超重擅自放行的後果

另外，在機場常可見到，旅客為了行李只超過三、兩公斤，就會和航空公司人員計較，可否免付超重費？這裡有一個嚴肅的問題是：

假如旅客託運行李超重許多，而原起飛地航空公司辦理行李人員，如果一時同情，沒多收超重費，私下放行時，會擔負什麼法律後果？

不久前，就有一件起站航空公司辦理登機手續人員，因一時同情，未向行李超重旅客，收取行李超重費，而在目的地站的行李工作搬運員，因搬運該超重行李而扭傷腰部，所以，就依法律途徑，控告該承運航空公司起飛站的工作人員，對該件超重行李，未按規定收取超重費，也沒另貼超重警告標記，而使他腰部扭傷。訴訟的結果，不問而知，該起站航空公司，付全部賠償責任。

所以，航空公司人員，如果向旅客收行李超重費，絕不是刁難，而是遵照規定同時，也是在保護他們自己。看了上例，大家就會更明白了。

避免雙重扣稅

國人如果攜帶在國內新買的電器用品出國，又擔心返國後，被海關誤認為是國外所買而要扣稅，怎麼辦呢？在此告訴你，解決的方法有二：

1. 將國內商店開給你的該電器發票，帶在身邊，足以證明不是國外所買的，就不用重複打稅。

2. 出國前，持該電器品向機場海關申報登記，他們會開給一張證明，返國後，向海關人員出示此證明，就不必再打稅。

登機門在哪裡？🎧
WHERE IS THE BOARDING-GATE?

S： Okay, sir. This is your boarding pass and baggage-checks.

P： Thank you. Am I through here?

S： Yes, and please go over Gate 20 for your departure.

P： Yes, miss. But how do I get to the Gate 20 from here?

S： After you get through the passport control and security-check,

" you'll be passing through duty-free area.

" You'll see the signs out there showing you how to get to Gate 20.

" Just follow the signs, you can't miss it.

P： What time do I board?

" Do I have time to do some duty-free shopping before boarding?

員：好了，先生，這是您的登機證和行李收據。

客：謝謝，我的手續辦完了嗎？

員：辦完了，請去 20 號登機門準備登機。

客：好的，小姐，但是 20 號登機門怎麼走？

員：您驗完護照以及安全檢查後。

" 您將會經過免稅商店區。

" 那有指示牌會告訴您 20 號登機門怎麼走。

" 只要遵循指示牌指示您一定看得到的。

客：我什麼時候登機？

" 我有沒有時間在登機前買些免稅品？

S： I suppose you can, but don't miss your flight.

P： No, I won't. It won't take long to shop.

員：應該有，但不要沒搭上飛機。

客：不會，我買東西很快。

 關鍵字詞 🎧

baggage checks　行李牌；託運行李之收據
Am I through?　我手續辦完了嗎？
security check　安全檢查

 TIP 小博士

尋找登機門
　　搭機前的最後一道步驟就是，怎麼找到登機門去登機？各大國際機場的登機門指示牌都做得又大又清楚，告訴旅客登機門怎麼走，所以找登機門應該沒有問題，只是，有些機場面積過於龐大，要走很遠才會走到登機門，有些甚至要搭乘機場專用車輛，才會找到登機門，所以，最好事先問問幫你辦理登機手續的櫃臺人員，登機門怎麼走，以免錯過班機。

 本篇相關字詞 🎧

international airport	國際機場	boarding gate	登機門
domestic airport	國內機場	gate number	登機門號碼
porter	行李員	window seat	靠窗座位
passenger terminal	客運大樓	aisle seat	靠走道座位
cargo terminal	貨運大樓	security check	安全檢查
airport bus	機場巴士	body check	搜身檢查

airlines counter	航空櫃臺	smoking area	吸煙區
check-in counter	登記櫃臺	non-smoking area	非吸煙區
passport	護照	duty-free shop	免稅店
visa number	簽證號碼	bank	銀行
air ticket	機票	money exchange	換錢
baggage tag	行李牌	departure time	出發時間
over weight baggage	超重行李	arrival time	到達時間
excess weight	超重行李	on schedule	準時
airport tax	機場稅	behind schedule	誤點
checked baggage	託運行李	delay	延遲
hand-carry bag	手提行李	cancel	取消
boarding pass	登機證	reservation	訂位
seat number	座位號碼		

Note

國家圖書館出版品預行編目資料

觀光旅遊實用英語／黃惠政著. -- 初版. --
臺北市：五南，2020.04
　面；　公分
ISBN 978-957-763-582-2（平裝）

1.英語　2.旅遊　3.會話

805.188　　　　　　　　108012910

1L9A　觀光系列

觀光旅遊實用英語

作　　者 — 黃惠政

發 行 人 — 楊榮川

總 經 理 — 楊士清

總 編 輯 — 楊秀麗

副總編輯 — 黃惠娟

責任編輯 — 高雅婷

校　　對 — 卓純如、盧妍蓁

封面設計 — 姚孝慈

出 版 者 — 五南圖書出版股份有限公司

地　　址：106台北市大安區和平東路二段339號4樓

電　　話：(02)2705-5066　傳　真：(02)2706-6100

網　　址：http://www.wunan.com.tw

電子郵件：wunan@wunan.com.tw

劃撥帳號：01068953

戶　　名：五南圖書出版股份有限公司

法律顧問　林勝安律師事務所　林勝安律師

出版日期　2020年4月初版一刷

定　　價　新臺幣450元

經典永恆・名著常在

五十週年的獻禮 —— 經典名著文庫

五南,五十年了,半個世紀,人生旅程的一大半,走過來了。

思索著,邁向百年的未來歷程,能為知識界、文化學術界作些什麼?

在速食文化的生態下,有什麼值得讓人雋永品味的?

歷代經典・當今名著,經過時間的洗禮,千錘百鍊,流傳至今,光芒耀人;

不僅使我們能領悟前人的智慧,同時也增深加廣我們思考的深度與視野。

我們決心投入巨資,有計畫的系統梳選,成立「經典名著文庫」,

希望收入古今中外思想性的、充滿睿智與獨見的經典、名著。

這是一項理想性的、永續性的巨大出版工程。

不在意讀者的眾寡,只考慮它的學術價值,力求完整展現先哲思想的軌跡;

為知識界開啟一片智慧之窗,營造一座百花綻放的世界文明公園,

任君遨遊、取菁吸蜜、嘉惠學子!